Barefoot Doctor

Books by Can Xue in English Translation

Barefoot Doctor: A Novel
Purple Perilla
I Live in the Slums: Stories
Love in the New Millennium
Frontier
Vertical Motion: Stories
The Last Lover
Five Spice Street
Blue Light in the Sky and Other Stories
The Embroidered Shoes: Stories
Old Floating Cloud: Two Novellas
Dialogues in Paradise

CAN XUE

Barefoot Doctor

A NOVEL

Translated from the Chinese by
Karen Gernant and Chen Zeping

A MARGELLOS
WORLD REPUBLIC OF LETTERS BOOK

Yale UNIVERSITY PRESS | NEW HAVEN & LONDON

The Margellos World Republic of Letters is dedicated to making
literary works from around the globe available in English through
translation. It brings to the English-speaking world the work of
leading poets, novelists, essayists, philosophers, and playwrights
from Europe, Latin America, Africa, Asia, and the Middle East to
stimulate international discourse and creative exchange.

Yale University Press books may be purchased in quantity for
educational, business, or promotional use. For information, please
e-mail sales.press@yale.edu (U.S. office) or sales@yaleup.co.uk
(U.K. office).

Set in Source Serif type by Motto Publishing Services.
Printed in the United States of America.

Library of Congress Control Number: 2021950216
ISBN 978-0-300-25963-6 (hardcover)
ISBN 978-0-300-27403-5 (paperback)

A catalogue record for this book is available from the British
Library.

10 9 8 7 6 5 4 3 2 1

Contents

Barefoot Doctor

1

The Barefoot Doctor
in Yun Village

Even when she was young, Mrs. Yi had been courageous, multi-talented, and well respected in Yun Village. She was the village's "barefoot doctor," a title given to her by the township government. At that time, the village was rather isolated, and it was short of doctors and medicine. When villagers were sick, they could only wait to die. The young Mrs. Yi went to the county seat for training in medicine. After six months she returned to the village and formally started her practice, including midwifery. Though the barefoot doctor earned only twenty yuan a month, about the same as a farmer, she was so dedicated to the job that she often forgot to eat and sleep.

She was a junior high school graduate. For a villager, this was almost as good as graduating from college. Ever since returning from training, she had applied herself to studying traditional Chinese medicine and Western medicine on her own. She recited the herb formulas, learned about women's genitalia, studied the treatment methods for different fetal positions, memorized a variety of herbal properties, practiced acupuncture and cupping, and so on. In the eyes of the villagers, Mrs. Yi was born to be a doctor.

There was not much basis for their opinion. When pressed, they would say, "The patients feel reassured with her. Just look at her hands." In fact, they were an ordinary countrywoman's hands, strong with prominent joints. Perhaps the villagers' faith in her rested on the strength of the hands? But women with strong hands were everywhere in the countryside. The Yun villagers often spoke vaguely; it was hard to guess what they meant.

Mrs. Yi did cure a lot of people's diseases, and she successfully delivered some babies. If a woman was experiencing a difficult labor, Mrs. Yi would urge the family to send her to the county hospital. Most peasant families couldn't afford to do that, and the woman and her family would despair. Mrs. Yi could only hope for a miracle while racking her brain to think of ways to alleviate the woman's suffering. This happened several times; each failure tested her will, as if she had died and come back to life. Except once, when it happened to a small woman nicknamed "Shorty." Throughout the night, Mrs. Yi sweated profusely as she applied hot compresses and used acupuncture. At last, Shorty successfully delivered a healthy boy. After the delivery, Mrs. Yi felt weak in the knees, almost fainting. She slept for three days and three nights.

The earthen house where Mrs. Yi and her husband lived was a little removed from the other cottages and backed up against the mountains. In front of the house a large herb garden had been planted. The many varieties of herbs grew quite well; they showed Mrs. Yi's deep commitment to studying medicine. Mrs. Yi not only planted Chinese herbs, she also made synthetic medicines. The big room in the back was filled with Chinese herbs and her decoctions. She made them to help the sick, of course, but mainly out of a desire to know more about how the two sides would interact when the herbs entered the human body. She often thought of such things. Sometimes, in the middle of the night, she would awaken with a premonition, get up, put on a coat, and do some research.

When she was busy in the herb garden, she frequently felt that the herbs were like her brothers and sisters. She bred them, put them into the human body, and blessed them as mankind's best friends. Recent data showed that though banlangen—isatis root—was good for eliminating inflammation, it could severely damage the kidneys. This saddened Mrs. Yi, because banlangen was one of her favorite herbs.

From thinking about this problem all day long, Mrs. Yi became a banlangen in her dream, waving slightly in the wind in the herb garden. She firmly believed that banlangen was the good friend of the human body, not only getting rid of viruses but also strengthening the immune system. Another of her favorites was the coralberry. It could bring fevers down rapidly. She also found beauty in the simplicity of its posture. Moved by its bright red beadlike fruit, she sometimes couldn't bear to pick it. Some of the herbs were transplanted from the mountains to the garden and were difficult to cultivate. In the first year, for example, only a quarter of the dwarf lily turf survived; it was not until the second year that the roots took hold and new leaves grew. The wild one was much more effective than the domestic one. Perhaps they were born to be friends with humans. Wave after wave of joyful reverie swept over Mrs. Yi.

"Hello—someone's coming to see you!" her husband called from the door.

It was the village accountant's son, Gray, a sallow eighteen-year-old with thin ears that were almost transparent. His expression was cold.

"What's wrong?" Mrs. Yi asked solemnly.

"Nothing's wrong with my body. I'm just bored with life," he murmured.

"Then don't come here. I can only treat some diseases. I can't change your life."

The boy looked at her sadly, and Mrs. Yi softened.

"Okay, go fertilize the herbs in the garden. Wait, Gray, does your father know you're here?"

"My father can't control me, but I think he agreed," Gray said as he walked out.

A smile rose on Mrs. Yi's face. She could see what Gray would be like twenty years from now. Would her son Shanbao be like this if he were still alive? Her poor Shanbao had been only a little more than two years old when disease snatched him away in a long, drawn-out process. Mrs. Yi had never again become pregnant.

While she cooked, Mrs. Yi was listening to Gray in the garden. From time to time she walked to the window to look out. Gray was working very hard among the herbs. The sun shone on his face, which was flushed with perspiration, and his expression had relaxed. Mrs. Yi realized that it was only after careful consideration that he had come to her. In the future, he would fill the void left by Shanbao's departure. Mrs. Yi was a little emotional but more exhilarated: she suddenly now had an assistant, a successor . . . How had Gray been attracted to her work? Today felt like a holiday to Mrs. Yi.

When the meal was almost ready, Gray had already finished his work and disappeared. He had done a good job, and Mrs. Yi had intended to invite him to stay for dinner.

Over dinner, Mr. Yi told his wife that Gray had said he was world-weary.

"'Why don't you take a look at my wife's herb garden?' That's what I said to him."

"Did he come to see it then?"

"Yes, several times while you were away."

"What do you think of him?"

"He's a promising young man. I'm almost sure of that now."

Mrs. Yi went to the herb garden in the moonlight to take a break from studying. At night, faint cries came from the village, not from the villagers but from underground. Mrs. Yi thought that in such a large village and among so many villagers, Gray was the only person who showed a particular interest in her work. He was so special!

On the edge of the garden the brocade grass and the pungent white *Polygonum* gave off faint fragrances. These two herbs clung tightly to the earth. Mrs. Yi felt a little sorry for them because of their pure and cautious nature. Even when she stepped on them, they didn't complain; they showed their love for her in silence. Under the willows in the distance, two crickets chirped ardently. Mrs. Yi had keen hearing; she bobbed her head, keeping time with their chirps. She saw again the image of herself years earlier: at that time, with a bamboo basket on her back and carrying a two-toothed hoe, she was seeking herbs in the mountains. To her the most beautiful scenes were the herbs which grew in lonely spots for the sick. The invisible link between herbs and people had existed since ancient times. Their calls were soundless, and it was only after trying for a long time that Mrs. Yi could hear these silent calls.

Wasn't it to cure Chunli's stomachache that the beautiful clematis showed up? As soon as Mrs. Yi saw it nodding in the wind to her, she knew the girl Chunli would be saved. Touching encounters similar to this one frequently took place on this mountain. In recent years, Mrs. Yi hadn't climbed the mountain to collect herbs as frequently as before because she could grow many of them in her garden and she wasn't as strong as she had once been. But the memory of that joy could still warm her heart and brighten her eyes. Seeking herbs on the mountain was quite different from picking them in the garden. The exhilaration of being a barefoot doctor could not be fully experienced unless one had searched for herbs in the mountains. People and herbs tacitly helped each other and shared the happiness of living in this world. It was probably this joyous atmosphere that had drawn Gray to her.

2
Uncle Ma

When Uncle Ma was alive, he often discussed his illness with Mrs. Yi. She loved this kind of discussion. Sitting in the yard where yellow and white chrysanthemums were blossoming, they chatted at intervals. In the sunlight the fat hens murmured in their sleep.

"Today I found the herb you need in the crevices of the earth in a stone cavern," Mrs. Yi said.

"You mean the mountain cypress?" Uncle Ma asked.

"That's right."

"Yes, I think it would help me. I remember the shape of the herb. It looked perfect, like a handsome young man. Ha-ha. Mrs. Yi, aren't the cypress's needles and twigs excited when you pick them?" Uncle Ma said as he stood up. He started pacing back and forth in the yard.

"I think they're really excited. Maybe they feel they're starting to travel. The herbs were throbbing in the palm of my hand like little fish, and I still feel that sensation," Mrs. Yi said. One side of her face felt hot.

"Like little fish!—that's exactly what I need to get better." Uncle Ma patted his big belly, which was swollen with ascitic fluid, and said, "This kind of plant absorbs the essence of the rock. I'm so lucky! Thank you very much, Mrs. Yi."

"You are a lucky man for sure, even when you're ill. You

see, now you have a precious friendship. Most people never get the chance to be friends with such beautiful herbs."

Uncle Ma nodded, and pointing to the butterfly on the chrysanthemum, he said, "We live at the foot of a mountain, and we have everything we need, don't we?"

"Absolutely. How do you feel now?"

"Never better! The mountain cypress can raise the dead."

Mrs. Yi laughed. She felt that he wasn't like a dying patient. She sighed, "Yun Village, how wise your villagers are!"

Uncle Ma calmed down. He remembered something.

"Mrs. Yi, when you approached that cave today, did you hear anything?"

"Ah, yes. I heard the clattering sound of falling sand and rocks."

"This is good! They can't wait. My wife is preparing the herbal medicine for me. I am also kind of impatient. It's wonderful to be alive, but even if I were to die, I would have no regrets."

Mrs. Yi looked admiringly at her patient, and thought to herself, This must be one of those happy encounters. How had the mountain cypress walked down the hill into the body of Uncle Ma? She thought of Gray again, and of the torment the young man had endured before making up his mind.

"Mrs. Yi, I will pray for you every day, even after I go to the other side," Ma said as he saw her out.

Mrs. Yi visited Uncle Ma every other day. She noticed that Uncle Ma's belly was swelling more and more, but his state of mind was better and better. Every time she saw him, he told her of good news like the magpie laying eggs, a seven-leaf flower growing next to the courtyard wall, or his deceased grandson coming into his dream. These were of course but sensory phenomena that occurred near death, but they were also happiness. The three of them—Mrs. Yi and Uncle Ma and his wife—shared this happiness. They didn't feel depressed. Mrs. Ma even set up a big mirror on the fence so her husband wouldn't have to take the bumpy path in order to see the woods on the other side of the road. Uncle Ma knew all about the living creatures in the woods, for he used to be a hunter.

"Mrs. Yi, the person whom he most admires is you," said Aunt Ma.

"Why me? I can't cure him!" Mrs. Yi replied with a big smile.

"That isn't the point."

"What is it then?"

"You've reassured us. You're the only one in the village who has done that."

"Thank you, I'm flattered."

"It isn't flattery. It's the truth."

"Thank you for telling me this. I'll sleep like a baby tonight."

Walking outside the fence, Mrs. Yi knew that inside the courtyard the Ma couple were watching her through the mirror. Her heart was still with them.

Uncle Ma died that night. No one knew the exact time because his wife happened to fall asleep, and their daughter was sleeping in the next room with her baby.

"Daddy left joyfully," his daughter said to Mrs. Yi. "Before going to bed, he drank the herbal concoction that you brought him. He said he was lucky because he wasn't in much pain."

Mrs. Yi's eyes moistened, but her heart felt very warm. He wasn't in much pain; it was probably the herbs that got him through . . .

Though his stomach had grown large, his body had shrunk

into a small one—the viruses had finally come to terms with him. What a generous man he had been! His face, now serene, revealed the secret of his heart: he had said good-bye to everyone. Aunt Ma did not cry; she bathed him and dressed him in his favorite flannel pajamas, the ones with the cherry pattern.

"I don't feel he's gone," said Aunt Ma. "He's talking everywhere in the house and the yard. He told me that even after he died I would have to boil herbal medicine for him once a month and pour it on his grave. He loved the smell. Mrs. Yi, will you grant his wish?"

Seeing Aunt Ma's earnest expression, Mrs. Yi nodded at once. "Of course! Don't you worry, I'll write a prescription for him every month!"

Uncle Ma was buried at the edge of the mountain cave— the place he had chosen. It was at the entrance to the cave where Mrs. Yi had found the mountain cypress. Mrs. Yi remembered this and said to herself, "Uncle Ma had a very good memory."

Sometimes Mrs. Yi was too busy, so she asked Gray to deliver the prescription to Aunt Ma. Gray was happy to accept this special mission. The holiday-like glow on his face made Mrs. Yi wonder. At last she couldn't help asking him, "Why are you so happy about this?"

"It is the noblest task in the world. Every time I hand your prescription to Mrs. Ma, I hear folksongs coming from the mountain, and the ground beneath my feet trembles slightly. Then I see the image of myself as a newborn. They say I was born in a woodshed . . . Mrs. Yi, why? Why was I born in the woodshed?"

"Because you couldn't wait, because you were so eager to come out to play with others. How is Mrs. Ma feeling these days?"

"She's fine emotionally. She said, 'I brewed his herbal medicine while he was alive, and I brew it now after his death, though less often. He's a thoughtful old man.' I saw her take her granddaughter to the grave."

"Ah, Yun Village!" Mrs. Yi sighed. She was meditating.

"I will listen to the words of the folksongs!" Gray shouted as he went out the door.

Mrs. Yi thought the whole thing over as she ground the medicine into powder with a roller. Unconsciously she said aloud, "Uncle Ma is representative of Yun Village."

"What did you say?" her husband asked from the next room.

"Are there more than two thousand people in our Yun Village?"

"Two thousand four hundred and thirty-eight. Why do you ask?"

"Uncle Ma is the patron saint of this village."

"So are you. As for me, I protect you only." Mr. Yi laughed.

"If people cared about herbs, the world would be a different place."

Mr. Yi said, "Didn't Uncle Ma also plant a lot of herbs? He learned to befriend viruses. Prolonged illness makes a good doctor. You can see how healthy Mrs. Ma is; this is because her husband created a good atmosphere for her. I really admire the man."

The husband and wife walked into the herb garden and sat on the wooden bench, unable to calm down for a long time. Mrs. Yi heard someone crying again, but the crying wasn't sad, just a gentle venting. But why cry? Was it because things were always changing, or because the loved ones always had to leave?

3
The Deceased Uncle Liang Shan

Uncle Liang Shan had been dead for several years. His widow, Mrs. Liang, lived with her son Songbao in an earthen hut at one end of the village. All year round, she sold roasted sweet potatoes in Yun Village. She had learned this business from her late husband. When Mrs. Yi arrived, she was treated with freshly roasted sweet potatoes.

"Why do men in Yun Village always live short lives?" Widow Liang asked Mrs. Yi.

"They worry too much. We women settle for what we can get, but men don't. Is Songbao taking after you?"

"Maybe," replied Widow Liang. "He's only fourteen, but I can already see that he's an optimist. He can't be held down."

"It doesn't matter how long one lives, does it?" Mrs. Yi said with a smile.

"Exactly! When Liang Shan was alive, he was so happy. He said he had been wandering around selling sweet potatoes. In those years, people didn't even have enough for meals—how could they afford snacks? His business hadn't been very good. But after he married me, life got better and better. He told jokes all the time at home, and Songbao could never leave his side. He never complained of his troubles. Perhaps that hurt his health."

"I don't think so. I think his rheumatic heart disease came from his drifting about when he was young."

"Maybe. Anyway, he was happy with me for the last ten years or so. It should have been enough for him, and he died a happy man and without pain. He wasn't a burden for others, either."

"He was a good man."

"Thank you, Mrs. Yi. I took the medicine you prescribed last time and feel much better now."

"It has birthwort in it, so it works better."

Mrs. Yi stood up to go. Widow Liang hated to see her leave. She held Mrs. Yi's hand tightly, looked into her eyes, and said, "Mrs. Yi, if it weren't for you, I might have gone with Liang Shan, and then Songbao would have been a miserable orphan. But now my stomach is almost better, and I'm ready for work. Songbao and I can't thank you enough."

"It's just my job. The herbs are really miraculous. This is the advantage of living close to the mountains."

The garden in front of the Liangs' house was planted only in sweet potatoes; it had no green vegetables. Mrs. Yi thought, Widow Liang must miss her husband very much to plant so many sweet potatoes. The villagers said she was seeing a chicken dealer, but she apparently still missed her late husband. As Mrs. Yi walked down the path in the middle of the sweet potato field, a warm current coursed through her heart, because in the twilight she heard the crying again. It didn't sound sad; instead it sounded a little joyful.

"Mrs. Liang, you're a remarkable woman," she sighed.

Outside the garden a woman came up to her with a big smile. She wanted to carry the medicine kit for Mrs. Yi.

"What is your name? Sorry, I've forgotten it."

"I'm from another village. My name is Mia. Chunli is my cousin. I admire your work and came to see you. I've been waiting here for you for a long time. You are so patient with sick people."

"Are you ill?"

"Not physically. My illness is in the mind. I am always afraid," Mia said.

"Of what?"

"I'm afraid my husband will cheat on me and fall in love with another woman. Mrs. Yi, you don't know our village. I wish our village were the same as your Yun Village. Uncle Liang Shan has been dead for several years, and his widow still grows his sweet potatoes. This reflects the morality of Yun Village. As for the herbs in your mountains, I've heard about them only recently from my cousin Chunli. Mrs. Yi, you're a miracle. Everything in this world is connected to your heart. I want to visualize life the way you do."

"Ha, Mia, you're so serious about life—in a good way. But I think a woman of your caliber can do better. You have to be relaxed in both mind and body. You have a lot going for you. Don't be nervous. Ha-ha-ha," Mrs. Yi laughed.

"Me, my caliber? Mrs. Yi, you must be kidding." Mia blinked in bewilderment.

"Yes, you are very capable. I can tell by your words. You are an earnest person. You have the ability to understand and appreciate people. You have good taste."

"Mrs. Yi, I also want to learn some medical skills from you. Unfortunately, I'm too late. You've taken Gray in as your apprentice. Do you think I can learn medicine by myself?"

"Of course. You should teach yourself. Did you finish junior high school?"

"Yes, I did."

"Then there won't be a problem. I can help you with the difficulties you come across in your studies. Okay?"

"Mrs. Yi, good-bye!" Mia suddenly ran away.

It seemed the young woman was in tears. Mrs. Yi was a little surprised. Why was she so emotional?

Mrs. Yi turned around and saw Widow Liang standing motionless in the sweet potato field. Looking farther ahead, she saw the chicken dealer and Songbao heading this way. Mrs. Yi left hurriedly.

It was getting dark. As she walked along the road, Mrs. Yi began to miss Liang Shan. She couldn't tell why the peddler who had been her patient made her so sad just now. His illness was incurable. She had become good friends with him and always brought him some Western medicine for emergencies. It was not entirely to treat him that she had visited him but mainly to talk with him and his wife. She liked his attitude toward life. She and Mrs. Liang both adored him. Each time she went home after seeing them, Mrs. Yi felt that her courage had been reinforced. She reflected that Yun Village men such as Liang Shan and Uncle Ma were just as wonderful as women. Now they were both gone and had left their wives behind.

"What are you doing here?" whispered Mrs. Yi.

"It's getting dark. I was afraid that you might run into some wild animals on the way." Her husband, Mr. Yi, whispered, too.

While Mrs. Yi was handing the medicine kit to her husband, she heard a series of gentle laughs; the sound seemed to be coming from the same person who often cried.

"Chunxiu—"

"Call me 'woman.' I like that," Mrs. Yi interrupted.

"Yes, woman. I saw that young woman on the road just now. Her name is Mia. She asked Gray about you."

"Looks like our ranks are expanding. She is an extraordinary young woman."

The light in their home was too dim because the small hydropower station in Yun Village had never been powerful enough. After supper the husband polished the large kerosene lamp. It was time for Mrs. Yi to do her research.

"This big fellow is more practical," he said.

"I burn a lot of kerosene for nothing every night," Mrs. Yi said apologetically.

"How can you say for nothing? Your career is flourishing more and more, and you're the leader of Yun Village now."

"Nonsense, I'm just a barefoot doctor. That's all. I wasn't aware of this until the last two or three years. I'm so glad they came to me. Our own child died, but now they've all become our children. And do you know what? I'm not sure when this began but my hearing has become so good that I can hear the dead talking."

They both laughed.

While his wife was doing her research inside, Mr. Yi went outside. Standing on the edge of the herb garden, he was looking at the sky.

An oblique shadow was approaching. It was Widow Liang.

"Hush, don't disturb your wife. I'm just bringing a woolen vest for her. Here, take it. How is she doing?"

"Very well, and she'll do even better with you people thinking about her."

"I don't know why I just want to think about her. She's my spiritual backbone. I have to go now. Take care."

Looking at Widow Liang's silhouette floating along the

path, Mr. Yi recalled the changes occurring in the village, especially in the younger generation. "Things are becoming the way you'd like them to be," he said to himself.

Like his wife, Mr. Yi enjoyed reading medical books, and in his spare time from farming he thought about herbs. Actually he had learned quite a lot about herbs. But he knew that his understanding of herbal medicine was different from his wife's. As he saw it, one needed to be "possessed" to penetrate deep into this field of research, but he wasn't possessed. He had just told his wife about this. He felt relieved.

4
Something Unpleasant

Gray hadn't shown up to work in Mrs. Yi's herb garden since the rainy day. Could he be ill? Not at all. He was healthy now. He could eat three big bowls of rice at one meal. Perhaps he was seeing a woman? This was possible: he'd been seen with a girl from another village. Mrs. Yi chatted with her husband about this.

"I am so glad for him. A young man like Gray will be good for Yun Village," Mrs. Yi said.

"I certainly hope so," her husband said in a tone that was a little uncertain.

And so Mrs. Yi had to go to the mountains alone, as she had before. Her husband couldn't go with her because this was the busy farming season. All he could do was pray for her safety. Sometimes Mrs. Yi had to go into the mountains because a critically ill patient needed a certain kind of herbal medicine that was better sourced in the wild than in her garden. It was only on Niulan Mountain that one could find almost any herb. Of course, they were not always easy to find. Often when she was about to despair, she told herself, "Hold on, hold on one more moment and you'll have a harvest." And it worked out every time. She sometimes felt lonely in the mountains without Gray. But she had been alone there before Gray showed up; she could get used to it again. Mrs. Yi stopped worrying and turned her attention back to the task at hand.

The herb she was looking for in the mountains was called patch-the-bones. In the shadow of the trees, her eyes became as sharp as an eagle's. She murmured something. It wasn't long before she found the herb on a tree trunk.

The drizzle thickened as she came down the hill. The path was wet and slippery. She sprained her ankle and could not move. She had to take out some of the bone patch herb that she had just picked, pound it, and apply it to her ankle. She could not bear to use more of the herb, because she needed it to treat Grandma Mao's legs.

Time passed. She still couldn't walk, and her clothes were drenched.

"Hi, woman, is that you?"

The sound of Mr. Yi's voice lightened her heart.

"Hurry and help me. I slipped."

Mr. Yi helped her slowly down the mountain. How strange—as soon as her husband came to help, she could walk by herself. She had heard people say that heaven never seals off all the exits. Tomorrow she would deliver the medicine to Grandma Mao. "The rain can't stop me," she said to herself.

"Ask Mia to make your deliveries for you tomorrow, okay?" Mr. Yi suggested.

"I'll think about it. I have to do some things by myself, you know."

After they got home, she changed clothes and dried her hair. Then she counted the herbs she had picked that day. She heard some wild thing making a noise behind the house, and asked her husband about it. He said it was a weasel trying to steal the chicken.

"I was worried for a moment on the mountain because it seemed my inspiration had vanished. I've always relied on inspiration to find herbs. I've never told you that, have I?"

"I knew that. So was it better without Gray?"

"I don't know. I can't tell. I just know that I haven't lost my inspiration. On the mountain, my thoughts about Yun Village were particularly clear. And when I looked up in a trance, I saw these herbs. They were so beautiful. They were stretching out their greeting to me." Mrs. Yi grew excited as she talked.

"I wish I could share the moment with you, darling. But it's impossible."

They ate glutinous sorghum buns for dinner. The freshly steamed buns dipped in white sugar tasted delicious. While eating, Mrs. Yi thought, The weasel didn't get the chicken. It must be very disappointed. The poor thing will be hungry on a rainy night like this.

"What are you thinking of?" her husband asked.

"The weasel. If only it had inspiration."

"I agree."

"Grandma Mao will be better off for a while."

"With you in the village, she has hope."

Both husband and wife brightened when thinking of helping Grandma Mao. This time last year, Grandma Mao had attempted suicide because of intolerable pain.

It had been raining hard. The weasel had probably left long ago, and the chickens were resting quietly in the cages. Her idea of having a successor was shattered, perhaps because barefoot doctors were burdened with worries, and it was human nature to seek an easier life, Mrs. Yi thought.

In the dark, while her husband was sleeping, Mrs. Yi began to roam the mountains. She didn't know exactly where she was going. The plants and the rocks were always illuminated by faint light that came from nowhere. Tonight she reached an unfamiliar place on the hillside where there weren't many trees. She felt that the herbs were all around her, some even right under her feet. She squatted down, and sure enough, she touched a poria mushroom. She harrowed the roots out. What a nice smell! Looking out by the moonlight, she saw porias everywhere. She kept digging. Suddenly she saw a dark hole in front of her. She was scared. Sitting on the ground she looked again: next to the hole was a grave. A giant spirit mushroom—*Ganoderma*—stood at the edge of the dark hole, emitting a faint light. She didn't dare touch the *Ganoderma,* so she picked up her basket and left. Her clothes were drenched in sweat. She got up in the dark to change.

"Woman, what are you thinking?"

"I think there are many things in the mountains that we have never seen."

"I think so, too. That's why you're inspired. The mountains are actually ourselves." He seemed very happy.

Mrs. Yi lay down again and quietly fell into a deep sleep, no longer dreaming of spirit mushrooms.

The next morning, they saw that the herb garden had been ruined. The footprints left in the earth were not those of wild animals, but of a human being—a grown man.

"Who would do such a wicked thing?" Mr. Yi felt puzzled and said, "It's as if there were deep hatred, but we have no enemies. It rained all night, and the man braved the rain to do this."

"What's done is done," Mrs. Yi interrupted him decisively.

The couple began picking up the pieces.

The sun was already high as they tended the last few plants.

Mrs. Yi returned to the house to cook breakfast. When

she put the pot on the stove, she felt a baby kicking inside her. Of course it was not a real fetus, it was just a feeling.

"Gray?" The name slipped from her lips.

"I saw him going to town with his girlfriend. He looked very happy," Mr. Yi said.

Mrs. Yi nodded. "He needs a girlfriend. Were they going to work in the city?"

"I think so."

The baby inside her kicked again. She was a little excited because the sensation resembled the way she had felt in her previous pregnancy. Was her Shanbao coming back?

She went to Grandma Mao's right after breakfast.

"I kept thinking of your coming today, so I woke up at three o'clock this morning," said Grandma Mao.

"Here you are, these herbs are all cooked. They're the last of what I picked from the mountain last month. Next time I'll give you some freshly picked herbs. You are very lucky."

"I kept thinking that if one only had hope, one would live well. I was waiting for you to bring me the medicine. That was my hope. Now that I've swallowed the medicine, I feel much better. Mrs. Yi, I watched you grow up. You're not an ordinary person."

After Grandma Mao drank the herbal medicine, her face turned ruddy. This surprised Mrs. Yi.

"I am an ordinary countrywoman. As a barefoot doctor I know some herbs, that's all."

"You don't just know the herbs, you actually command them. I've heard them talking inside me."

Grandma Mao stood up on crutches. She was all smiles.

"Mrs. Yi, you can bring the dying back to life!"

She took several steps around the room. Mrs. Yi rushed to help her sit down again.

"You're not an ordinary person," Grandma Mao said again. "When I was a child, there was a mudslide on Niu-lan Mountain. We survived the disaster, but then a plague came and killed more than half the people. After the plague, I went to the mountain and saw that the grass and trees were no longer the same species. I knew my legs would be cured when I heard that you had been picking herbs from the mountain and making medicines from them. You see, after so many years, I'm still okay, aren't I? And it's all because of you!"

"Is that true, Grandma Mao? All the plants are new varieties after the mudslides? Are you sure?" Mrs. Yi stared at Grandma Mao.

"Believe me, dear. I know because at that time, I picked wild vegetables on the mountain every day."

They smiled at each other, and warmth welled up in their hearts.

"Grandma Mao, are you confident about my work?"

"Not only am I confident about your work, it's mainly because of you that I've stayed alive. Just think, I need herbs for my legs, you go to the mountains to find herbs, and the mountains grow those herbs for you to pick. What a great game it is! Life can be such fun—who can bear to give up life? I often think that from the very beginning, it must have been arranged that Yun Village would have you!"

"You are really wonderful. I didn't know I was so lucky. Today, your words inspire me. As I sit here with you, I see many things on the mountain that I've never seen before."

Carrying her medicine kit on her back, Mrs. Yi left. Grandma Mao held the door and waved to her.

As she walked along the country road, Mrs. Yi kept marveling at the curative effect of herbs. For patients with chronic diseases, herbal medicine generally didn't take effect for at least a day. Perhaps it was because Grandma Mao was very familiar with Niulan Mountain that her body reacted unusually well to herbal medicine. It was remarkable. Caught up in this vision, Mrs. Yi giggled. For the time being, she forgot the unpleasant things that had happened in her garden in the morning. Perhaps, she thought, the truth would come out in the end.

5
Aunt Yossi and Her Eccentric Daughter-in-Law

She met Gray on the road. His girlfriend was with him, and they were in high spirits as they walked to town. He looked happy and healthy, wearing a white shirt and carrying a load of chestnuts on a shoulder pole.

"Mrs. Yi, this is my girlfriend Spoon. I'll call on you in a couple of days," Gray said.

"Oh, she's very pretty!" Mrs. Yi said heartily, "Gray, you look good, too. Are you going to get married?"

"Not so soon. I won't think of getting married before I've accomplished something."

Gray's bold words stunned Mrs. Yi because he used to be very shy. Apparently love could really change a person.

"We shouldn't waste Mrs. Yi's precious time. She's busy. Good-bye, Mrs. Yi," said Spoon, urging Gray to walk faster. They were soon far away.

"They're a perfect match!" Uncle Ma's wife had approached and was speaking to Mrs. Yi.

"The boy is very lucky. He wanted to learn medicine from me, but I'm glad he's striking out on his own now," Mrs. Yi said.

"Is that so?" Aunt Ma looked inquiringly at Mrs. Yi. "It's hard to understand a Yun villager's mind." She sighed softly, and said again, "He is so young, he has a long way ahead."

What did she mean?

Mrs. Yi wasn't worried about Gray. He was happy—that was enough for her. Every youth had a long way to go; Gray would be no exception. A good, simple young man like him should have a good future. Maybe Aunt Ma was a little pessimistic. Her worries about Gray came from caring, Mrs. Yi knew.

"How time flies!" Mrs. Yi sighed.

Aunt Ma invited Mrs. Yi to drop in at her home.

"It's cold inside. Let's sit in the yard."

Aunt Ma brought out two cups of sesame bean tea.

"Yesterday when I took medicine to his grave, he didn't say anything. Is he mad at me?"

"I think he must be content to see you come, and there's no need to say anything."

Aunt Ma was relieved to hear that.

The courtyard was spacious. Sitting there, one could see a large expanse of sky. Mrs. Yi hadn't noticed this before. No wonder Uncle Ma had sat here every day: his mind must have wandered around the world, just as he had wandered about in the woods through the reflection of the mirror on top of the wall. Uncle Ma, you surely knew how to enjoy yourself in life. Mrs. Yi believed big-hearted people were blessed, and Uncle Ma was one of them.

"He has moved to a better place, and left me here alone."

"It's good here, too, isn't it?"

"It's all right here, but he's gone."

"You can find another good man to take his place."

Aunt Ma giggled as if considering that possibility.

Mrs. Yi saw a long row of seven-leaf flowers standing next to the wall like guards. After she stared at them for a while, her eyes reddened with tears.

"I know he can't return, and I'd like to find another man, but where—?"

Mrs. Yi knew Aunt Ma wanted to say, "Where is there a man as good as he was?"

"You'll have to find out. There's a big world out there."

As Aunt Ma walked her out of the courtyard, she heard Uncle Ma murmuring.

"Listen, isn't he talking?" Mrs. Yi whispered to Aunt Ma.

"That's because you're here." Aunt Ma's voice was even softer.

Mrs. Yi went to visit her next patient, Aunt Yossi, who was suffering from bone cancer. Mrs. Yi treated her conservatively with herbal medicine. She was trying not to give her morphine too soon.

"Aunt Yossi, are you home?"

"Oh, here's my niece! Come on in, please."

Aunt Yossi liked thinking of Mrs. Yi as her own niece. Recently she had often consulted with Mrs. Yi about her will. She thought Mrs. Yi was the only one she could trust. Yesterday afternoon, Ginger, her second daughter-in-law, told her that Mrs. Yi wanted to use their free-standing lean-to for storing herbs. She laughed and said loudly, "I built the lean-to, and I haven't used it much. It would be perfect for Mrs. Yi to use!" Her daughter-in-law was dumbstruck and hurriedly backtracked: "I was just making a wild guess." The old woman immediately said, "It's all right. That reminds me. I need to find someone right away to draw up my will. I want Mrs. Yi to have the lean-to after I die. You are a thoughtful person. You have such a good heart. You'll always have a good life." When she said this, the daughter-in-law began to cry, saying, "Mom, please don't die."

Ginger went outside. While Mrs. Yi and Aunt Yossi chatted

with each other inside, Ginger was making coal briquettes for fuel. Aunt Yossi couldn't bear the cold, so they needed to burn a lot of coal in the winter.

The young woman rolled her eyes and smashed her shovel in an outburst of rage. Aunt Yossi's voice came through the window: "Ginger is a wonderful person. You must look after her two daughters after I'm gone."

"I know she's wonderful. She works so hard to support this family," Mrs. Yi said.

When Ginger heard this, her legs gave way and she sat down on the ground. She wondered what this barefoot doctor was up to. Would she really take care of her daughters? She thought and thought, and concluded that this was possible, because the doctor was on such good terms with her mother-in-law.

The two voices inside the room dropped, and Ginger could no longer hear them.

This is what they were saying: "My dear, one night recently I took an aimless walk in the woods. I arrived at my old home. The house was dark, and some people were standing outside, but I didn't see a single familiar face among them. So I withdrew. When I returned to the woods, it was daybreak all of a sudden. Tell me, dear, how long do I have?" Aunt Yossi looked puzzled as she told of her experience.

"That's very good." Mrs. Yi also lowered her voice. "It seems you'll eventually return home safely, but not so soon. You have to wait at least a year or two. About your granddaughters, you have my word."

"Thank you. You've reassured me."

While they talked, Aunt Yossi was holding Mrs. Yi's hands. She was so familiar with this pair of hands, which not only often checked her pulse but also gave her massages. These were the hands of someone dear to her.

"I've always wanted to ask you, what do you think of the vitality of Yun Village?"

"Very strong, obviously," Mrs. Yi said definitively.

Aunt Yossi beamed with joy. Patting Mrs. Yi's hand, she nodded: "Good, good! I think so, too. Someone said that in our Yun Village yin prevails over yang, and the good is not strong enough to eradicate the evil. That's complete nonsense. Yun Village is very old. An old village doesn't usually lose its way. My grandfather told me that among our ancestors there was an herbalist just like you . . . I sit at home and wonder, Back then, what did Niulan Mountain look like? My dear, after I die, will you come to visit me on the mountain when you're free?"

"Of course. In the end, I myself will return to the mountains."

"Then we have a date. Shhhh, keep your voice down so that my daughter-in-law won't hear. Young people shouldn't hear this kind of thing. I can talk with you because you're a doctor."

As she watched Aunt Yossi swallow the herbal medicine, Mrs. Yi's throat also moved—as if the herb had entered her own body. She hoped that the little plant would soon do its work.

"The vitality here is strong indeed. Poverty can never beat us," Aunt Yossi said. "But a bad thing happened last week. A toon tree I planted suddenly died. I had planted it in the backyard where the soil is good. How could this happen? I was worried, so I lifted the soil with a shovel to find out. I found a stone slab one foot down in the earth! I planted this tree with my own hands. Who would bother to cram a stone slab under the root? Alas! Alas!"

"Don't be pessimistic, Auntie Yossi. Even in a good place, some confused people might do evil things. It doesn't matter. You can always plant a new tree," Mrs. Yi comforted her.

Aunt Yossi wanted to show Mrs. Yi the tree hole, so Mrs. Yi followed her to the backyard. The hole had not yet been filled in. Because she had been so sad, Aunt Yossi had left it that way—wide open.

"A miracle! Absolutely a miracle!" she shouted, swinging her shovel. "That slab is gone! Dear, the person who did this must have regretted it. That's good! That proves that the vitality of Yun Village is just fine."

"Of course we're okay, for Niulan Mountain is protecting us. You see, everything we plant here grows well, and our young generation is ambitious," Mrs. Yi happily agreed with her.

As they sat on the bench looking at the hole, they were recalling the setbacks and the happy moments of their lives. Aunt Yossi confided that she wanted to knit sweaters and caps for her two granddaughters before she died, five for each of them, with even stitches and new patterns. She was working hard, as if it were a major project.

"Your vigor reflects the character of our Yun Village," Mrs. Yi said.

Aunt Yossi went into the house and took out a bag of dried sweet potatoes which were almost transparent. She gave it to Mrs. Yi. "How I wish I could go to the mountains with you to collect herbs!" She was almost in tears. Mrs. Yi left hurriedly.

"Wait, Mrs. Yi!" The daughter-in-law caught up with her.

"Will you really take care of my two daughters?" she asked.

Mrs. Yi looked at her and nodded earnestly.

"In that case, I will change. I want to be a good person," she said shyly.

"What's the matter with you? You're a very nice person."

"Thank you, Mrs. Yi. I always thought that since I wasn't from Yun Village anyway, it didn't matter how I behaved. I'll change, I swear—"

"Oh, sweetie, you don't have to swear. Let me tell you one thing: I like coming to your home very much, because it's an auspicious home."

"Do you really think so?"

"Absolutely."

"I shall be too happy to sleep tonight! Please come more often!"

"I will!"

Parting with this fickle young woman, Mrs. Yi felt relieved. She thought, How forgiving Aunt Yossi must be if she can get on well (at least on the surface) with this difficult daughter-in-law! Yun was a large village built at the foot of the mountain. The village had been growing bigger and bigger. Every year, more and more newcomers showed up. Mrs. Yi often ran into strangers in the village. How could this poor and obscure village be so attractive? For example, it was said that Spoon, Gray's girlfriend, came here on her own and fell in love with Gray right away. She would never leave again. Didn't this prove the vitality of Yun Village? The concept of a village's vitality was hard to define, as mist is, but it was definitely a fact.

Mrs. Yi took a bus to the county town to buy medicine.

Not many people were riding the bus, so everyone had a seat. Next to her was a peasant woman with a little girl.

"Your little daughter is adorable," Mrs. Yi said to the mother.

"But she doesn't eat properly. Yanzi, do you hear me? The doctor says you won't grow up if you don't eat!" the mother said to the girl with a smile.

"I don't want to grow up!" The girl rolled her eyes at Mrs. Yi. "It's too hard to be a grown-up."

"She has a point. She's a little thinker." Mrs. Yi looked at the girl curiously.

The mother and daughter soon got off the bus, leaving the seat next to Mrs. Yi empty. Suddenly, someone spoke to her from the empty seat.

"Mrs. Yi, did you notice . . . ," a man's voice whispered.

"Notice what?" Mrs. Yi asked softly.

"The child who just got off told the secret of generations of Yun Village."

"Her point was fair enough. We adults do work really hard. But who are you?" Mrs. Yi asked blankly to the air.

"I'm the kind of invisible person who's not supposed to be seen. Sorry, I have to get off now."

The bus stopped. Mrs. Yi bent to look but did not see anyone get off.

After arriving at the town, Mrs. Yi was in a trance as she went to the herb market to buy some traditional Chinese medicine. And she was in a trance as she took the bus back to Yun Village.

What happened in the afternoon seemed unreal to her. Were there actually some invisible people in Yun Village? How did the man manage to become invisible? Maybe he wasn't invisible. Maybe he had just sat in the back, and she hadn't noticed him? While in town, she had also sought out the former barefoot doctor training center. The place was deserted; one-third of the red-brick building had collapsed. An old man on the second floor beckoned her. He was the former director of the training center, but now he couldn't even speak clearly.

"Are you still holding on? I knew back then that you had potential."

"This is my life, director. How are you?" she asked, concerned for him.

"You're determined to do it all your life? Good. I'm dying. I often dream of the good old days. I remember that the sight of blood used to make you sick, but later you got over that. You, you have potential . . ." He coughed violently.

Mrs. Yi walked a good distance, the old director's voice ringing in her ears. He used to be a capable, middle-aged doctor specializing in obstetrics and gynecology. Mrs. Yi had learned midwifery from him. In those days, she had had sort of a crush on him. Mrs. Yi shed tears as she recalled the old days.

Was she afraid of hard work? Of course not. It apparently gave her something to look forward to. What kind of something was she looking forward to? Hadn't even her baby Shanbao left her? But as soon as she got down to work, she felt an indefinable anticipation. Perhaps this was what the director meant by "potential."

6
Gray's Abnormal Behavior

"I'm getting old," Mrs. Yi said to herself. While she was delivering the baby for Aunt Yossi's other daughter-in-law that morning she felt dizzy and nearly fell. Then, with great effort, she steadied herself. Not long before, she had been planning to teach Gray midwifery. Now should she consider Mia instead? But this girl hadn't come to Yun Village for a long time. Perhaps she had fallen in love with someone, as Gray had? Or even gotten married?* Life was unpredictable. For instance, she had never expected that the director of the training center would turn out the way he had. She had gone back to the training center several times before but had never seen him. Had he been hiding from her? Alas. She should visit him more often.

"Tell me, darling, will I ever have some days off?"

"Perhaps. Once you have an apprentice, you won't get so tired. But woman, can you stand to be idle? I don't know what's going on with Gray. He might be a little confused by now," her husband said.

"He's not confused at all. He looked very happy. He's a lucky man."

"But I'm not sure about his girlfriend Spoon's personality."

* Author's note: Mrs. Yi has forgotten that Mia is married.

"Why do you think there's a problem? She's so young. Don't listen to what other people say."

"Okay, I agree with you, Gray will be on the right track."

"Absolutely."

As they talked, it grew dark. Mrs. Yi sighed that time went by so fast in the country, and said she liked country life because every day was so full. Even if one made a mistake, it could be easily corrected. There was no time for regrets. Mrs. Yi had never complained about anything. For example, it was fine for Gray to come to her, and it was fine for him to leave. Whatever she experienced—the excitement she shared with Gray or the blueprint she had designed for his future—was fine with her.

"But I'm getting old," Mrs. Yi said.

"Well. We need to groom a successor quickly."

While the husband was lighting the kerosene lamp, his tall figure was reflected swaying on the wall. Mrs. Yi remembered a lot of the past. She suddenly wondered, If Shanbao were still alive, would he become a barefoot doctor?

Later that night, Mrs. Yi's reading of the medical journal led her thoughts to the countryside far, far away. The journal introduced several rare herbs which didn't grow on Niulan Mountain. One had to go early in the spring to the mountains in the northeast to pick them. These herbs were very potent, probably because they'd been isolated from people for so many years that they had accumulated a great deal of energy. She knew she could not go to the mountains in the northeast, but she was so fascinated by such things that she kept repeating and memorizing the properties and growth habits of those herbs, and the right season for picking them.

Her husband was asleep. While he was snoring, the weasel was making noise once more. It came almost every night. How tenacious it must be!

"Who is it?" Her husband was talking in his sleep.

"Relax, just the old friend again."

Mrs. Yi went outside and saw a man standing in the pale moonlight. Was it Gray? The man soon disappeared like a shadow. It couldn't be Gray.

Mrs. Yi didn't see the weasel, but she knew it must be hiding nearby. She was full of pity for the weasel. The pity she felt for the weasel was the same as the pity she felt for her Shanbao. The chickens were silent, perhaps terrified. Like everyone else, Mrs. Yi raised chickens and ate them. She couldn't explain why she felt sorry for both the weasel and the chickens.

The herbs in the garden were thriving. Was it because of the good soil or because of her careful cultivation? She knew some people disliked the smell of herbs, but she had always been fascinated by their powerful fragrance. She often smelled them in her dreams as she traveled through the mountains and forests. Once, some herbs in her garden had withered because of over-fertilization. Unable to sleep, she had arisen at midnight and gone to the garden. She took a flashlight with her. All night long she squatted there and observed carefully. Under her care, the herbs finally came back to life. The herbs were like children to her: she needed to give all her attention to looking after them.

The person appeared again. He was leaving. It was indeed Gray. Mrs. Yi thought, This young man was really genuine: he became a barefoot doctor because of love, and then he gave up the job because of love. A young man like this would not have an easy life. She did not see his face, but seen from behind she felt that he looked sad. It could just be her imagination. Why did she think he was sad? Hadn't he already found his love? He should feel very lucky.

"I saw Gray in the garden just now," she said in the darkness.

"Really?" Mr. Yi woke up. "What's he up to?"

"Just came to take a look, I think. He's a good kid."

"But I suspect he had something to do with the previous destruction."

"Don't say that. Let's go to sleep."

Mrs. Yi was in a very good mood, so she fell asleep immediately. But unable to fall asleep again, her husband quietly dressed and went out. At first he couldn't believe his eyes, so he rubbed them and looked again. Yes, it was Gray. Had something happened to him?

"Gray, it's midnight. What are you doing here?"

"I came to check on them. They keep bothering me," Gray mumbled.

"Do you mean the herbs?" Mr. Yi whispered.

"Yeah."

"You can come any time during the day. Mrs. Yi would really like that."

"But I betrayed them. I'm ashamed to come during the day."

"Gray, feel your chest—is your heart beating fast?"

"I don't have to feel it, Mr. Yi, it almost jumps into my throat."

"You are a fine young man. Mrs. Yi is right about you."

"I have to leave now."

"You can come again during the day. Don't be shy. Look at the lily turf. It loves you."

As Mr. Yi walked home, a chicken broke free of the coop. It was walking calmly in the moonlight. What was going on?

Was it looking forward to being caught by the weasel? Mr. Yi put it back into the chicken coop. He made sure the coop was closed tightly. When he did this, the chicken made a terrible noise, as if a weasel was biting its neck. Mr. Yi shook his head with a wry smile: things were so ridiculous.

"Why didn't you just let it be?" Mrs. Yi said to her husband with a smile.

"You heard it all? The longer I live, the more complicated I become." Mr. Yi was a little depressed.

"For people living in Yun Village, it's better to be a little complicated. I heard Gray whistling all the way home. Let's get some more sleep."

They fell asleep almost at the same time, but not sound asleep. They both walked in the darkness, and both saw the moon, the boars, and the pale gray lake shining in the moonlight. It was not often that the two of them had the same dream, maybe once or twice a year. They called it a link dream. A link dream was sheer happiness, because you always felt that a person was next to you, and this person saw what you saw, and you remembered where the other person came from in the previous dream.

The chicken made noise again outside the house, as fiercely as before. It was probably just a drill. The bird liked to amuse itself. But this time, neither person in the bedroom heard anything, as they were falling into a deep sleep.

7
The Turning Point
in Mia's Life

Mia was not from Yun Village. She lived in Deserted Village in a neighboring county. The name didn't fit the village, for it was lively and the villagers were very close to one another. The doors of all the houses were open during the day, so it was easy for villagers to visit back and forth. Mia was a sensitive woman. For many years, though she lived in a congenial family where her husband loved her, her son clung to her, and her sisters were close to her, she had somehow felt that this life was not right for her or that it was even toxic. She had recently been imagining that her husband, Lohan, was planning to walk out on her and their young son, and run off with another woman. Of course she had never talked about her fears with others in the village. All day long so many people dropped by that she had little time to think about this. The anxiety lingered, however, and at times she stared at her husband in despair, finding it difficult to hide her feelings.

"Mia, do you have something on your mind?" Lohan asked solicitously.

"No. What makes you think that? I'm fine!"

"Just a guess. How's it going with the barefoot doctor?"

"I don't know exactly. I'm concentrating on studying acupuncture and haven't been in touch with her for a while. She must be doing well as usual."

"Why don't you go to Yun Village and visit her? I think you'll get along with her."

"I will. Maybe after a while. She's so busy that I hate to disturb her."

Lohan ran an oil extraction plant in town. All he wanted was to make more money in order to provide a better life for Mia.

When Lohan went out to work, Mia stayed home. She was such a capable woman that housekeeping wasn't enough to fill her day. The village loafers often stopped by to play with her four-year-old son, Milan. Sometimes Mia liked to shut the door for a quiet moment and read a little. But the village women wouldn't leave her alone. They knocked, and Milan raced to open the door. "Milan, Milan, would you marry my baby girl?" They laughed, the boy laughed, and Mia laughed, too. The little boy was adorable. Mia felt sorry for him.

These happy days flew by. Mia turned twenty-eight. Once, she had gone to Yun Village to visit relatives and had seen Mrs. Yi walking on the narrow path with a medicine kit on her back. Mia's cousin Chunli said the woman was the barefoot doctor of Yun Village. It was the first time that Mia had heard the term "barefoot doctor." Looking at Mrs. Yi's receding figure, Mia actually felt panicky. She had experienced this panic before when she was a junior high student. On her way to school, a bird nearby made a strange noise: *chi, chichi, chi, chichi* . . . but she didn't know where the bird was. Whenever she heard the bird, she felt panicky. After she got married, the bird disappeared, and she had never felt this way again. Was this barefoot doctor the bird?

Chunli told her that the sweet fermented rice was ready to eat, and they should hurry home.

"Are you interested in practicing medicine?" Chunli asked.

"I'd like to be like this doctor."

"Let me show you her herb garden. Let's just look at it from the outside. We shouldn't waste her precious time."

They stood on the slope looking at the herb garden. Mia wasn't just panicking now, she was choking.

"Mia, are you sick? Why are you so pale?"

"Let's go," Mia said, taking a deep breath.

"Are you allergic to herbs, Mia?"

"Oh, no, I love herbs. They seem to be my destiny!"

"People in Yun Village respect Mrs. Yi very much, but I don't understand why no one wants to be her successor." Chunli looked puzzled. "Too bad I don't have the aptitude. I'd love to do this work!"

After they ate the fermented rice, their faces reddened. But Mia was in a bad mood. She looked into her cousin's eyes and said vaguely, "I'm already twenty-eight. How strange."

"You're very pretty, Mia. Twenty-eight is the best age for a woman," Chunli said admiringly.

"Ah, but why am I feeling at a loss?"

"It's because you're obsessed with the idea of being a barefoot doctor. You need more time to think it over."

"Chunli, you know me best, you have to save me. I'm sinking."

"Hold on to me. You won't sink."

Mia got home at dusk. From a distance she shouted, "Milan, Milan."

Her little boy ran out of the house, and—wailing—he threw himself into her arms. Mia cried too.

Afterward, Mia wondered why she had cried as if she were going to abandon her son. Of course she wouldn't abandon him. Her son was her life blood.

The next day, Lohan said to Mia, "I've always thought you hit it off with that Mrs. Yi. You can have your career and family at the same time. I've given it a lot of thought: I don't have to expand the oil business. I'll support you by spending more time at home."

They drank silently to a career which hadn't yet started.

"I didn't see your true character before. I'm sorry," Lohan said.

"I didn't see it myself. Until I stood on the hillside and saw the herb garden . . . actually now, I still don't know exactly what it was, but I want to make a change. Oh, I feel terrible."

"You still have time. Don't worry, Mia, I've got your back!"

Mia was strongly motivated. She studied day and night. Her sense of urgency increased when she heard that Gray had left Mrs. Yi. She also took a day to visit the kind director of the former barefoot doctor training center in the county. He was now a sick old man.

"At that time Mrs. Yi was about your age, or even a little younger." The old man spoke hoarsely, by fits and starts. "She was a natural for this occupation. Her hands seemed glued to the baby when she delivered it, and her movements were perfectly coordinated. She was the daughter of the forest, and everyone could see this . . ." He was interrupted by a violent cough.

"Director, you'd better have a rest. I'll come to see you another time."

As she walked out, Mia turned and looked at the partly collapsed red-brick building of the barefoot doctor training center. She wept.

Two dark-complected middle-aged women caught up with her and took turns speaking with her.

"Young lady, are you here to study medicine? Now . . ."

"Have faith in yourself, young lady. Though this place appears to be decaying, a great woman doctor was trained here, and her name was . . ."

When Mia was about to ask them a question, they ran off and were soon out of sight.

"The good old days will come again . . ." The wind carried their voices to her.

What a beautiful career—exactly what she'd been yearning for. She hadn't gone to see Mrs. Yi yet, because she didn't feel well enough prepared. She vowed to herself, "I will be indomitable." The old director had said that Mrs. Yi was the only trainee who had persevered until today. The words touched her, and she immediately conceived of an herb garden, not in her front yard but on a hill. She would fill the barren hill with herbs. She wanted to enlist the young people of the village to help.

"I love the old director. He's the last of the old guard. If he dies, there will be no more people like him in the world."

Mia felt a little nervous when she said this to her husband.

"Aren't there also you and Mrs. Yi, my dear? Now I can see your potential."

Lohan's words echoed throughout the room, and Mia felt herself getting stronger. Although the old director's words were sentimental, his tone—containing an ancient fervor—had told her how much he trusted Mrs. Yi. Only insiders could understand the passion. Mia didn't really know what it was, but she longed for it.

"I'm going to lease the hill behind the village," she said to Lohan.

"Good for you! That's ambitious. I'll help you."

"I feel blessed to have such a like-minded husband."

"Milan, come here, come and meet the future barefoot doctor!"

Their son Milan came running over and climbed onto his mother's lap to kiss her.

"Oh, I feel much better now," Mia said. "So many people are sick in our Deserted Village—we do need a hill full of herbs. In a few days, I'm going to learn how to grow herbs."

"Since ancient times, various kinds of herbs have grown on Niulan Mountain in Yun Village. Our Deserted Village is not so lucky. But Mia has ambitions. She can build a hill of herbs." Lohan was speaking slowly and thoughtfully. He was smiling and looked very happy.

"Lohan, do you really believe in me?"

"I didn't understand you before. Now I do. You're an herb hill."

"When my mother was alive, she told me stories about herbs. I didn't really understand them then . . . One day not long ago, I went with Chunli to see the herb garden. I can't remember the exact circumstances, yet I do recall that I interacted suddenly and strongly with the medicinal herbs. I was so shocked. I seemed to be facing a life-or-death choice . . . Mrs. Yi—she knew everything from the beginning. Unlike her, I wasn't sure at the beginning, and I didn't figure it out until recently."

Mia had spoken quietly. Lohan listened and nodded.

"It isn't too late," he said. "You aren't a person who acts on whim. You aren't very sure of yourself because you haven't done it yet. No one is absolutely sure of a career before it has begun."

Mia smiled.

8
Mia and Lohan Go into Action

Mia borrowed some medical books from Mrs. Yi. On her way home, she saw a man sitting at the roadside counting money. It was Gray. He looked up and smiled.

"How's your business going in town?" Mia asked him.

"Not bad. Spoon is good at it. We're going to hire some help."

"Congratulations."

"Congratulations for what? Congratulate me for breaking away from my dream?" said Gray blankly, blinking his eyes.

"Wasn't it your dream to start a small business?"

"I thought so at first, and I was really into it . . . but I don't know why, now I feel it can't match *that kind* of dream. You know what I mean. Still, I don't want to turn back, either. What's wrong with me? Mia, I hear you're going to plant herbs. I'd like to give you a piece of advice: you must be very careful because some weirdo could destroy you. It's dangerous to be unconventional in a place where everyone holds grudges."

"Okay, thank you for your advice. But tell me: I am doing a good thing—why should anyone destroy me?"

"You don't understand. But maybe there's no point in trying to. I'm not sure. I have to go home now."

Gray put his money away and headed off in the opposite direction.

Mia was a little confused by Gray's words. Maybe he was right about grudges in everyone's heart. But why didn't these people pursue their own dreams? Was it because of inertia or restlessness? That's right, Gray had been restless just now. He was probably confused by a lot of things.

Mia sympathized with Gray, but at the same time she couldn't help feeling a little pleased. She saw that she could take over the space that Gray had left open. When he talked of people with grudges, did he mean himself? No, he was pursuing his own happiness. His business was picking up. He wouldn't hold grudges. Although Mia gave it careful thought, still she couldn't figure out what Gray meant.

She recalled Gray sitting at the side of the road counting bills, and felt that this was a little strange. It seemed to be another Gray, whom she didn't know. Gray had once dreamed of being a barefoot doctor, but he had given up.

Before Mia got home, Lohan had already signed the lease for the hill. From now on, the hill was theirs. Their son Milan ran around the room shouting, "We have a mountain, we have a mountain . . ." Mia smiled broadly as she picked up her son, although tension was building inside her.

"I have to learn cultivation techniques from Mrs. Yi first," she whispered to her husband.

"Relax. Do whatever you have to do. I'll support you 100 percent."

"How did you know that I'm nervous?"

"I'm your husband. We're all in, aren't we?"

"Yes, everything is difficult in the beginning. I've learned a lot from Mrs. Yi."

Someone came in without knocking. It was the village barber, a gloomy fellow.

"Hi, your barbershop is doing very well recently, isn't it? Even people from neighboring villages come to your shop for haircuts," said Lohan, handing him a cup of strong tea.

"The barbershop is no big deal. I just get by, day in and day out," he said over his tea.

"That's not true. People love the haircuts you give them," Lohan said.

"Doing good deeds is risky these days." The barber squinted, as if recalling some painful experiences.

What did that mean? Mia thought. Why did he, and even Gray, think that doing good was dangerous?

All three of them stopped talking, and the room became very quiet. Mia heard some big birds flying outside, circling round and round.

The barber suddenly stood up and went out without saying good-bye.

"Someone broke his leg before he moved here. That's why he is crippled. Why would someone hurt such a good man?" asked Lohan.

"I've had warnings from two people today, both about planting herbs, I suppose," Mia said.

After their little boy fell asleep, the couple went outside hand in hand.

The hill behind their house was glowing hazily, even shimmering. They stared in awe. Did it recognize its new owner? This hill had originally been owned by Yang, an old widower who lived at the other end of the village. Yang didn't plant anything on the hill, but he went up there every day. He looked around and squatted down to talk to the weeds and the little fir trees. Mia's impression was that Yang was an interesting man. He was also sick. In the springtime, his left leg was swollen like a bucket. When Mia offered to lease the hill, he agreed at once.

"How much do we owe you then? Tell me what you want for it," Mia asked him in trepidation.

"Money? I don't want your money. It's yours now," Yang answered calmly.

"But this—this isn't right. It's your property."

"I've done nothing with it. I don't deserve it. I'd be happy to give it to you and your husband for free."

"In that case, then, I'll work it out with Lohan and give you some money anyway."

"As you please. I don't care, really. What do I want money for?"

When Mia told her husband this, Lohan was silent for a long time before saying, "Yang is the soul of our Deserted Village." Neither of them felt that Yang was like others living in today's society. He was more like an ancient wanderer who had settled down in the village.

"Listen!" Mia whispered.

They heard Yang's indistinct voice. On such a night, under such a hazy moonlight, listening to such a voice . . . the couple was deeply intoxicated.

"Would it be a mistake to turn this hill into a garden of herbs?" Mia hesitated.

"No. It can only get better. You see, isn't it welcoming us? Yang is discriminating, and he chose us. We are lucky," Lohan said.

"Ah, you're a clear thinker. Perhaps you should be a barefoot doctor?"

"When you become a doctor, I'll also be half a doctor. It's a spousal benefit."

"I am the one who gets the spousal benefit, my dear. Sorry I didn't see your merit sooner."

"Don't say that. I didn't see your true character, either, did I?"

They heard Yang's voice from the hill, again. But was it really Yang?

"Lohan, how can a dream come true all of a sudden? I feel like crying."

"But you don't have time for crying now. You may cry later."

When they reached the edge of the hill, Yang's voice died away. It seemed that it wasn't Yang just now, because the light in Yang's house was still on. Could the hill be imitating Yang's voice? When Mia asked this, Lohan was moved. He hugged his wife tightly.

Then they climbed halfway up the hill and sat down to watch the night scene.

"Mia, I heard you say something just now."

"But I didn't say anything," Mia whispered.

"Ah, it must be it, then. It was imitating you."

"Oh my God. We've become its owners all of a sudden!"

Mia sat on a stone, feeling both excited and frightened. But she soon started worrying about her son Milan, and they hurried back.

The door opened, and Milan stood in the doorway.

"Milan, my baby!" Mia picked up her son and patted him on the back.

"I heard a lot of people talking, so I got up to take a look." Milan yawned.

"Go back to sleep, they're all gone now," Mia said sadly.

When they were in bed, Lohan said in the darkness, "Milan may become your successor someday."

"Lohan, I can't forget the old director of the barefoot doctor training center. He's the kind of man you meet once and never forget. Oh, what will the future bring?"

"Don't think too much. Let's take it one step at a time. Just now on the hill, I silently spoke to our hill in my heart. No, I should say I communicated with it, because it responded. So I'm relieved. Now I can see the *Mosla* all over the hill. The light-violet color is very like the way you described heaven the other day . . ."

Lohan fell asleep as he was talking.

"He's so happy. He is so easily satisfied," Mia said to herself.

A question lingered in Mia's mind: If she fell into a trap, would the mountain help her? It was a long time before she fell asleep—

9
Mrs. Yi's Daily Work

"She's very heroic." Mrs. Yi was moved. She said to her husband, "As if God had arranged it—Gray dropped out halfway, and Mia stepped in."

"The conditions in Deserted Village are not as good as in Yun Village, but she is young and she'll survive," her husband said.

Mrs. Yi's heart was like a sunny day in May. After breakfast, carrying her medicine kit on her back, she set out to see Sangyun's baby. Sangyun was Aunt Yossi's older daughter-in-law.

The baby slept in a bamboo cradle. The baby was very beautiful, although his face was still a little yellow.

"Mrs. Yi, I couldn't have made it without you," Sangyun said, weeping.

"Nonsense. Why are you crying? It's never easy to give birth to such a beautiful baby. Smile. Listen to me: smile!"

Sangyun smiled through her tears and said happily, "I didn't expect him to be so nice-looking. It's because of the good fengshui here . . ."

Mrs. Yi uttered "ah" in alarm when she saw a snake slipping away from under the cradle. It didn't get very far. It hung from a wooden beam and seemed to be watching the baby. Sangyun looked up a little and smiled gently at the snake. Mrs. Yi wondered if the snake was waiting for her to go. It must have a special relationship with this family. She stood up and said she was leaving.

"Don't rush off. Please have some sweet dumplings before you go," Sangyun said anxiously.

"Another time. I'm kind of busy today."

Sangyun walked her to the gate, and said, "Please don't be offended. The snake is our patron saint. You haven't seen it before because it was hiding. When my baby was born, it got bolder and started living under the cradle."

"It's a good sign," said Mrs. Yi excitedly. "Your baby has been psychic from birth."

"You must come back for dumplings."

"I will."

Recalling the experience of delivering the baby, and thinking of the snake, Mrs. Yi sighed emotionally.

On the traditional memorial day, most villagers visited their family graves in the morning, and so the village was quiet. Worried about Aunt Yossi's condition, Mrs. Yi went to her house. Aunt Yossi's second daughter-in-law, Ginger, greeted her.

"My mother-in-law just fell asleep. She had a rough time last night. I gave her the medicine you prescribed, and she went to sleep. This medicine really works. Please prescribe some for me, too. I don't sleep well, either."

"Nonsense. How can I give you the same medicine? You're young and healthy—why can't you sleep at night?"

"I worry all the time. My mother-in-law doesn't notice anything going on in the house. Everything is going to be stolen."

"I don't think there's anything valuable in your home," Mrs. Yi laughed.

"A penny is money to us folks." Ginger blushed.

"You don't need any medicine. Just relax and you'll be fine."

"Perhaps. But I'm always tense. Someone's trying to hurt me."

"What makes you think so?"

"Just because—Oh, I can't explain. I don't have much education. I'm all mixed up."

"Why don't you learn to read and write? You're clever and kind. If you could read and write, you'd have a wonderful life."

"Are you making fun of my stupidity?"

"Of course not. I have to be on my way now to see Aunt Lian. Don't forget to tell your mother-in-law to take the medicine, and don't forget what I said—learn to read and write."

When Mrs. Yi turned and looked from a distance, she saw Ginger complaining tearfully to another young woman. Her weeping was audible from far away. Mrs. Yi got goose bumps. The young woman must have been in great pain to cry so brokenheartedly. Ginger is a complicated person, Mrs. Yi thought. Perhaps I hurt her feelings just now. How thoughtless I am! Most villagers here couldn't read and write. She should have known that Ginger wasn't likely to learn, either (unless she had some special motivation), but she gave her the unwelcome advice anyway. No wonder she felt despair. Mrs. Yi felt bad and sped up to get away. She sensed that the two women were staring at her and inwardly cursing her. Her sunny mood was gone, and her footsteps became a little sluggish. She felt that Yun Village was dismal. "Ginger,

I know you're in pain, but why didn't you tell me? Did you think I couldn't understand you? No, you're wrong. Completely wrong." She conversed silently with Ginger. In a moment she was off on a side path, in front of Niulan Mountain.

When she came back from Niulan Mountain and hurried to Aunt Lian's home, Aunt Lian had just died.

"My mother wanted me to thank you very much. She kept repeating your name till the end."

Tears streaming down her cheeks, Aunt Lian's daughter held Mrs. Yi's hand tightly.

"You are my mother from now on. You meant more to my mother than anyone else."

Mrs. Yi couldn't say a word; her heart hurt.

Aunt Lian's eyes were half closed, and Mrs. Yi closed them gently for her.

On the way home, Mrs. Yi kept hearing Aunt Lian saying, "I can't wait for you. Where have you been? I can't wait . . ." Mrs. Yi answered in her heart, "Where could I be? It was someone in need who held me up, so I missed seeing you off." But then she wondered if Ginger had really needed her help. Maybe not.

"Woman, you don't look well today. What's the matter?" her husband asked.

"I am getting old. I can't tell what's real and what isn't . . . Aunt Lian is dead."

"Ah . . . You didn't see her at the end?"

"No. I lost my way on a side path and when I came to my senses and arrived at her house, she had left. I was so stupid . . ." She began to cry.

"Don't cry, don't cry. Niulan Mountain planned it this way, so the two of you would think of each other in two different worlds. This way, Aunt Lian will never be forgotten."

"You have a point." Mrs. Yi stopped crying and began to recall, "No wonder I was daydreaming all the way to Niulan Mountain. In fact, Niulan Mountain informed me about Lian's death. Oh, Lian, we were closer than sisters!"

"That's a good thing about living in Yun Village—What shouldn't be forgotten will never be forgotten."

Mr. Yi handed her a bowl of hot soup.

After drinking the soup, she felt much better.

"You don't have to worry about Ginger. Over time, she'll grow up," Mr. Yi said.

There was a noise outside the door. Someone was there.

Mrs. Yi opened the door. It was Lian's daughter Qiu.

"Qiu! Come on in. You must feel terrible. Do you want to talk to me?"

"No, that isn't why I'm here. Mrs. Yi, I want to ask you: in the future may I help you take care of the herb garden?"

"Of course. You have a lot of housework of your own. Aren't you afraid of getting worn out?"

"No, I'm not. It's what I want to do, and it was also my mother's last wish. I've always wanted to learn more about herbs. This is very useful in life."

"Okay, thank you very much, Qiu!"

"I ought to thank you. Ah, my mother showed me a way out!"

When the girl left, Mrs. Yi stood in the doorway with her husband, looking at Qiu's lonely figure for a long time.

"She grew up all of a sudden. She loved her mother so much that she loved me, too."

"Do you hear someone talking in the mountains?" Mr. Yi whispered.

"Yes, but I can't hear what he's saying."

"Every time someone dies in Yun Village, someone talks

in the mountains. Now you've got another apprentice. They come to you of their own accord. This girl is better than Gray."

"But Gray is good, too."

The turning point had arrived unexpectedly. Mrs. Yi's migraine eased immediately.

In the middle of the night, Mrs. Yi heard the voices from the mountains again. One voice she caught clearly was that of her son Shanbao saying, "Mom, may I sleep with you?" Tears of ecstasy welled up in her eyes, and she fell blissfully asleep amid the vague murmurs.

The chicken moaned in the beautiful moonlight. It seemed to be longing for something. What could that be? The weasel had left, deeply disappointed, and had not returned.

In the small decrepit building in the county town, a fantasy had taken hold of the old director's mind. He saw a big bird flying to Yun Village. It was a huge carrier pigeon with an urgent letter tied to its leg. The old director couldn't remember when Chunxiu had last visited. Was it five years ago? He was so pickled in alcohol that he forgot many things. But the carrier pigeon was flying to Yun Village, and he could see it clearly from his doorway. Behind him, someone whispered, "Yun Village, the ideal home!" He sprang from his cane chair and staggered out of the room.

Young girls in white smocks ran toward him from all sides.

"Do I see what I think I'm seeing? Are you my girls?" he asked loudly.

No one answered him. It was dark again, and he could no longer see anything.

But a timid girl's voice rang out.

"It's me, director! I—I want in. My name is Mia. Do you

remember me? Mrs. Yi will come to see you soon. She's been awfully busy recently, and so I've come instead."

Mia helped him go inside and made a cup of strong tea for him.

"Thank you, Mia. I can't see you, but you remind me of Chunxiu back then. How are your hands? Are they strong?"

"They're okay. I'm exercising them."

The old director laughed and began to drink the tea.

"Thank you, dear. Go home and rest. I know life is hard for you right now."

Even a long time after Mia had left, the old director was still talking to the wall: "Is it Chunxiu? Are you all right? Can you keep going? There's a loose stone here. Be careful not to step on it. Yes, over there . . ." He thought Mia and Mrs. Yi were the same person.

He sat in the dark, climbing mountain after mountain.

Waking up in the morning, Mrs. Yi said to her husband, "The old director sent me a message. The letter is lying at the front gate."

She ran to the gate and picked up the colorful feather.

She thought for a while and then said, "And I heard Mia talking. What a night!"

"The old director sincerely wishes you happiness," her husband said with a smile.

"Look, isn't it—"

They saw Gray at the same time. He was bending over, weeding the garden.

"Gray! Come inside and take a break," cried Mrs. Yi.

He straightened up, as shy as he had been on his first visit.

"I must finish this first. Someone is going to take my place, isn't she?"

"No one has taken your place here. You're both welcome.

The more help, the better. With the village population increasing, we'll have more work to do," Mrs. Yi said with a smile.

"Is it true?" Gray blinked his eyes. "You don't mind my betrayal and you really will take me back? But I'm a different person now."

"Nonsense. How different can you be?"

"Let me finish this work. It's only work that can put my mind to rest."

"Okay, sure . . ." Sobbing emotionally, Mrs. Yi went inside.

"The kid is unpredictable," Mr. Yi said.

"He's very thoughtful. He would make a good barefoot doctor."

Mrs. Yi was thrilled by the succession of changes in her life. In all these years, no one had ever wanted to be her successor. It was as if people thought she was destined to be alone. Fortunately, her husband was at her side.

"I think he has cleared his mind after this interlude. Those who can change for the better are more precious than others. Yun Village's vitality is reflected in these young women and men . . . What will it be like in another ten years?" Mr. Yi said, looking out the window. Gray was weeding there.

"In another ten years or so, everyone in Yun Village will be able to die with dignity!"

As she said this, Mrs. Yi laughed heartily. What was dying with dignity? As soon as the question came to her mind, she thought of Tauber—one of her patients for many years.

Tauber was the only successful businessman from Yun Village. He was a bachelor, and he was rich—by Yun Village standards. In other words, not really rich. Who would have thought Tauber would suffer from a terminal illness in his old age? After being diagnosed in a big city hospital, Tauber resolutely gave up treatment and returned to the village. He hired some craftsmen to help him build a three-story wooden house in a scenic spot on Niulan Mountain, and then he moved in. The air in this new home was fresh and warm. The water was connected to the mountain spring. Thinking that kerosene was not a pollutant, he lit the kerosene lamp at night. A village youth, who was also his admirer, took charge of his daily needs.

Living in the mountains, with birds, animals, flowers, and trees for company, Tauber spent his days reading. Five years passed in the time it takes to pour a cup of tea, and instead of dying as the doctors had expected, he became more and more vigorous. Only Mrs. Yi knew that his illness was still progressing, though surprisingly slowly. Of course Tauber knew it himself, but he was particularly cheerful about it.

"I'm on top of the world when I wake up in the morning and find that I am not about to die. If it weren't for this disease, how could I be as happy as I am now? What do you think, Mrs. Yi?"

"Of course, a blessing in disguise is a common occurrence in life. I'm so happy for you."

Life would have been perfect for Tauber if he hadn't had to take these anti-inflammatory drugs for cancer, thought Mrs. Yi. But no one's life was perfect. Tauber did live a full and happy life, and above all, a dignified one. It seemed that a dignified death required money, as well as the help of medical staff. She recalled her former patients, some of whom died with dignity (not as much as Tauber, of course), but their families had made enormous sacrifices. Some patients' deaths could only be said to have been miserable; speaking of dignity was out of the question. Mrs. Yi kept reflecting on their hopelessness as they neared death.

In that warm wooden cabin, Mrs. Yi often had lengthy talks with Tauber about life and death.

"Mrs. Yi, you are a great woman! I have long wanted to tell you what I think of you. Your relationship with Niulan Mountain shows your greatness. By contrast, when I was young, I totally ignored our mother mountain. I was an idiot then. It wasn't until I became terminally ill that I saw what I had missed in life. What was I doing all those years? I wasted so much time." He shook his head vigorously.

"Ah, Tauber, sooner or later, people do become aware. Your life is wonderful now. Don't you think?"

"I was just going to say that. How did life get so good? In the morning when I was walking on the mountain road, I couldn't help kissing the daisy at the roadside. I was so moved that I wept. I've never cried like this. And you, Mrs. Yi, you are an angel. I heard your steps while you were still at the foot of the mountain, and I thought to myself that this great woman was chosen by Niulan Mountain, and she's the only one who knows where the wonderful herbs grow. You are the only insider."

"No, you're wrong, Tauber. There are several insiders now. I haven't had time to tell you that some young people are joining me . . ."

"Mrs. Yi, do you see my tears?"

"Don't, please don't cry . . . You mustn't be emotional. I'm leaving now, Tauber. Good-bye!"

She ran out of the cabin. When she turned around, she saw Tauber watching her from a window on the third floor. She said to herself, "Tauber, how lucky I am to have shared with you the greatest happiness of your life. Niulan Mountain is fair to each one of us." When the words came to her mind, she found herself in tears—tears of happiness.

A clever little rabbit was guiding her, as if afraid that tears would blur her vision. The white clouds drooped low, and the branches of the trees hid in the clouds. At this moment, Mrs. Yi saw the story of Yun Village.

After the excitement on the mountain, Mrs. Yi felt a little unwell. Again she sensed that she was growing old. But her heart was still like a sunny day. Someone took her medicine kit from her and held her hand. Of course, it was her loving husband.

Mrs. Yi told him that when she went to Tauber's cabin, Tauber was sleeping on the ground next to a jujube tree in front of the building, oblivious to the dirt. Afraid that he might catch cold sleeping on the ground, she woke him up. Tauber got up and said, grinning, that he was feeling the heat of the mountain. "It is so warm!" Tauber sighed. He also said that various voices came to talk to him every night. He thought this must have been arranged by Niulan Mountain, for he would soon be inside it. He felt that he had enjoyed enough sweet happiness over the years, and he was content.

Listening to her, Mr. Yi was fascinated and kept nodding his head. Soon they were home.

Gray was sitting on their doorstep.

"Gray, why are you still here?" Mrs. Yi asked.

"I was reading medical journals for a while. It's beautiful here. I saw geese just now."

"Go home, Spoon is waiting for you," Mrs. Yi said.

"She went back to her hometown the day before yesterday."

"Do you miss her?"

"Yes, I do. I've got to go now. Bye!"

The couple looked into the garden, and found that Gray had done his work very well, and that all the herbs looked cheerful. Mrs. Yi murmured, "He saw the geese, and he was

thinking of Spoon. Poor boy. Spoon didn't want him to practice medicine because it was too hard . . . Spoon is a beautiful girl."

"That beautiful girl broke his heart," Mr. Yi whispered.

"Not everyone can appreciate the happiness of barefoot
doctors," Mrs. Yi gently reproached her husband.

"Alas, the young generation," they said in unison.

10
Gray's Adventure

A warm breeze was blowing. Summer was coming. It was the best season in the mountain area. How many years had gone by? People in Yun Village didn't count the passing years. Many villagers, especially seniors, didn't know exactly how old they were. They were too busy enjoying life to reflect on past mistakes. So they didn't remember much. Mr. and Mrs. Yi were no different. Mrs. Yi vaguely knew that she was more than fifty, but she wasn't sure how many years over fifty. Her mother, who had died long ago, had never made it clear to her. One exception, however, was Gray. Not only did he remember his age, he remembered every important event in his life. This young man was meditative, indecisive, and remorseful. These days, Gray worked in Mrs. Yi's herb garden and read some medical books in his spare time. But he had not yet made up his mind whether to become a barefoot doctor. He liked herbs, Chinese medicine, acupuncture, and the strong smell in the pharmacy. But he didn't like patients, and he thought that people who were sick had character flaws. He believed that it was character flaws that made people physically sick.

Mrs. Yi gradually got used to Gray's personality. She decided to let things take their course. After making this decision, she calmed down. She was going to observe these two young persons, Gray and Mia.

One time in the middle of the night, Mr. Yi happened to see Gray sitting in the pharmacy: he had opened all the herbal medicine drawers, and lit a bundle of herbal moxa cones, which he knew were used in moxibustion therapy. A strong medicinal smell filled the room. The air was almost suffocating.

"Are you sick?" Mr. Yi whispered to him in the dark.

"Oh, it's you, Mr. Yi! No, I'm fine. I just wanted to dream about herbs, and I came here on an impulse. I did fall asleep for a while just now, but I didn't dream of herbs."

"Maybe it isn't your time yet. When it is, you'll be with them every night."

"Really? Is that true for you and Mrs. Yi?" Gray asked eagerly.

"Basically so. If you miss them, they'll miss you, too."

"How can they miss me? They aren't human and have no thoughts."

"Nothing to do with thoughts. You love them, and they know."

"I just love them. I can't help it." Gray frowned.

He got up and left for home. In the moonlight, Gray suddenly looked like an old man, walking as if a little lame.

"I know he's different from us, but I still like him." Mrs. Yi suddenly spoke up from the dark corner where she'd been standing all along.

"He's a deep young man," said Mr. Yi.

Returning to their bedroom, they shone a flashlight on the wall clock. It was three in the morning. They heard a sad song in the north wind.

When Gray neared his home, he ran head-on into the deceased Uncle Ma. Gray's heart was pounding.

Ma made a strange gesture as he passed by Gray. Gray smelled herbal medicine on Ma's clothes.

"Uncle Ma, wait a minute!" Gray shouted desperately to the white figure.

But Ma did not even turn his head.

When Gray got home, the living room was dark.

"Did you see him, Gray? I mean Uncle Ma," his mother asked.

"Yes," Gray answered softly.

"He wanted to talk to you, but he couldn't. He probably wanted to repay Mrs. Yi's kindness to him."

"That's what I thought, too. I'm not cut out to be a doctor."

"So you've changed your mind again?"

"Not yet. I'm going to bed, Mother."

"Go to sleep. Niulan Mountain will bless you."

Gray took off his clothes and then put them on again because he heard the weasel stealing his chicken. He raced out and grabbed a big bamboo broom. The weasel ran away. When he went to close the coop, however, the old hen pecked him hard on the back of his hand. It bled, and Gray froze, puzzled. What did this mean? The old hen could not possibly regard him as a weasel, for he was the one who often fed it. Did it resent him for meddling?

"What are you thinking about? Don't waste your time," said his mother, standing at the window.

Gray went to his bedroom and bandaged the wound. Spoon's scent still filled the room. Thinking of her young, fragrant flesh made him shudder. But Spoon wouldn't return. Mother was right: there are some things you can never figure out. He didn't know why Spoon had come to Yun Village, but they had really hit it off. Gray had never expected to fall out with her.

He took a sip of cold water and went to bed. He tried to fall asleep, but the chickens in the coop made so much noise that it seemed as if the weasel were attacking them nonstop. Maybe he shouldn't have interfered just now.

As he was falling asleep, he saw himself in his own herb garden. A dirty beggar with ulcers on his leg was sitting among the herbs. In a muffled voice, Gray asked him to leave, but the beggar was unfazed. When Gray started dragging him away, he bit Gray. Gray shouted and almost fainted. Just then he woke up: it hurt where the hen had pecked him.

He remembered that the herb garden was full of small purple flowers. What was the name of this herb? He lit the kerosene lamp and checked the herbal medicine handbook. He couldn't find it. Dismayed, he thought he didn't have what it took to be a barefoot doctor. Just now he was disgusted by the sick beggar. Mrs. Yi never reacted the way he had. Mrs. Yi was made of different stuff, while he was just a country bumpkin. But the herbs, those beautiful herbs, kept him from giving up.

By the time he got up in the morning, the wound on the back of his hand had scabbed over. Although it was itchy, it didn't have to be bandaged again. Apparently, what had happened last night wasn't serious.

At breakfast, Gray bent his head to eat porridge. His dad looked at him from across the table.

"Gray, Old Onion asked me if you could help him with acupuncture. His back hurts a lot. He knows you're studying to be a barefoot doctor, and he said you could practice on him."

Gray was embarrassed. He hated Old Onion. The old man smelled so bad that he couldn't bear to go near him. Gray had only practiced acupuncture on himself, and he didn't want to do it on anyone else, especially an old man like Onion.

"I'd love to, Dad. But I'm not good enough. I'm afraid it might go wrong. I'm still young. I have a lot to learn from Mrs. Yi. I can't rush this kind of thing."

"Relax, Gray." His dad laughed. "I'm just testing you. I've been wondering, Can Gray really help people? What will he be like as a doctor?"

"Don't be so condescending," Gray said angrily. "Why can't I be a doctor? Aren't I learning to be a barefoot doctor? Aren't I the only one in this village doing that? Maybe you also look down on Mrs. Yi? Didn't you see her for your tooth-ache not long ago?"

"Oh, no. You misunderstood me. Mrs. Yi is from another world. I'm just a little worried about you. Go on doing what you're doing. I'm 100 percent behind you."

"Thanks, Dad."

Gray put down his chopsticks and slipped out of the house. He was a little afraid of his dad. Dad's old eyes could read his mind. He had hooked up with Spoon, given up his medical studies, and started a small business. Later, he broke up with Spoon and went back to work in Mrs. Yi's herb garden. Dad had never said anything to him about any of this. Just now Dad had pointed out his weakness—his lack of interest in helping sick people. Thinking about his future, Gray felt a little dejected.

Today he planned to go to the mountains alone to look for an herb called "ancient mountain dragon." Mrs. Yi had given him rough directions. As he passed through the village, he noticed that people were giving him strange looks, and they were all staring at the basket on his back. He felt these people were looking down on him just as Dad was, and thinking he would never become a doctor. He lifted his head, squared his shoulders, and walked quickly toward Niulan Mountain.

As he climbed to the cliff, he became nervous. Mrs. Yi had told him that the ancient mountain dragon grew in this area. He looked around blankly, feeling that this place halfway up the mountain was not at all like the environment in which the ancient mountain dragon should grow. There were some big trees here, but too sparse for a forest. The soil underneath the trees was poor and dry, the kind of red earth with so many stones mixed into it that even weeds rarely grew. He was surprised to find such a large barren space on Niulan Mountain. In his memory, there was fertile soil everywhere on the mountain.

Gray walked around the cliff several times, but he didn't find a trace of the ancient mountain dragon. Why? Hadn't he been paying close enough attention? Bracing himself, he tried again. He sniffed around, imagining that he was a wolf, and he even climbed more than ten meters up the cliff. Then he cautiously descended. As he sat on the ground, he thought of Mrs. Yi and of Dad's comment that she was "from another world." He was a little discouraged and a little suspicious. If there was no ancient mountain dragon here, shouldn't he leave this spot and look elsewhere? This thought struck his muddled mind like a shaft of light.

He left the cliff and continued climbing up the mountain. Just then he saw Niulan Mountain's other face. It was no longer the mountain he had known. Stony red earth was everywhere, and neither shrubs nor grasses grew under the trees. The trees had very few leaves, and some of them were even bald. Looking at the dark branches made him shiver. "Ah, ah . . . ," he gasped. The farther up he went, the bleaker the scene became. When he neared the top of the mountain, he gave up hope and decided to go home. He did not understand how Niulan Mountain could have changed so much. He had climbed the mountain six months ago. At that time, it was not at all like this. Halfway down the mountain, he came to the cliff again. Someone spoke to him.

"Gray, did you come to collect herbs? So did I."

It was Old Onion.

"Ah, it's you, Grandpa Onion. I went up the hill just for fun—"

"For fun? Then why did you bring a bamboo basket? Collecting herbs is important work; you shouldn't be ashamed of doing it."

Embarrassed, Gray wanted to slip away, but Old Onion blocked his way.

Onion approached Gray. Gray was surprised that the old man was no longer dirty and smelly. He looked tidy and fresh in his light-blue shirt. Onion put his arm around Gray's shoulder and said affectionately, "Gray, how about going treasure hunting with me today?"

"Grandpa Onion, where are we going?" asked Gray hesitantly.

"You don't have to worry about it. Just come with me, ha-ha-ha! See, down there next to the cliff. Isn't that the herb you're looking for?"

Sure enough! Gray was ecstatic. He ran over to the ancient mountain dragon herbs and dug them up and put them in the basket.

"Grandpa Onion, did you call them out? I've been searching all around here. Why didn't I see them? I'm so hopeless!"

"In fact, you had already seen them. Look, there are more." He pointed under the big tree.

Under the tree was a ditch, so the soil was more moist, and there were more of the ancient mountain dragon. The herbs were so beautiful. Gray's heart was beating fast.

"Don't dig them all up. Save some for the future," Onion admonished him.

Both excited and ashamed, Gray dug up the herbs.

As they descended the mountain, Onion seemed distracted. He slipped and would have fallen if Gray hadn't steadied him. He gasped.

"Gray, have you ever been to Magic Spring?"

"Magic Spring? I've never heard of it. Where is it?"

"I don't remember exactly. So many years have passed. Let's go this way."

Before Gray knew it, Old Onion had led him into the dense, dark woods. Onion walked in front. The woods had no path, and Gray wondered how Old Onion knew where to go. Did he know that there was a path ahead? Or could he tell the direction even in the dark? This was so fresh and novel to Gray that he forgot about Magic Spring. But suddenly Onion stopped and groaned. Gray saw that a python had wrapped Old Onion around a maple tree trunk.

"Grandpa Onion . . . you . . . ," Gray stammered.

"Gray, help! I can't breathe. Get rid of it with your hoe . . ."

Gray dashed over and struck the python with the hoe, violently and blindly, again and again.

"Good, good . . . ," Onion said lazily, as if enjoying himself.

The python loosened its grip and slithered slowly away through the dead leaves on the ground. Its body was smashed.

"Oh, it's okay now. Grandpa Onion, are you all right?"

"Of course I'm fine. With you here, I'm safe. I've been to

Magic Spring just now. What a wonderful view! I'm a little selfish, don't you think?"

When Old Onion said this, Gray smelled the fragrance of honeysuckle on his body. He remembered having smelled this fragrance in the past in the early morning sun. The old man's thin figure in the light-blue shirt was full of life.

"Grandpa Onion, I'm the selfish one. To tell you the truth, Dad asked me to help you with acupuncture, but I refused because I'm not interested in patients."

The old man burst out laughing, startling several large birds, which flew out of the woods with a loud crackle. Just then, Gray noticed the python lying motionless in the distance.

"I'm so sorry . . . ," murmured Gray.

"Gray, you are really a good boy!"

"But I'm world-weary sometimes."

"That's because you're too young. When you become a barefoot doctor, you'll be just fine."

In the dense, dark woods, Gray suddenly heard Onion saying good-bye to him. Before he knew it, the old man was gone. All at once, Gray felt nervous. Just then, the ancient mountain dragon in his basket stirred and made a rustling noise. What lively herbs! Where were they so impatient to go? The herbs calmed him. Suddenly he saw the familiar path where he had walked with Dad when he was a child . . .

"Gray, you are very much like a real herbalist now!"

His dad greeted him at the door—something he had never done before.

Gray set the basket down. Lying on the bamboo recliner, he felt relaxed from head to foot.

His father looked through his herbs and commented, "Niulan Mountain was generous to you."

"Dad, I plan to go to the mountains every other day."

"Really?" Dad looked at him. "You can only do what you can."

"I know. I don't feel tired at all. I want to exercise my will."

"Exercise the will? Are you really going to do that? This is frightening!"

Gray didn't dare look at Dad. He didn't understand what Dad meant. He had only blurted out that he wanted to exercise his will—why was Dad making such a fuss? Were there dangerous wild animals in the mountains? He'd never heard that.

In the evening, lying in bed, Gray recalled his adventure with Onion on the mountain. Was it a real python? Of course it was. But when he saw it for the last time, the wounds on its body had seemingly healed completely. What kind of self-healing ability was that? Somehow as he thought and thought, he felt that the old man and the snake had some kind of mutual understanding. Gray envied Old Onion because he could walk back and forth in the dark forest like an immortal. No wonder Dad had asked him to do acupuncture for Onion. Perhaps Dad was giving him an opportunity to learn from Onion?

The next day, Gray went to the mountain again. With no difficulty, he collected a lot of dominoes. This spooky herb was a cure for tuberculosis. Gray attributed his success to his liking the shape of this plant. He was particularly attracted by the mysterious little dots on its leaves. Could the dots be the historical records of Yun Village and Niulan Mountain? And they could actually cure disease! This sort of thing aroused infinite reverie in him.

"Gray, you are really remarkable. You've learned so fast," said Mrs. Yi appreciatively.

"But I don't think I can be a doctor."

"It—it doesn't matter. You'll get used to it. Most doctors aren't born to be doctors."

"Thank you, Mrs. Yi. I think there's a huge difference between you and me."

"Don't take me as a benchmark. I also got where I am through practice, and even now, I still feel inferior. Just do your best. That you like herbs so much is a powerful advantage. I didn't like being a barefoot doctor at first, either, but I was curious about human birth, so I've been doing this work ever since. I have no intention of giving this up."

While working in the garden, Gray thought to himself, Were the herbs in the garden and those on the mountains growing because they loved the sick? Why did he love herbs but not the sick? Recalling his experience with Old Onion, he felt that he had taken a great interest in the old man, but it wasn't love, at least not the love that Mrs. Yi had for her patients. It was instinctive fear that had driven him to strike the snake. Had he felt something besides fear? He wasn't sure. He wasn't well enough educated to figure out such a complicated question. When Mrs. Yi told him to adapt to this profession gradually, was she pinning her hopes on him? But she didn't try to come after him when he left last time without saying good-bye. Now he felt a vague impulse to do acupuncture for Old Onion and see what kind of mystery the old man's body was. Onion complained of pain in his back and legs, but he didn't seem to be in pain when he was entangled with the python.

Mr. Yi came back from the field. He said to Gray, "Grandpa Onion is going on a trip. He wanted me to tell you that he wouldn't return for a while."

"Why tell me?"

"I don't know. He may regard you as his grandson. This old man knows herbs better than Mrs. Yi! Mrs. Yi learned from him."

"My goodness! Yun Village is full of hidden talents."

After work, Gray walked home with his head down. On the way, he suddenly heard Spoon talking: "Some things look good, but they aren't."

He raised his head and looked all around. He saw no one.

Was Spoon speaking to him from far away? Was he in a good position now, or not? Spoon hadn't been gone long, but his memories of her had faded. Gray was surprised: Was he himself a cold-blooded animal? Indeed, only herbs excited him now. After two trips to the mountain, he realized that he was still a son of Niulan Mountain. On the mountain, just a quiet passion was what he wanted most. Now Old Onion was much more important to him than Spoon. Day and night, he involuntarily recalled the adventure with Onion as if he had been possessed. Grandpa Onion wanted him to know that he had left. Did he mean to leave Niulan Mountain to him—a new hand—to deal with alone?

Sitting in the dark bedroom, he thought about the hint Old Onion had given him.

"Gray, why don't you turn on the light?" said his dad, standing by the door.

"I want to clear my mind."

"Have you got an idea, then?"

"No. Especially about the python. Did Grandpa Onion summon it?"

"Very likely. Grandpa Onion can do anything."

His dad went into the living room. Gray felt a chill. There was one more thing that he couldn't figure out: Grandpa Onion was usually a dirty old widower who smelled bad. Why did he change into a different person on the mountain? Was he usually disguised? But as far as he could remember, the old man never pretended or told lies. He wanted to go to his house to find out the truth, but the old man had gone away.

Gray saw a shadow swaying at the window and went over there.

"It's you, Spoon!" he said excitedly. "Come on in."

"I won't come in. Do you miss me?"

"How can you ask such a question? Of course I do."

"But it doesn't do any good, right? I've got to go. Bye!"

"Good-bye." Although Gray opened his mouth, he said this silently. Strangely enough, once Spoon left, he didn't think about her much. He was thinking about Grandpa Onion. Years later, when he was old, would he be like Grandpa Onion? If only that were true! Grandpa Onion could walk around in the dense forest just as easily as if he were at home. The woods were his second home. The python had probably made a deal with him. So was it possible that what had appeared in front of him was just a show—a false performance that had become true? Gray still remembered his despair at that time. He had brandished the hoe and nearly injured his own feet. At that moment he felt that it was not the old man who was going to die, but himself—the python was so scary. The feeling was so real.

Another person appeared at the window. It was not Spoon this time but an old woman.

"May I help you?" Gray asked.

"You've brought out all those old things by going up the mountain. I'm your second aunt on your mother's side."

"Auntie! They said you were lost . . . It's been years!"

"It wasn't true. How could I get lost? I just like to amuse myself in the mountains." The woman giggled.

"So do I, Auntie. Will we see each other in the mountains?" he said earnestly.

"It's up to you. Gray, will you become an old mountain man someday?"

"You mean like you and Grandpa Onion? That's what I dream of being!"

"I've heard from Grandpa Onion that you're going to be a barefoot doctor. If so, I'll see you around."

With that, Second Aunt disappeared from the window. After a while, Gray saw a little light flashing on that road. Was it the torch that Auntie was carrying? It turned out that she had been in the mountains all along. This was good news for everyone. He hoped he would run into her in the mountains, but he was a little afraid because he wasn't sure she was a real person. Maybe she had become a mountain spirit. He had heard old people say that the girls in Yun Village were very wild, and if they were dissatisfied with their lives, they would disappear. But he didn't know anyone who had disappeared and then returned later to visit, as Second Aunt had just done.

"Gray, are you still awake? Who are you talking to?" he heard his dad say.

"Second Aunt."

"That's good, go on talking with her. She's a little lonely in the mountains."

"So you know she's in the mountains."

"I've known this right along. Now that you've become a barefoot doctor, you're going to the mountains all the time . . ."

Dad's voice grew thin, as if he had gone far away. Where was he talking?

In the end, Gray couldn't keep his eyes open. He threw himself into bed and fell asleep. By daybreak, Auntie still hadn't let him go. She kept talking to him.

11

Something That
Mrs. Yi Can't Forget

With Yun Village's wonderful natural environment, why were there as many sick people there as in the city? Mrs. Yi had been giving this question a lot of thought. In fact, the Yun villagers paid attention to hygiene and had never eaten poisonous mushrooms. Although they were poor, their lives were not boring: all the villagers had their own hobbies and pursuits. But the diseases, mostly chronic diseases, did not leave them alone. People in Yun Village were optimistic. If they had no acute pain, they didn't think of these chronic afflictions as serious diseases. They thought of them as minor problems that most people had.

Mrs. Yi slowly figured out what caused the villagers to be sick: some people got sick because of hardships in their lives. They lacked time and the right conditions to protect their health. But most didn't have particularly hard lives. They got sick because they had been longing for something. They often wanted to achieve a certain level of success in their endeavors. Though they couldn't explain what success was, everyone understood it. Communicating with each other stimulated everyone to demand more of themselves. Whatever they were doing—farming, making tofu, hairdressing, or building houses—the villagers worked so hard day and night that their health gradually deteriorated. It was only after getting old that they started paying attention to their health. Some of them took a turn for the better. The only thing others could do was change their attitude toward aging and live in peace with disease, as though they were living with friends. As Mrs. Yi saw it, those old people, such as Uncle Ma, Aunt Yossi, Tauber, and others, had the air of the ancient saints. When she delivered herbal medicines to ease their ailments, she often had pleasant, illuminating chats with them. She felt lucky: it was inspiring to be around such wise people. She used to ask herself, "What did they think of *that thing?*" Later she found the answer: they had kept it in mind all their lives, they had never allowed themselves to forget it. It was the precondition for every day's activities, and gradually they came to a thorough understanding of it. It was through associating with these elderly patients that all the doubts in her mind were resolved, and she found her own solutions in her early middle age. She probably would never fall seriously ill, yet because of benefiting from these people's experiences and wisdom, she was at ease with *that thing*. She felt blessed.

Tauber lay on the cane recliner under the pear tree in full bloom. Mrs. Yi sat beside him.

"One day last week, I felt it coming. I had finished my tea and picked up *Ancient Egyptian Civilization*. After I read a few lines, my vision blurred. Someone behind the house was calling me, 'Tauber, Tauber,' and the voice was familiar. I thought, Was that it? I didn't expect its voice to be familiar. I've enjoyed life long enough. Now it had come. I felt relieved. Then someone tugged at me, and I woke up again. I found that I was the only one in the room, and the book was still on the table. So I picked up the book and continued reading. It looks like it will be gentle. Won't it?"

"I'm sure it will, Tauber, because you've already rehearsed for it. I'm not worried at all for you. Niulan Mountain will help you. I just hope you are happy every day. Please tell me, Tauber, do you think our civilization in Yun Village is the kind of civilization that will have a future?"

"Of course. People in Yun Village are working on it, and I believe in them."

They fell silent. Later, Tauber and Mrs. Yi agreed that they would meet under the pear tree in the future after they were separated, and continue to discuss this profound topic that brought them so much happiness.

Talking with Tauber was Mrs. Yi's favorite thing to do, and she wished she could be like him someday. In general, Tauber's terminal illness was not a punishment for him but rather a reward for his hard work in life. How contented and grateful he had been during his last ten years on the mountain! The mountain had already seeped into his body and soul before he melted into it. With such a full life, what else could one want?

"Woman, did you say Tauber would give us his cabin when he died?"

"Yes. But we may not be able to enjoy it. Living in the mountains isn't convenient, especially as we get older and need help which we can't afford," Mrs. Yi said.

"Yes, we don't have that kind of money. Living in the village is just fine."

"A lot of people care about us here. Our life is so secure, and we're so good at taking care of ourselves. We'll probably never get sick even at the very end."

Mrs. Yi smiled as she daydreamed about their old age. Yun Village was home. They should be all right. People and things would never get lost in Yun Village. Hadn't even Gray's second aunt returned to visit? At night, the mountains were so alive! Tauber was blessed.

"Oh—Ah—!" Mrs. Yi groaned.

"What's the matter? What happened, woman?" Mr. Yi ran over and asked.

"I tried acupuncture on myself. I was afraid Grandma Mao couldn't stand it."

"Are you sure now?" Mr. Yi's voice quivered.

"Yes, I am."

After extracting the silver needle, Mrs. Yi felt happy for Grandma Mao, and for the success of her treatment plan.

"Why didn't you try it on me?" her husband grumbled.

"I was afraid you wouldn't be able to describe the sensation precisely enough. You're not as sensitive as I am."

"That's true."

It was windy outside. When the wind blew, they always heard a lot of people walking toward the mountains and some people singing as they walked. They knew these people weren't real people, but close enough. Mrs. Yi once again felt that Niulan Mountain was "the land of joy."

"No one buried here will be lonely."

"We won't, either. The problem of finding your successor has been solved, hasn't it?"

"It's strange that I don't worry about it at all. I feel as if I know who it will be."

"That's because you have faith in Yun Village."

When the couple hugged each other and came to the window, the marching crowd had disappeared. It was very quiet except for the thin voices of the newly hatched chicks.

———

Whenever Aunt Yossi felt a little better, she sat up straight on her cane chair. Recently she'd been having more frequent pain and shorter intervals between these attacks. But she still seized these brief breaks to enjoy life. As long as she didn't give up the fight, she thought, the pain would be bearable. Every attack of pain was followed by a reprieve, and that in itself was something to be grateful for. She kept a notebook handy and made notes as soon as the interval came. At such times her mind became extremely active and clear. She was the head of the family, and she wanted to sail the boat into a safe harbor before she died.

"My dear niece, I made it again. Am I not going to die? Ha-ha."

"Maybe," Mrs. Yi said. "Anything is possible."

"I don't intend to live forever, but every time I get through it, I'm very happy, just like someone turning a profit in business. Life is amazing, isn't it? I can chat with you here again. I am very comfortable. And you brought me some more painkillers."

They held hands and gazed at each other.

"You—certainly—look—good," Mrs. Yi said.

"I woke up last night, laughing, because I heard it promising me some more days. I mean Niulan Mountain. Of course, a day is never all happiness, but every day always holds something good. Life is like this, too, isn't it?" Aunt Yossi said.

"You're a hero."

"I'm not special. Most Yun villagers are the same. Crying is not in our nature. Sitting here noting the family affairs and waiting for you to come, I feel as if I'm celebrating a festival. Ha, you've brought a merry festival to me! "

At this moment, second daughter-in-law Ginger stuck her head in the window and cried out, "Mom, I'm scared!"

"Don't be afraid, my dear, everything will be all right," Mrs. Yossi said kindly.

She turned to Mrs. Yi and said, "If I do not die this time, I will make some dumplings for you. I've asked my son to buy glutinous rice. Just now I dreamed of making dumplings."

Stretching out her arm, she asked Mrs. Yi to help her stand up. Then she began to inch her way into the yard. Ginger covered her eyes; she couldn't watch.

Mrs. Yi supported her. Filled with joy, they moved to the long wooden bench and sat down side by side.

"I'm overjoyed," the old woman whispered.

"Me, too." Mrs. Yi shivered.

At the same time, they saw a group of people happily passing by outside the gate.

"It's Grandpa Qin's relatives escorting him to the mountains. He is eighty-five years old. That's a long life," Ginger said.

"He was an experienced fisherman, and he had so many good days . . ."

Saying this, Aunt Yossi fell into a reverie. She paled.

Mrs. Yi motioned to Ginger. They gently lifted Aunt Yossi up, carried her inside, and put her into bed. Aunt Yossi's body became very light.

Mrs. Yi gave the medicine to Ginger and quietly told her how to use it. The young woman glanced sharply at her. Mrs. Yi felt the hostility and was depressed. Why did she do that? What was going on in her mind?

"I'll come again tomorrow."

"Will you still come after she dies?" Ginger asked tartly.

"Of course. That's what your mother wished. But perhaps not so often."

"This, this . . . Why? You don't have to."

"I do, because you are also my family."

"Oh, I see. Mrs. Yi, I'm afraid."

"Of what? Afraid to see dead people?"

"Yes, and I'm also afraid of death. I can't sleep at night. I think I must have a heart problem."

"Who's the doctor here?"

"You are, of course. Do you agree with me?"

"No, you're wrong. People here love you. I do."

"My heart is beating very fast. You love me? I need some time to think it over. Will you come tomorrow?"

"I will come."

Mrs. Yi looked around from a distance, and saw Ginger standing there watching her. Ah, Ginger had been married into Yun Village for so many years, yet her ideas were still very different from those of Yun villagers. Mrs. Yi shivered, she was so worried about this young woman. She wanted to shout at her, "Death is not so terrible, my dear. You're wrong!"

Walking in the field, feeling the warm south wind blowing, Mrs. Yi recalled something from the past. Once when she was about eight years old and her mother was still alive, some grown-ups were sitting outside, talking. They probably thought she was asleep in the inner room because it was late at night.

"Is she going to get better?" a neighbor asked.

"There's no cure. We have to let things run their course," her mother sighed.

She cried loudly.

Mother burst into the room and held her so tight—as if trying to push her back into the womb. "It'll be all right, it'll be all right . . . ," Mother repeated, and put a piece of rock candy in her mouth. Sucking the rock candy, she finally realized that she wouldn't die soon.

Recalling this remote past helped Mrs. Yi understand Ginger's fear. She was not a local, and her attitude toward death was different. Mrs. Yi planned to be in touch with this young woman more in the future and help her out.

"Mrs. Yi, are you going to the county town to buy medicine?"

"No, I'm going to see my old teacher." She wanted to cry.

She finally came back to the old barefoot doctor training center. She had been too busy to do that for a long time.

The old director of the center stared at her as if she were a stranger.

"Director, you are my pillar. You . . ." She was too emotional to go on.

"You used to come here frequently. But I can't remember your name right now. It doesn't matter. You've run into difficulties, haven't you?" he said, leaning close to her.

"I am Chunxiu. I used to be your favorite student. Someone in Yun Village is threatened by death. She can't adapt and lives in a hell of her own making."

"Ha-ha-ha, I remember now. Yes, you are Chunxiu, I entrusted you with my hope for the future. Did someone tell you of the pain in her heart? I think she loves you."

"But I feel she doesn't love me. She's afraid."

"That is love. You are her hope, just as you are my hope."

"Director, do people come to see you at night?"

"Yes, quite a few. It relieves my loneliness. Do you understand this, Chunxiu?"

"Yes, director, I understand now. I need to let her know that I really love her."

The old director clapped his hands and said happily, "Good, you are really the daughter of Yun Village! People are constantly coming down from the mountains, and they come here to talk to me. It will soon come."

"You're so calm!"

"It's nothing to do with being calm. I have just become familiar with them. Listen—"

Mrs. Yi didn't hear anything, but she did smell a faint odor of Lysol.

"Is there a doctor among them?" she asked.

"Of course. It's no coincidence."

The old director pointed to a box on the table and said it was a gift for her.

She opened the box carefully and saw a big handful of dried wild rose petals.

"I picked these roses for you on Niulan Mountain, but I didn't have the courage to present them to you. I was a respected director at that time . . . It doesn't matter now. They're coming for me soon, anyway. Chunxiu, I am proud of you."

The director waved Mrs. Yi away.

Sitting on the bus in tears, Mrs. Yi opened the box and sniffed the dried flowers. She imagined how happy the flowers would have been when the director picked them. How long had this love lasted? Would it last forever in the mountains? It turned out that he knew everything! At that time, she thought nobody knew the secret. Alas, how wonderful youth was! She had a presentiment that the old director would go away soon, but why was she sad? No, maybe she wasn't sad, just reluctant to let him go . . .

It was dark before she returned to Yun Village. Someone was heading up the path with a flashlight. It was the young man who was taking care of Tauber.

"How is he?"

"Perhaps the moment is near, either tonight or tomorrow."

"I have to go home first to put my things down, and then I'll go up the mountain with my husband. I want to keep him company during his last hours. Thank you for telling me that."

"Thank you, Mrs. Yi. You're Tauber's favorite person."

After eating dinner, the couple hurried up the mountain.

As they neared Tauber's cabin, they saw the light. The night birds were fluttering in the woods, squirrels were running along the path, and the mountains were a little restless. A question came to both their minds at the same time: Were these omens of the coming event? When they pushed the door open, the fragrance of fresh flowers wafted out. Oh, there wasn't a hint of depression in this atmosphere! Good for you, Tauber!

He was half-lying in bed, and the wide-mouthed vase on the table was full of wildflowers.

She held his hand and noticed that he was short of breath.

"I . . . I don't feel any pain," he said to the couple. "Many familiar people over there are calling me . . . It's good to have you here."

"We'll see you off," Mrs. Yi whispered in his ear.

"Something small came in."

"It's your bird. It also came to see you off. You are blessed," Mr. Yi said at the bedside.

"I see them. They are walking over the cliff. I'm going to sleep. Good night, you . . ."

He fell asleep. Mrs. Yi wiped the cold sweat from his forehead with a towel. Mr. Yi dressed him in new pajamas and new cloth shoes.

The couple could see no suffering in Tauber's calm expression. Outside the house, all kinds of birds and animals clamored, as if a festival were starting.

The door opened, and the young man who had been taking care of Tauber came in, followed by several other men. The young man said that they were all Tauber's friends, coming to see him. They looked at him one last time and agreed to take him into the mountain the next afternoon. One older man said admiringly, "It was a pleasant and refreshing departure."

Going down the mountain and returning home, Mrs. Yi felt the clear night sky open up. Everything was quiet except for the tiny insects. She sighed, "What a dignified death!"

"Nothing could be more touching," her husband agreed.

Beside the herb garden, the couple saw the weasel. It was lying on the ground, dead. Next to it was the black-and-white chicken, also dead. The chicken's neck was snapped off, but they found no wound on the weasel's body. How could it be dead?

They went into the house to fetch a basin, and placed the two dead animals in it. They would bury them the next day.

"We need to pull together," Mr. Yi said.

Looking at her husband, Mrs. Yi felt her heart tremble with love.

She didn't expect to be as lucky as Tauber when she died. That day was still far off, and she was determined to wait calmly. Right now, she had a lot of work to do. She had no time to grieve.

12
Mia Is Taking Off

Mia diligently taught herself medicine and herbs, and she went with Mrs. Yi twice to deliver babies. Her performance was remarkable. She was neither nauseated at the sight of blood nor frantic. Mrs. Yi was secretly surprised by this young assistant's inner strength and capability. She felt that Mia was much better than she had been at the same age. She asked, "What did you feel, Mia?"

Mia thought for a moment, then said, "I felt myself being born."

"A perfect metaphor!"

On the way back, Mia had so much to say to Mrs. Yi, but she didn't know how. Mrs. Yi's determined face while delivering babies was freeze-framed in her mind. She couldn't help being excited as she recalled the moment. She murmured, "Yun Village . . ."

When Mrs. Yi heard her, she laughed and said, "Yun Village is not the only place with barefoot doctors. The old director told me that barefoot doctors were once practicing in every corner of the vast countryside. Although many places are better off now, and villagers can go to the cities for treatment, the old occupation hasn't disappeared."

At the intersection, they separated. Mia was reluctant to part with her mentor.

"Mrs. Yi, do you think my plan to cultivate the barren hill is feasible?"

"Yes. But this kind of work requires unshakable determination."

Mia walked very fast. She was so overcome with emotion today. Her heart had beat like a drum when she saw a baby born. It had been so exciting, so intense that she was speechless when she entered her cousin Chunli's house. That's where she was staying. Chunli gave her a cup of tea; she drank it silently.

"I saw a lot of things today," Mia said at last. "I saw the history of Yun Village from the mother in labor. I never cared about that before. We were nervous, but we knew exactly what to do. I was surprised by my own performance. This was probably because of Mrs. Yi. She's closer than my own mother, and I could follow her to the ends of the earth . . . The woman in labor was so beautiful."

"You and Mrs. Yi are very much alike," Chunli said with a smile.

"No, not at all. She is unique. Now if I close my eyes and think of her, I don't know how to describe her. I lag far behind her." Mia closed her eyes.

"I love Mrs. Yi, too—love her from a distance."

"I really feel happy now."

They went outside for a walk around the pond. The frogs in the pond began singing in unison, and the smell of procreation was everywhere.

"People say our Yun Village has very strong vitality," said Chunli proudly.

"History unfolded before my eyes in the delivery room. I'm going home tomorrow. I really don't want to leave Mrs. Yi. But I miss Milan, too. Oh, dear."

"You can always come again. Do you see the lights on the mountain? They were hung there by a friend of Tauber's. They were business partners, and born in the same year. He got here too late to see Tauber. He stayed in the log cabin, and hung the lights in the woods. He thought that at midnight he could follow the lights to meet his old friend," Chunli said.

"These lights are much brighter than ordinary lamps! They will probably come into our dreams. When I was a kid, I once fell into a pond; in that moment I saw the same bright lights. Oh, their friendship is so moving! Yun Village is great."

"Deserted Village is the same. When you become a barefoot doctor and your herb hill is thriving, you'll discover the mysterious greatness of your village."

"Thank you for saying that, Chunli. You're the one who set me on the right track!"

The next day, carrying her belongings, Mia was in high spirits as she went home by bus.

The rosy-faced girl next to her was younger. She told Mia that she was going to Blue Mountain. There was a clinic at the foot of Blue Mountain. The old doctor in the clinic had fallen ill and could die at any time. She was going to learn medicine from him. Mia asked her where she got the information, and she told her it came from a medical journal. Mia mentioned the name of a medical journal she had borrowed from Mrs. Yi. The girl confirmed that it was the very one, and this piece of news was in the most recent issue.

"I'm taking everything I need with me. I'm prepared to stay for a long time, maybe forever. My mother was worried about me. She was in tears when I left, as if I would die over there."

"What do you think of being a doctor?" Mia asked.

"I don't know. I just heard it was tough. That's the kind of life I want to live."

Unlike Gray, this girl looked very stubborn, and her eyes were determined. She was a bit like Mrs. Yi.

The girl would have to ride the bus several more stops after Mia got off. She said it would be dark before she could reach Blue Mountain, and then she had to find the clinic in the dark. But she believed that there would be good people to help her.

"My heart has flown to the foot of Blue Mountain!" she said.

"You are very brave! You're a wonderful girl!"

After getting off the bus, Mia was still feeling warm all over because of encountering the girl. In the vast wilderness, at the end of the horizon, she saw many little men coming toward her. Were these people coming from a certain legendary clinic? Was the place where Mrs. Yi had been trained a branch of that clinic?

When Mia was a child, her family was better off. She had kept a pet white rabbit. One night, the rabbit was attacked by a feral cat. Mia woke up and blocked the large cat in the hallway. The feral cat went mad and bit her leg. Mia was enraged, shouting and kicking at the cat until Mother came over and beat it away with a pole. The rabbit died, and it took more than a month for Mia's leg to heal. Her mother said, "How brave you are! You're a wonderful little girl!"

On her way home, Mia recalled this bloody tragedy and her feelings at that time. Suddenly she realized that she was destined to choose her career today.

Standing at the end of the road were Lohan and Milan. Milan looked a little thinner.

Gathering Milan into her arms, Mia turned her face and wept.

"Good news, Mia. Three young people volunteered to help you with the project. One of them is experienced in gardening," Lohan said.

"Lohan, dear, I owe you so much," Mia choked up.

"Don't say that. That's what my life is all about."

As they passed by the hill, they heard a lot more noise than usual.

Not until Mia was sitting at the table did she feel that her soul had come home.

In the dark, she told Lohan about the girl she met on the bus.

"She's walking alone at the foot of the mountain at night. *Fear* is not a word in her vocabulary. She's a certain type of person, but I can't tell what that type is. Meeting her wasn't just a coincidence. Do you feel it, Lohan?"

"Yes, I do. I wish I could see the old doctor. What you just said reminded me of something. I've noticed that those of us who live in the countryside always have a chance to meet a certain type of person, and I can't say what type that is, either, but I knew what you meant right away. Mrs. Yi falls into that category. Now you, Mia, are in the process of becoming like these people. There may be more than one of that kind of clinic: there may be many more scattered around the country, hidden in the foothills of various mountains."

"You're so nice, Lohan. Good night." Mia suddenly fell asleep.

Her dreams were uneventful. Under the gray sky, she walked ahead.

When Mia saw Gray again, he looked much different. His shoulders were broader, and there was a thin line on his forehead. Mia felt that his palms had grown larger and his joints were starting to protrude. He's shaping up, Mia thought.

He was working in the herb garden. There was a passion in his skillful movements, as if the herbs were his lovers. Mia was awestruck.

"You're here." He straightened up and said, "Mia, do you need my help? I can fill your hill with herbal fragrances!"

"Of course. I'm an amateur. I need an expert like you."

"No one is an amateur in this line of work, Mia. Once you start working, you'll learn everything on your own. That's what Mrs. Yi said," Gray said brightly.

"Gray, you look completely different." Mia's eyes were full of admiration.

"Mia, I'd like to ask you a question. You don't have to answer it. Will a true love, like the love between you and Lohan, ever change?"

"I'm willing to answer you: I think everything in the world may change. But love—if it is true love—may not change so easily. Gray, why do you have to break up with Spoon for the sake of your career? What a shame!"

"She's the one who wants to break up with me. She can't put up with my studying medicine."

"I'm sorry, I shouldn't have asked. Good-bye, Gray."

This encounter with Gray shook Mia greatly. There weren't enough barefoot doctors in the world, and they were facing endless challenges with little help . . . Gray had held out so far, but could he hold out to the end? Had he paid too big a price in sacrificing his love for the cause? Mia had met Spoon: the girl was an ardent canna that could change Gray's temperament. But did Gray need to be changed? Life held some problems that were hard to solve, but Mia was not one to hesitate. Following the vague summons in her heart, she moved ahead.

Herbs had been planted on her hill, and they were growing well. She and Lohan often went to the hill at night, and they noticed that the voices on the hill had died away and it had become quiet. What was going on?

One time they met Yang, who was sitting on a rock smoking a pipe.

"Uncle Yang, you should come to the hill more often. I think it is upset," Mia said.

"Ah, Mia, the hill is waiting and processing," Yang said happily.

"Really? Ha, I'm relieved!"

"I told it just now, 'The couple is making a home for you! You're so lucky.'"

They invited Yang to go up the hill with them to see the herbs.

The moon was bright that night. As soon as Yang appeared among the herbs, the earth stirred. The indistinct human voices and animal voices mingled, as if saying, "Long time no see! Long time no see . . ."

Mia stood there motionless, listening so rapturously that she almost forgot that Lohan and Yang were there. She was trying hard to recall an event, but no matter how hard she tried, she could not recall it. Yang came over to her, his white beard fluttering so that he looked like an immortal in the moonlight. In a daze, Mia said to Yang, "It hasn't acknowledged us, Uncle Yang. Have we done something wrong?"

"Mia, you've done a great job! What you're doing is innovative. It can't wait to join your cause. I heard it murmuring just now."

Yang laughed and patted Mia kindly on the shoulder.

Mia let out a long sigh. She felt all her pores open up, and joy fluttered like a bird in her chest.

"Look, this is banlangen, this is, this is . . . Oh, I love these herbs so much. They're more beautiful than anything else! Come and join us in our work, Uncle Yang . . ."

"That's what I'm thinking, Mia! You're talented and ambitious! It was waiting here all along until you and Lohan came. You are its lucky star."

Lohan came over, gasping for breath. He said, "Uncle Yang, someone just pulled at my foot, right next to the field of lily turf. What's going on here? Is it trying to send me a message?"

"It's long been customary for it to send love by dragging the other's feet. It is in love with you!"

"I see. Can you tell it we love it, too?"

"It already knows. Just now it was startled awake."

The three of them sniffed the intoxicating smell of the herbs and breathed deeply. But Mia soon became restless and worried: Milan was at home. What if he woke up and no one was there? Ah, wasn't that Milan?

Over there, in the field planted in green chiretta, Milan's little figure fluttered.

"Milan . . . ," Mia cried out. Her voice was shaking.

"Don't worry," Yang said with smile. "I asked the little friends underground to bring your son here. See how happy he is!"

"What do you mean by the little friends underground?"

"The owls. Your son is so brave."

Lohan picked Milan up. Milan fell asleep again on Lohan's shoulder.

"Milan . . . He thought he was dreaming. How nice. Thank you, Uncle Yang. May I ask you a question? How many years have you been looking after this place?" Mia said.

"Maybe more than thirty years. But I can't say I was looking after it because I didn't create anything. It was never truly looked after until you came here. Listen, Mia. Do you hear all the sighs of admiration?"

Mia heard a great many people yawning, which sounded very comfortable. The hill was going to fall asleep.

When they got home and opened the door, a voice came from the darkness: "There was a carnival over there tonight."

The voice sounded like the old director's. Did he know everything she was doing? She thought it was possible.

After settling Milan in bed, the couple ecstatically made love. When they climaxed, they heard the hill murmuring.

"He's still alive, he promised me," Mia said to herself before falling asleep.

13
Angelica Joins In

The girl Mia met on the bus that day was Angelica. It was dark before Angelica reached the foot of Blue Mountain. She asked directions along the way. Blue Mountain was high and gloomy in the night, and the wind from the mountains was a little eerie. As she scrutinized the majestic mountain in front of her, she was at a loss—no one could tell her where the clinic was, much less anything about Dr. Lin Baoguang. But Angelica wasn't panic-stricken: sizing up the immediate situation, she decided to spend the night in the open air and look for the village the next day.

Near the edge of the mountain stood a maple grove with dead leaves all over the ground. Angelica gathered up the leaves and sat down on them. She took out her dry food and her water bottle, and ate slowly. When she finished eating, she fell asleep contentedly.

Every now and then, someone beside her would ask the same question: "Are you here to see Dr. Lin? Why are you looking for him?"

Angelica gave an impassioned answer to the man's question. She felt herself becoming eloquent, but she couldn't hear what she was saying. In this way, passionately and somewhat mysteriously, she explained her motives for coming to Blue Mountain.

"Who are you, please?" she asked, turning to the invisible man.

"Ha-ha, haven't you figured it out? Who else do you think I could be?"

"Are you Lin—Dr. Lin Baoguang?" she asked hesitantly.

The man made no answer. In fact, Angelica felt that no one was near her, and she was not fully awake. She decided to go back to sleep. For some reason a vague hope rose within her, and she fell asleep with the rising hope.

When she awoke in broad daylight, birds were singing in the trees, and a mountain spring was gurgling to her left. A man was chopping wood not far from her. Angelica jumped up in excitement.

"Good morning. Do you live near here, sir?" Angelica asked loudly.

Wearing a dark-blue work shirt, the man came out of the woods. He looked at her and said, "I live fifteen kilometers from here next to the river. I'm preparing firewood for the old people's home for the winter. And you? Are you looking for Dr. Lin Baoguang?" he asked with a smile.

"Ah, how did you guess that?"

"People who look like you come in search of the old doctor all the time. But the old doctor has been missing lately. Some people say he is dead, but I feel he is still alive. Have you seen the clinic?"

Angelica was taken aback and looked in the direction he pointed out. Sure enough, she saw a small gray-brick house deep in the woods. This was great! After thinking for a second, she asked uneasily, "Sir, you say people who look like me often come to see Dr. Lin. What do you mean by 'look like' me?"

"That's an interesting question. It's just my personal feeling. I think you all look alike."

"I see. Good-bye, sir!"

Angelica walked happily toward the little building.

When she pushed the door open, she smelled herbs. This was one of those houses with a front room and a back room. In the front room were a large table, some chairs, and a filing cabinet. Angelica figured this was an examination room. There was nothing in the back room but an empty wooden bed. When Angelica opened the glass door of the filing cabinet to look at the files, she found that the papers were damp. It seemed that no one had lived here for a long time. Her eyes clouded over, and she couldn't read the words on the papers. She wondered, There were no herbs in the room, so where did the smell come from? Just then, someone knocked gently on the door. It was the woodcutter.

"I was a little worried so I came to check on you. What do you think of this place?"

"Is this house for me to stay in?" asked Angelica, bewildered.

"Who else? Look, there's a fireplace. I'll stack some firewood here for you. Here's a kerosene lamp, and here are some matches. Ha-ha, I have to go now. I'll bring more firewood for you tomorrow. Have you seen the bedding? It's inside this cloth wrapper."

Angelica suddenly spotted a large bundle of things hanging from the beam.

"What's your name, sir? Why did you bring me firewood?"

"My surname is Firewood. Please call me Uncle Firewood. Why did I bring you firewood? Because Dr. Lin's cause is mine as well. That's what I think anyway. Good-bye now. I'll come again tomorrow."

Angelica took the bedding out of the wrapper, and carried it to the wooden bed. Everything was new—sheets, a quilt, and a pillow. They all smelled of starch. There was also a mosquito net. And when she turned around, she saw the bamboo poles for hanging the mosquito net. What was going on here? Was there someone else who cared about Dr. Lin's cause? Angelica excitedly hung up the mosquito net, and all of a sudden the back room became animated. A face appeared at the window. It was a woman.

"Good morning, Miss Angelica. I've brought you some pancakes," said the woman.

"Good morning, ma'am! Thank you so much! But I haven't done anything yet."

"You're welcome. We all knew you were coming, and we knew your name when you were still on the way. We live in the historic Blue Village. My name is Blue."

Blue smiled, revealing her white teeth. She was an attractive woman.

Angelica was hungry. Moved to tears, she ate two big pancakes, and then wiped her hands on the white towel. Blue was looking at her curiously.

"Miss Angelica, look," she said, standing next to the window. "That little white hut over there is your bathroom."

"I still don't understand," Angelica said, blinking. "It's like I'm in a dream. What's going on? How did you know about me?"

"You subscribe to the medical journal, don't you? We sent out messages and you received them. What a splendid way to communicate. When I was a child, there wasn't much information in our poor mountain village, so I waited and waited with a few other people until we totally despaired . . . What am I rattling on about?"

She laughed and said she had to return to the village.

Angelica walked her to the end of the path and watched her disappear into the woods. How strange! There was no path in the woods. Where had she gone? Three black ravens, not at all afraid of people, came and pecked at Angelica's shoelaces to loosen them, and then flew away together. Watching the scene in surprise, Angelica laughed out loud. When she bent over to tie her shoelaces, she saw a crystal stone. There was a dark hole right in the middle of the huge crystal. She looked at it, shivered, and sat down on the ground.

"Hello," said a middle-aged man above her.

"Who are you, please?" Angelica was still shaking.

"I am the publisher of the medical journal, and I am delighted to see that you have made contact with the villagers! You, Miss Angelica, are our hope."

"Thank you for the compliment. But I don't understand. Actually, I haven't made contact with the person I want to find. I'm still looking . . . But what is this?"

She pointed at the dark hole, eyes wide with horror.

The man smiled and said, "So you've found it! You'll be all right. On my way over here, I was worrying that you might change your mind. I didn't expect you to be so mature."

"No, I'm not mature at all, I haven't figured out—"

"No need to be modest. You've done very well. I have to get back to deal with the printing arrangements. We'll meet again. Would you like that?"

"Of course, yes!" said Angelica, with tears in her eyes. "Today—oh, is it morning already? How beautiful it is today! May I have your name, please?"

"My name is Wind. You may imagine me as a gust of wind. Look—"

The man disappeared.

When Angelica returned to the cabin, an old man was sitting at the diagnostic table.

"Grandpa, are you a patient? Are you waiting for Dr. Lin?" Angelica asked him.

"I'm waiting for you, the one who's going to be a doctor," said the old man kindly.

"Oh, thank you! I'll do my best."

"Why don't you sit down and feel my pulse?"

The old man extended his arm to her. Angelica involuntarily pressed her fingers on his pulse as if she were a doctor. Touching that powerful pulse, Angelica immediately saw farmhouses, cattle, and green rice paddies. She and the old man looked at each other across the hill. She heard her own thin voice.

"Grandpa, I am Angelica. Do you hear . . ."

Then, with a splash, she returned to the table and faced an empty chair.

What a magical pulse, thought Angelica. This place was like a kingdom with secret passageways to all parts of the world. In front of the window, acacia trees peered inside, as if to tell her a great secret, or to warn her . . . The old man might or might not have heard her, but Angelica felt this was communication that stirred the heart. Who was Dr. Lin Baoguang?

Without giving it any thought, she turned again to the filing cabinet to look through the files. The words had disappeared from the pages; now the papers were all blank. A current swept through Angelica's body, and she felt connected to this house. "Mom, don't you worry," she said quietly. "I'm learning to be a doctor. Many people count on me."

In a desk drawer was a stethoscope. When she put it on, she heard thunder and rain. Another man was sitting at the diagnostic table.

Angelica looked at him: this man had no distinct silhouette.

He was giggling.

"Do you think I'm naive and ridiculous, brother?"

"No, not at all. I'm just happy for you. We love you so much!"

"Thank you. But I haven't done anything for you folks yet."

"You don't have to do anything. It's enough that you're here."

"Why are you leaving so soon?"

"I just came to check on you, and now that I know you're all right, I can go. Good-bye."

Leaning against the door, Angelica saw an old man walking briskly up the hill. This man didn't look sick, so he couldn't be Dr. Lin.

"How should I start practicing medicine?" Angelica asked herself.

Although this visitor and Blue had both said that she didn't have to do anything—it was enough that she was here—Angelica still felt a little uneasy. She wanted to go to the mountains to collect herbs, but she was afraid of losing her way. Besides, she didn't know anything about medicine yet, so her top priority was to find Dr. Lin Baoguang.

"Why don't you go to the village to look for him? Everyone in the village knows him," Blue said.

But Blue had left without telling Angelica how to get to the village.

Angelica thought for a while and then set out with a bag on her back. She walked along the path beside the mountain and did not see anyone for a long time. Some small birds with colorful necks chirped in front of her. These sounds lifted her spirits. There were trees all around, but no houses in sight.

She was a little tired, but she had to keep going. Where was Blue Village?

"Blue Village is the kind of place that exists in people's hearts."

The same person was talking to her again. Angelica assumed it was Dr. Lin Baoguang.

"Yes, you are right . . . ," she responded inwardly.

So what would a village look like if it were in people's hearts?

Angelica finally saw a man sitting on a stone stool by the roadside. Apparently he was suffering from abdominal swelling. He gazed at the fallen leaves on the ground, and he looked happy. Angelica heard Blue talking somewhere.

"He's my husband, a true optimist."

Angelica thought this optimist would have no interest in her. But when she passed by, the man said, "Are you here to replace old Dr. Lin Baoguang?"

Angelica stood still, her heart surging.

"How can I—replace? Can you please tell me where he is?"

"No." He shook his head. "Sorry. Nobody knows where he is. We respect his privacy."

"I stayed in his clinic last night."

"That means you're his replacement," he said reproachfully.

"Maybe I am. But how can I . . . I don't know medicine."

"We need more than medicine." He pointed at his bulging stomach.

But Angelica had no idea what he meant. Blue Mountain and this Blue Village were so profound.

"Our illnesses aren't so painful. Okay, good-bye."

With that, he lowered his eyes.

As Angelica walked on, she whispered, "Optimist, optimist . . ."

Gradually, she lost her confidence. Would she ever arrive

at Blue Village? There were always the same woods, always the same pattern of stone roads. The small birds with colorful necks were far away; she could only faintly hear their call. She consoled herself that she would not get lost—she could always go around the mountain and return to her starting point. Why should she be worried? As soon as she got flustered, she grew angry with herself all over again. Even the man with ascites sat calmly at the roadside, while she was a healthy young person—why panic? As if arguing against herself, when she saw a path into the mountains, she took it.

But what kind of path was this? It was narrowing. Before she had walked a kilometer, it was totally blocked by a tyrannical parasitic banyan. Angelica had to turn around and head back. She realized that at the foot of Blue Mountain one couldn't wander around as one wished. She had to either feel her way forward or retreat.

She returned to her original spot. It was strange to see Blue's husband again. He was still sitting at the roadside but not in the same place. He was playing with pebbles. He tossed the shiny pebbles in the air and caught them one by one.

"Mister, can you tell me why I can't find Blue Village?"

"It's pointless to look for it." He stopped playing and looked at her sternly. "I am Blue Village. Couldn't you recognize me?"

"I—oh, I kind of get it now. I love you, mister."

He smiled and motioned to her to keep walking.

Angelica walked for a while. Suddenly she felt her heart filling with joy. "I love Blue Village so much! Oh, I—" How she longed to tell someone! But there was no one near her, only a small bird hopping in the tree.

Blue suddenly appeared on the road.

"I've brought you some food." She pointed at the basket.

"I've been out for a long time. How did you find me so quickly?"

"Look, isn't that your clinic?" She pointed to the right.

"Oh, so it is! It seems I've been walking around in the place I started from."

"It's all right, newcomers always do."

Blue took out steamed buns and broth from the basket and set them on a stone table beside the road.

"I can't let you bring me food all the time," said Angelica, embarrassed.

"It's a job Dr. Lin assigned to me."

Under Blue's urging, Angelica ate the buns and broth.

"Blue, may I make a request of you?" Angelica asked.

Blue avoided her gaze; she was a little uncomfortable.

"I know you want to go to the village, but it isn't a place you can go just because you want to. Ah, it's a long story . . . To tell you the truth, Angelica, we have no fixed abode. Our Blue Village is such a secret place that it can't be found on the map. Only the clinic is always here. It is the mark of Blue Village, and the treasure of Blue Mountain . . . Dr. Lin left, and you came. You now belong to Blue Mountain. You are a pearl. I have to go back now to look after my husband. He was very impressed with you."

She packed her basket and disappeared into the woods.

Angelica returned to the clinic. She'd walked a lot today, but apparently she'd just been circling around the clinic. Blue Mountain, Blue Village, the old doctor Lin Baoguang, the publisher of the medical journal, Blue and her husband . . . Angelica tried to link them together, but she couldn't find a way to do that. For some reason, the beautiful young woman she met on the bus kept appearing in her mind. Was she an insider, too? Angelica felt her blood boiling. She was transforming her life. A cause was opening up before her and waiting for her to join in. She'd been searching for this for years, hadn't she? Look at that acacia: Wasn't it sending her noontime's message?

Little birds with black crests chirped merrily.

Once more, Angelica heard the voice which she had thought was Dr. Lin's.

"When you enter the mountains, hold your head high as you walk ahead."

The sound echoed at the window, and Angelica saw the acacia tree nodding.

Angelica thought that she could not break out and arrive at Blue Village because she didn't have the faith that she could do so. If she had lived like Blue and her husband, perhaps she would have been sitting in the Blue villagers' homes and chatting with the villagers. She had been a little indecisive since childhood. This time she had surprised her mother by going away from home. What kind of life were Blue and her husband leading? Angelica couldn't tell, but she knew that they were very different from her. Angelica wasn't sure whether she would eventually fit in at Blue Village. She wished so much that old Dr. Lin Baoguang had appeared before her.

Angelica stared at the window, but the voice stopped.

In her imagination, the people in Blue Village were cooking dinner, and the cooking smoke was curling up from the kitchen chimneys in the valley. It was a bucolic scene of a farming village. She made up her mind: at sunrise the next day she would take one direction and charge into the mountains with her head held high.

Dusk came, and all kinds of little birds hopped about

among the branches. The copperwood looked very lively, but the acacia tree was a little sleepy.

"Who wants to come in?" cried Angelica mischievously.

No one answered. She took the dry food out of her knapsack and laid it on the table. Then she filled a glass of water (she believed it was spring water) from the faucet in the room. She was about to sit down to dinner.

"What a wonderful life!" she sighed.

Then she remembered Blue's husband sitting by the roadside playing with stones. She thought, Late-stage liver ascites disease was nothing to a Blue villager. A feeling of fearlessness came over her.

14
Kay Comes to Yun Village

"Just now I saw a star fall down. I think it was him."

"So shall we go to the county seat?"

"No, no. He told me not to go to his place again. He said my concern for him would make him uneasy six feet under. 'You must never come back.' That's what he said."

"We, I mean you, did just as he said."

Mrs. Yi was silent. Thinking of her old mentor who had suffered so much, she began to cry.

Her husband stroked her back and whispered, "Don't cry, woman, you're a hero far and wide. I always think that you are unbreakable. You have been tried and tested over and over, but you've never given up. Everyone dies. The wonderful old man nurtured such a remarkable student as you. He can rest in peace now."

Mrs. Yi stopped crying and turned to pack the medicine box.

"Are you going out at this late hour?"

"I'm worried about Grandma Mao. Her mood was swinging between joy and misery."

"I'll go with you."

Taking a flashlight, the couple walked out into the night. They noticed someone following them. It seemed to be a man.

"It must be Gray," Mr. Yi said with a smile. "He's observing us, trying to learn how to care about his neighbors. This boy will soon be ready."

"He has a great father," Mrs. Yi said.

The dog barked softly twice, and the couple entered the house.

Gray stood outside in the moonlight. His chest heaved with excitement.

After a while, Spoon also appeared.

"Do you mean it when you say you'll die if you leave the herb garden?" Spoon whispered to him.

"Yes."

"I've changed my mind a little. I've lost interest in life since I left you."

"Oh?"

"I'm thinking, perhaps we could live like the couple inside the house?"

"You? Could you do that?"

"I can try."

Inside, Grandma Mao groaned in her bed.

"I feel so good! I really don't want to die. Mrs. Yi, please tell me, how did this little silver needle loosen the knots in my body? I see it swimming inside me. Is that your magic power? The joy . . ."

As soon as the treatment ended, Grandma Mao turned over and got out of bed. Without using a crutch, she went straight to the table and sat down. Mrs. Yi looked at the old woman anxiously.

"When you stuck the needle in me a moment ago, I went back to my old home. So many acquaintances gathered around me, and they said to me in unison, 'Grandmother, you're home now. You'll be all right.' I lay in bed, crying. It was so comfortable . . ."

On the way home, the couple walked slowly, looking at the moon. They wanted to prolong their walk.

So many years had passed. Although Yun Village now looked different, its core remained the same as it had always been.

Mr. Yi sighed softly, "What a magical job!"

Mrs. Yi turned away to smile gently. She said to herself, "He was right, the old director would rest in peace." She thought of earlier years when the old director had been young and vigorous.

"The knot inside me has also loosened," she said.

"A ball of phosphorescence has been watching us from the mountain for a long time," her husband said.

"Director, sir, your cause is making great progress in Yun Village!" Mrs. Yi shouted toward the mountain.

They got home at last. At the gate, the black-and-white chicken came staggering out to meet them as if it were drunk.

"This chicken is very romantic," Mrs. Yi said.

"It makes me feel ashamed. Why can't I face the fact that it's also needy?" Her husband was distressed. She comforted him: "It happens all the time. You're human, and humans are too complicated. People can't easily see the animals' motives."

What a lovely night. Before falling asleep, Mrs. Yi kept thinking, The chicken has seen the weasel. Life goes on and on. Niulan Mountain had given these two small animals a chance.

For a long time they hadn't heard anything about the death of the old director. Quite the opposite: an acquaintance unexpectedly told them the old director was still alive and was getting better.

When Mrs. Yi heard this, she clapped her hands in delight. She said to her husband, "The director couldn't bear to leave his cause. For now, all he can do is pray for us. To tell you the truth, sometimes when I recall the past, I wonder how we got through all those years. We always worked independently in the village, but suddenly two fine young people came to join us. It's like a dream. I never expected that."

"But I did." Squinting, Mr. Yi said, "You didn't expect it because you're too busy, but I have a lot of free time. I've been observing, and so I realized long ago that this was possible."

"Then tell me, why did they join us?"

"Because they were desperate. They probably had been desperate for a long time."

"Oh, darling, you're so perceptive."

"I'm an ordinary person. You're the one with talent in our family. You've become the light of our Yun Village that illuminates the young generation's hearts. Ha-ha, am I right?"

"But my heart is often in the dark. How could I illuminate others'?"

"You became a light without being aware of it. It happens all the time."

"Okay, let's drop this subject and get down to business."

There was so much to do. These days, Mrs. Yi had more and more energy. She no longer felt exhausted, and she looked prettier than ever before. She jokingly referred to herself as a "young-old." When she was free, she looked at Niulan Mountain and recalled the times she had spent on it. She felt that the mountain had made her a certain promise.

In the middle of the night, a white-haired old man often recited a spell for her. She knew the spell was inviting her to go to the mountains. She couldn't make up her mind whether to do that or not. She had misgivings: What if she met the director in the mountains, wouldn't she be breaking her promise? Niulan Mountain had great confidence in her, but that didn't mean she was allowed to burst into the mountains. Communicating from a distance was more beneficial for both body and mind. She heard herself saying to Mia in the darkness, "Your son is a priceless treasure." Moved by her own voice, she wept. What strong material this beautiful young woman was made of!

"Darling, what's under the ground?"

"It's moonlight all over—no, it's Niulan Mountain."

"You're so good at guessing. I can't do that."

"Go to sleep. You have a lot of work to do tomorrow."

"Okay."

They fell asleep at almost the same time. That often happened.

In the morning, as soon as Mrs. Yi opened her eyes, she said, "Mia's son is really priceless."

"Sure he is," her husband responded, with his eyes still closed.

Outside the window the cuckoo was calling, urgently.

After eating breakfast and tidying up the house, Mrs. Yi went to Aunt Yossi's home.

As if by a miracle, the cancer cells in Aunt Yossi's body had recently stopped making trouble. Mrs. Yi had even stopped treating her. Of course the old woman was still weak.

As soon as Mrs. Yi walked into the yard, she heard Ginger's loud voice: "Mother, you can't trust the herbal medicine. And not the doctor, either! I've been watching your treatment for a long time, and I've always thought something was wrong with it—"

"Nonsense!" Aunt Yossi said weakly.

Mrs. Yi hurriedly faked two coughs. Her face was burning.

Aunt Yossi held her hand, and said, "I feel no pain at all today. Oh, thank God, is it because I saved the elm tree?"

Foreboding surged up in Mrs. Yi's heart.

"My daughter-in-law doesn't think clearly. She didn't know what she was talking about. She's embarrassed and went to hide. You don't mind, my dear, do you?"

"Of course not. Ginger is a strong woman. She takes good care of you. How kind she is! I appreciate her very much."

"My day is coming soon."

"Yes. You may rest assured that I will take care of everything."

"I trust you 120 percent. It's amazing that I feel no pain at the last moment. Maybe it's the magic of those herbs. I'm going to give you that lean-to to store herbs, and Ginger agreed. I've put it in writing. Oh, how comfortable I feel . . . My dear niece, give me a hug. I'm going to close my eyes now. On the other side of the bridge are the mountains. All the people from my old home are coming. I can't see them clearly, but I can smell them. My home village produces mugwort, and they all smell of mugwort. Son, are you here, too? Take my hand . . . This is Mrs. Yi."

Aunt Yossi passed away contentedly in Mrs. Yi's arms.

Weeping uncontrollably, Ginger told everyone who came to the house of her mother-in-law's virtues.

"She was an indomitable woman, not even afraid of death . . . I've never seen anyone like her. My heart died with her—what can I do?"

She wailed loudly, making everyone nervous. Finally, her husband had had enough and dragged her away.

Mrs. Yi looked at Aunt Yossi dressed in her burial clothes. For a moment, the old woman opened her eyes and made a face, then closed her eyes again. The room felt creepy. Ginger, of course, was showing her devotion to her mother-in-law, but to Mrs. Yi there was always a hidden meaning in Ginger's words. Was this connected with the lean-to that

Aunt Yossi gave her? Ginger's incoherent complaints terrified Mrs. Yi, and she almost fainted. Luckily her husband caught her.

"Let's go home," he whispered.

Her husband gave her his arm as they left. Outside, Mrs. Yi's tension was allayed only after she took a few big gulps of fresh air.

"I never had a grudge against anyone," she said.

"Her words came from love. She loves her mother-in-law as much as you do."

"I can understand her. Aunt Yossi did embody the age-old character of Yun Village."

While Mrs. Yi was talking about Aunt Yossi, she felt a rough palm stroke her cheek. She sank into memory and made up her mind: since her close friend had entrusted her rather eccentric daughter-in-law to her, she would do her best to carry out her wishes. Since Ginger loved her mother-in-law so much, the dead woman could act as a bridge between the two of them. Mrs. Yi regretted that she had been a bit stiff in her interactions with this young woman. As a barefoot doctor, she did not really understand human feelings. Compared with Aunt Yossi, she was still a student.

She heard murmurs from Niulan Mountain.

Not long after Aunt Yossi's body was taken to Niulan Mountain, a person who had been missing for years suddenly broke into Mrs. Yi's life. She and Mrs. Yi had been close friends when they were young. Her name was Kay, and she had been a capable young woman with endless energy. She and Mrs. Yi had quickly become the backbone of the clinic. But then tragedy struck. When the girl climbed up a cliff to collect herbs, she lost her footing, fell down, and broke her spine. From then on, she was confined to a wheelchair.

While Kay was recuperating, Mrs. Yi spent many days and nights with her. She worried a lot about her friend's injury and racked her brain to think of ways to ease her pain.

One day when Kay was feeling better, she washed her face and combed her hair early in the morning, waiting for Mrs. Yi to come.

"I'm going to the South China Sea tomorrow," she told Mrs. Yi with a smile. "It's a secret. I'll leave early in the morning; there's no way you can see me off."

Mrs. Yi stared at her friend for a long while, and then blurted out a question: "Kay, do you regret being a barefoot doctor?"

"A little. But I've figured it out. Maybe I'm not cut out for it. You're the one best suited to being a barefoot doctor. I used to envy you a lot. Good-bye, I'll always be your friend."

Mrs. Yi did not see Kay off. Colleagues at the medical center said Kay was missing. Mrs. Yi had never received any news of her. In sorrow, she had buried the memory of this friend.

Now she arrived while Mrs. Yi was grinding herbs with a roller in the back room. Kay limped into the room on crutches. Her skin was very dark, and the wrinkles on her face were as deep as if carved by a knife. Was this really Kay? Of course. She called Mrs. Yi "Chunxiu."

The two women embraced and cried.

Mrs. Yi treated Kay to tea and cookies.

Kay said quietly, "Just now I rented a house in your village for a clinic. I've been engaged in this work all these years—what else could I do? I will work with you."

"Oh, Kay . . . Oh, Kay . . . ," Mrs. Yi said tearfully.

"I came back to you because the fishing village where I

was living was swept away by a tsunami. I can't bear to even think about this tragedy. I've had nightmares for the past two years."

As she spoke, Kay crisscrossed the room, and her crutches clattered. When Mrs. Yi asked her to sit down and eat, she replied, "I can't sit down."

Mrs. Yi could see that Kay was very excited and thinking clearly.

"Yun Village is lucky to have you. Kay, what are you holding?"

"I hold my destiny in my hand. See, it's jumping! I can't let go!"

She raised a fist to her eyes and gazed intently.

"I have to go back to my clinic, Chunxiu. Maybe I'll have some patients today. No, please don't walk with me. If you do, the villagers will think I'm incapable of practicing medicine on my own. In fact, I've been studying hard all these years, just like you. Soon after the injury, I realized that I was destined to be a doctor. It explained why I could ignore the danger on the cliff."

Kay left. Thinking of Kay's experience, Mrs. Yi's anxiety gave way to a smile. How had Kay struggled out of the mire of life and grasped the light? Could it have something to do with a magical herb or a silver needle? Perhaps, when she was about to abandon the world of herbs, herbs had come to haunt her and had established an even closer relationship with her? Mrs. Yi couldn't calm down for a long time. She whispered inwardly, "Kay, Kay . . . A miracle!"

The door opened—Mr. Yi was home.

"Your friend has become an expert on calluses and other foot diseases!" he said.

"Oh, you know more about her than I do!"

They looked at each other. Mrs. Yi smiled through her tears.

"Darling, why am I so emotional?"

"She's come back, hasn't she? Isn't that wonderful?"

"Yes and yes, it's great! I have to go to work now. I can't fall behind her."

Mrs. Yi went into the back room and resumed grinding the herbs. Her thoughts returned to previous years. She and Kay had saved a passerby who had had an electric shock and lost consciousness. They became very strong at that moment, quickly positioning the dying person. Chunxiu had performed CPR. It was the first time she had found the power to bring the dead back to life. Before long the man sat up by himself, grumbled for a moment, then stood up and walked away. The two girls were speechless for a long time.

"Perhaps this man was playing dead?" said Kay hesitantly.

"Perhaps, but what an inspiration it is to save someone's life!"

"There seems to be nothing we can't do."

They had laughed and joked along the road. When they reached the medical center, the director greeted them at the gate with a smile. He said they deserved an award.

"We did what we're supposed to do. Why give us an award?"

"Do you know who that man is?" the director said solemnly.

"I don't know. Does it matter?" Chunxiu was puzzled.

"He's an old widower who lives alone in the neighborhood. You performed CPR and saved his life. What a miracle! This doesn't happen every day!" The director was flushed with excitement.

"It's not a big deal," Kay and Chunxiu said together.

But the director insisted that it was a miracle. He had a

silk banner made and hung it in the girls' room. The banner was embroidered with gold characters: "Heal the wounded and rescue the dying."

Mrs. Yi remembered that Kay had shrugged and said, "Why go to all that trouble?"

What a fiery era it was! She and Kay were both burning brightly, and they felt there wasn't time enough for everything. Mrs. Yi often asked herself later, "Was it because Kay was too impatient that she fell from the cliff?" This question made Mrs. Yi's heart ache, but she couldn't help thinking about it over and over. Kay was passionate. When she saw the crag-bean vine (*Millettia reticulata*) beckon her from an earthen hole at the edge of the cliff, she climbed over without hesitation and slipped. At that time Mrs. Yi also saw the strange expression of the crag-bean vine in the wind. It was a cloudy day, and she heard someone playing an *erhu* in a nearby bamboo grove.

One time after the accident, Chunxiu climbed the cliff again and found the earthen hole. It was black inside. She summoned the courage to probe into it many times, but did not reach the crag-bean vine—the hole was empty. She shivered: Was that beautiful herb but a mirage? Did it exist or not? But she didn't dare raise this question with Kay then, and didn't dare raise it now, either, because the weird plant had completely changed Kay's life. At that time, Kay just felt it was bad luck, and very unfair. Chunxiu felt the same. They were so young then. But seeing her now, Mrs. Yi felt that Kay had changed completely. She was confident, self-sufficient, and fearlessly moving ahead. So what had the crag-bean vine's weird expression actually meant all those years ago?

Rain was pouring down when she bottled the herbal powder. Mrs. Yi was worried that Kay's rented house would leak, so she pulled on her rain boots and walked out with an umbrella. She soon found the house. Before she had even knocked on the door, she heard Kay shouting, "Come in!"

Kay was treating Mrs. Fish's diseased foot. Eyes closed, Mrs. Fish seemed to be enjoying the treatment.

"I'm telling her the story of the fishing village," Kay said to Mrs. Yi. "There was a man who always took away all my hopes and then forced me to find new ones. I'm used to these ups and downs."

"Kay is my savior," Mrs. Fish moaned happily.

After expressing her gratitude, Mrs. Fish left.

In the rumbling thunder, the silhouette of Kay's face softened. She became almost beautiful. Mrs. Yi couldn't hold back from saying what she had buried in her heart for decades. "After the accident, I returned to the cliff. I fished in the hole with my hands, but I didn't find the crag-bean vine. But back then, we both saw it at the same time, didn't we?"

"Yes, we did. Perhaps I took the herb away with me. For decades, it never left me—not in the daytime and not at night. How else could I be who I am today?"

Kay laughed brightly. Mrs. Yi also smiled.

Kay stretched out her hands, and Mrs. Yi held the warm, dry hands and exclaimed to herself, "These hands are really big and powerful like men's hands!"

They sat opposite each other in silence, both recalling the past.

"You . . . ," Kay said first.

"You . . . ," Mrs. Yi responded.

"The fishing village was the reflection of Yun Village," Kay said.

"Under the rosy sky, I cast a net from your fishing boat," Mrs. Yi said.

Mrs. Yi heard a man sigh in the inner room.

"Who is he?"

"My patient and my husband. He and I are both survivors from the fishing village."

"Dear Kay, so you have found your happiness. Please accept my belated congratulations."

"Thank you, Chunxiu. I also congratulate you. As soon as I entered Yun Village, I felt that you were surrounded by happiness. At that moment I understood everything."

They thought of the old director at the same time, and of the bright-colored banner. Suppressing the impulse to cry, they pretended to be recalling the happiest things in the world.

A noise came from the inner room. After a while, the man staggered out. He had a full beard, and his eyes were cloudy.

"Hey, you—" he said, pointing to Kay.

When Kay approached him, he slapped her, knocking her to the floor. Then he looked at Kay in surprise as she struggled on the floor. Mrs. Yi hurried over to help Kay up, and she was punched in the back, too. Grimacing in pain, Mrs. Yi still managed to carry Kay to the couch.

The man groaned and returned to the inner room.

"He's suffering a lot, isn't he?" Mrs. Yi asked Kay softly.

"Yes." Kay nodded. "A huge wave swept his son away. When he had a seizure, he did not recognize me; he thought I was the sea. We are survivors."

"Poor man."

"He's my patient, and I'm in love with him."

Mrs. Yi shivered and gripped Kay's hand. She saw some figures reflected in Kay's pupils.

"Come in!" Kay shouted.

It was Mr. Yi. He set a basket of food on the table.

"Here are some buckwheat buns for you. Please eat them while they're warm."

Kay clapped her hands happily and shouted, "Honey! Come here and have a buckwheat bun!"

On their way home, the rain stopped, and a rosy cloud floated in the sky.

"They love each other very much," Mr. Yi said.

"You saw it at a glance. I'm not as perceptive. I never knew that Kay had such a deep, loving heart. And no wonder—I don't pay close enough attention."

"We can see people's true temperaments only in special circumstances."

"You're almost a shrink now."

"That's because my wife's a doctor."

As they walked, they discussed how to reconcile Gray and Spoon.

"Why did they break up in the first place? It was wrong. It wasn't principled."

After saying this, Mrs. Yi sank into meditation. She felt that they were discussing a big problem, infinitely big. She could not define what the "principle" was, but still she thought it was wrong for the young couple to have broken up, and that disturbed her.

"Our team is growing by the day." Mr. Yi changed the subject. He wanted to say something positive. Let time solve the mysteries of life. Wasn't there an old saying that "everything will be all right in the end"?

Mrs. Yi understood her husband, and smiled. She began to remember something else.

"The old director could also make mistakes in judging people. He always valued me more than anyone else, and he didn't know that Kay was the real star of hope."

"I should say you and Kay both excel, in different ways. Now that you are both here, Yun Village has become even stronger."

"You are so kind, you always encourage me. Look, it's just turned dark, and the ball of phosphorescence has come out. It seems that the old director has just realized that all his former students are now grown up. He is so happy."

As they passed the window of Sangyun's house, they heard the newborn's powerful cry. Mrs. Yi felt her heart beat violently in her chest, and she vividly remembered the scene not long ago when she delivered the baby.

"An old farmer from somewhere else introduced a new kind of herb to me. It is commonly called stop-bleeding grass (like *Aspilia Africana*), and it's truly miraculous. I put it in the medicine cabinet . . ."

Mrs. Yi heard her husband talking from far away; his voice faded in the wind. Once again she felt the strong vitality of this place.

15
Gray Is In

Gray learned acupuncture by practicing on himself. He thought he was ready to treat Grandpa Onion's lumbago when he returned from afar. He felt that Grandpa Onion hadn't really left Yun Village: he was just hiding somewhere to watch him closely. Grandpa Onion had reason to watch him because he was in a transition. In some ways he was becoming a better person—for instance, he was missing Grandpa Onion more and more, as if Old Onion were his own grandfather. But in other ways he felt he was getting worse—his attitude toward Spoon, for example. Deep down he still loved her, but when they were together he would suddenly retreat into his shell. He was absentminded when talking with her, and even totally ignored her. What he was most passionate about was collecting herbs, and he went to the mountains every two or three days. So were the herbs changing his nature? When he was alone in thought, it occurred to him that herbs were not only healing the sick, they were also secretly shaping people's dispositions. Indeed, the charm of the magical little grasses was irresistible.

"Gray, can you fix my leg?" Dad asked.

"Your leg is a little inflamed. You must have a cold."

As the needle was inserted, father and son both felt their

bones tingle. Dad groaned contentedly and said, "Son, you're a man now . . ."

"Dad, you've come back."

"Yes, I'm back. My son is a doctor now."

Looking at Dad, Gray felt that his father had a childlike attachment to him. It was a strange feeling for him. Dad had been a spectator, watching him grow up. Now he was a man and Dad a child. Life was interesting. He used to be indifferent to life, narrow-minded and poor at observing.

"Dad, tomorrow I'm going to Deserted Village to help Mia with her herb hill."

"I see. Everybody needs you now. There's been a lot of noise on the hill lately, and one day I saw a silver fox come out of a hole there. Mia is doing a great thing."

"A silver fox?"

"Yes, I didn't believe my eyes, for that kind of fox is only legendary."

"There are so many things we haven't heard of before."

Birds woke him up the next morning, and he jumped out of bed.

"Yun Village is awake—it's really awake!" he said.

"Gray, don't shout, you'll frighten the birds away!" said Mother. "The magpies were arguing. I was worried about them just now."

Gray was in high spirits as he took the bus to Deserted Village.

He had been there long ago, but the village he saw now had completely changed. The tiled houses were low and hidden from view by the trees. You couldn't see them if you didn't look carefully. He didn't remember Deserted Village looking like this. Had the bus taken him to another village? There were several hills around. Which one was Mia's herb hill?

"Young man, where did you come from?" Someone was talking in the woods.

"I'm from Yun Village. I'm looking for Mia."

"Yun Village! That's a good place. Come in and have a drink with me."

Gray didn't see the man. He followed the voice through the woods and went into a house.

"May I have your name, please?"

"My name is Yang. Come on in, have a drink."

Gray couldn't hold much liquor. After two cups of rice wine, he was already a little drunk.

"D-do you live here alone, Yang?" he asked.

"That's right. I didn't get married because I wasn't responsible enough. You've come a long way to help our Mia. You came here to help Mia, and I've also become a beneficiary. I knew this was my lucky day when I saw you looking about outside the woods just now."

"Oh, oh, I see!" Gray couldn't get a good look at this old man. "Wh-what you said m-makes m-me very happy. Where is Mia? I have to go look for her now!"

He put his hands on the table to push himself up, but he fell and blacked out. The last thing he remembered was the delicious rice wine.

Yang tied Gray's hands and feet with a rope that he had prepared. Before Yang gave the hill to Mia, he had received a message there. The message was vague. By analyzing it carefully, he got the general idea: somebody from Yun Village was coming to destroy Mia's project. So as soon as he saw Gray today, he decided this was the bad guy. Mia was taking good care of the herb hill, and she had learned a lot about herbs by consulting an old farmer. She didn't need this guy's so-called help. It wasn't help at all. It was a conspiracy.

When Gray woke up at midnight, he was lying on the ground, unable to move.

"Yang! Where are you!"

"Shut up!"

"Help me, Yang!"

"You're the only one who can save yourself."

"Of course I want to save myself. I've made a lot of mistakes, Yang. I used to be a bad man full of conspiracies. But I've changed. Since I began to collect herbs in the mountains—ah, I don't know. Anyway, you must be familiar with collecting herbs, aren't you?"

"I wanted to break your leg, because you were going to sabotage Mia's work. But I was a little surprised when you suddenly mentioned collecting herbs. Do you do that often?"

"Sure I do! I've even found domino grass. You can ask Mia about this. Oh, God, please untie the rope. I can't stand the pain. I think I'm going to faint."

Yang smiled and untied him. Looking at him doubtfully, he asked, "Is our Mia an associate of yours?"

"She's a good friend of mine."

"Are you learning to be an herbalist, too?"

"I'm not very good at it, but I'm working as hard as I can. Yang, take me to Mia."

"Listen, Mia is coming."

But it wasn't Mia who came in. It was Grandpa Onion. He patted Gray excitedly on the shoulder, and said, "Good boy, you're really somebody now. I'll tell your father that you haven't let him down. You're an ambitious young man."

The two old men looked at Gray appreciatively, their eyes shining with warm, moist light.

Gray stared at them for a moment, and then he suddenly understood a little something. He couldn't help crying emotionally, and he remembered many things. Yang said, "You see, Onion, this young man understands everything now. He's cut out for it, isn't he?"

"Of course. Why else would he have gone up the mountain? The day I found out he was going up there, I waited for him in the woods for hours!"

Hearing Grandpa Onion talking, Gray stopped crying. He wondered, How had Grandpa Onion known he was going to Niulan Mountain to collect herbs? It was really amazing. He had been thinking long and hard about what happened that day, and now he had the answer. But was it really true?

"Grandpa Onion, I can do acupuncture now. I can give you an acupuncture treatment someday."

"You see, Yang, I've got everything I want. Oh, no, I can't stay with this boy. I must keep my distance from him . . . Yang, send him away!"

Yang came up to Gray and shouted at him, "You get out of here, now!"

Gray left the house dazed. He walked through the woods and came to the road. The houses in Deserted Village were hidden in the dark; only the lights flickered like the blinking eyes of ghosts. A cold wind was blowing, and Gray's legs were shaking. He quietly cursed himself.

A shadow appeared on the road. It was a man.

"Who are you looking for?"

"I'm looking for Mia."

"You can't just go looking for her. Is there some particular reason you need to see her?"

"She asked me to help her plant herbs."

"I see. You can leave now."

"Why would I do that? I haven't seen Mia yet."

"You can't. Didn't I tell you this a moment ago?"

"You did. But . . ."

"Back off. Now! Or I'll beat you up! Damn it!"

Gray ran away in a panic. In the dark, he couldn't distinguish directions, and he didn't know where he was.

When he slowed down and stopped, he saw the hill in the moonlight.

Ah, banlangen! Ah, plantain! Ah, monkey grass! Ah, heartleaf! Ah, spider fern! Ah, ardisia! Ah, motherwort . . .

Gray crawled on the ground, listening to the voices of the herb roots. His pores were dilating. He felt that he was melting into the soil. These were Mia's herbs. They were as dear to him as Mia was.

"This guy doesn't give up easily."

Gray heard the man talking somewhere. He stood up and whisked the dirt off his coat. He glanced around but didn't see the man.

Looking down at Deserted Village on a night like this, Gray was confused. He saw only some lights flickering in the woods. No people were visible. Neither were houses. He thought, Mia is such a straightforward, naive young woman, how can she live in such a creepy place? If the village is really haunted, then how can the existence of this herb hill be explained? Thinking about what had happened just now, Gray felt that he himself was the problem. He was too shallow, and he had only a superficial understanding of the work. He didn't know its inner secret. Obviously Mia knew more than he did. Gray believed that both Grandpa Onion and Yang were profoundly engaged in this cause, and that's why they were so serious. One lived in Yun Village and the other in Deserted Village, but nonetheless they had come together, hadn't they? They even talked the same way!

As Gray went down the mountain, he felt that some of

the conventional wisdom he had absorbed was shaken. After one strange thing after another happened to him, he had now become very dissatisfied with himself. Indeed, he was a half-hearted person, and a loner who loved almost no one. How could Spoon trust him? Living with him, she would feel bored, tense, and even hopeless. Spoon had been right to leave him. He hoped she would never look back.

He returned to the road. He decided to walk along the road until dawn, and then take the bus back to Yun Village. It was clear that he was not welcome in Deserted Village, where people weren't compatible with him. But to his relief the villagers (including Grandpa Onion) were passionate, even fanatical, about his pursuit. What kind of place was this Deserted Village? And what else set Mia apart from him besides being more conscientious and determined? Oh, Mia, were you hiding in order to teach me a lesson?

He didn't meet anyone on the long walk. Somehow, the lonelier he was on the road, the more he felt this was a friendly place. Maybe he was far away from Deserted Village, and maybe the villages along the way were hidden like Deserted Village. Is this what Grandpa Onion meant by "putting distance between them"? How interesting! Occasionally a couple of the villagers poked their heads out of the trees, took a look at the sky, and then disappeared. They didn't pay any attention to Gray.

He boarded the bus. Through the window, Gray looked wistfully at the partially exposed hidden houses here and there, as if they were telling him something.

"Gray, did you learn a lot on this trip?"

"Dad, why are you here on the bus?"

"Because I was worried about you. But now I can see you're quite self-assured."

"Me? Yes, maybe a little. No, not really. I'm not confident at all . . . What's going on in Deserted Village? Can you tell me, Dad?"

Father and son looked at each other and laughed at the same time.

"Gray, why don't you ask it? Perhaps it can tell you." Dad pointed to the goose in the basket next to him.

Gray squatted down, and put his cheek against the white goose's neck. He felt a warm wave wash over him. When the goose looked at his eyes, Gray clearly saw the eyes of Grandpa Onion.

"Dad, it told me. I'm sure now."

On the way back, Gray fell asleep on Dad's shoulder. It was the first time in his life that he had had such intimate contact with his father, and he was bewildered by the unfamiliar emotion he was feeling. He dreamed that Dad kept calling, "Gray, Gray . . ."

Gray didn't wake up until the bus stopped. His father motioned him to get off.

A woman nearby said to his father, "Is this your son? He is very shy. Perhaps he has never gone out alone before?"

"You may say that." His dad nodded. "He's a homebody. But he's an adult now, and he may do some great things. Who knows?"

The woman made a face at Gray, and Gray blushed. Suddenly he felt that the woman was familiar. Oh, it was Mia's cousin, wasn't it? He recognized her, but he hadn't spoken to her—he hadn't spoken to many people in the village.

"Well, you've raised a promising son," the woman said solemnly, nodding her head.

"Cousin, where is Mia?" Gray blurted out.

"Look! Look!" cried the woman. "So he's not shy at all! Oh, he wants to get to the truth! He's just like my cousin Mia!"

Then the woman darted away by the fork in the road.

Father and son walked home in silence.

"Dad, what do you expect of me?" Gray said at last.

"Son, I'm not expecting anything in particular of you. How can you assume that about your father? You're going your own way now, aren't you? That makes me happy. Is this happiness a kind of expectation? Some people say I've cultivated you. That's nonsense."

"I'm sorry, Dad. I can say it now, I want to say it now: I love you, Dad."

"Okay, okay, I know you do. Did you think I didn't know? You underestimated your father."

"But I didn't love you in the past."

"No, you've always loved me. When you were three years old, I had a sore on my foot. You sobbed and sobbed when you saw it."

Gray looked up: the scenery in front of their home had turned hazy. He wondered what his three-year-old self had looked like. How could he forget all about his childhood, but remember some other things so well?

Father and son entered their home. Gray noticed his mother putting something away in the drawer.

"Mom, are you working on something?"

"Yes, I'm using small sandbags to exercise my eyesight. I want to help you. Gray, when you were practicing acupuncture, I always watched you. I wanted to see those things inside the human body. I threw the small sandbags rapidly, and my eyesight improved a lot." She was grinning.

"Thanks, Mom."

The family of three sat down to dinner. When he was half-finished, Gray set his chopsticks down and said, "What's the matter with the herbs Mia planted?"

"Are they different from Mrs. Yi's?" asked his mother.

"Yeah, they're very different, but I also feel they are so familiar. Just like, just like some exotic plants growing in the front yard. I think they may have feet."

"You're crazy!" Dad laughed and laughed.

Gray was embarrassed, but he went on talking. "Are herbs all over the world related?"

"Of course they are!" Mother responded warmly.

Lying in his bedroom, Gray was unable to sleep. He heard someone talking in the yard.

"You visited them, and they're coming to visit you . . ."

"Who's that?" Gray shouted.

"I come from Deserted Village . . ."

He got up and looked out the window.

He saw a face with the nose flattened against the windowpane.

"Do you want to speak to me?" asked Gray.

"Don't talk. I'm watching you. I'm from Deserted Village."

Gray felt uncomfortable. He wanted to duck, but would that seem too affected? If he stayed where he was, he had to stare the man in the face. He said to himself, "Fine, I can just as well observe this guy from Deserted Village." Had he come to exchange ideas with Gray? Gray had met some people in Deserted Village but didn't feel he could communicate with them. He could hardly understand their language. Living in Yun Village, which was not an isolated place, Gray had frequent contact with outsiders, yet he could not understand the people in Deserted Village. What about Mia? Hadn't he become good friends with Mia? It never occurred to him that Mia had come from such a foreign village. If he saw her again, he would ask her a lot of questions.

"The muscles in your left cheek look a little tight," the man said.

"Your nose is swollen," said Gray, tit-for-tat.

"Dear me, you knew what I meant at once. What did you see in Deserted Village?"

"What did I see? The moonlight, the herbs . . . Wait a minute. Did Mia send you?"

The man left the windowpane and turned his back to Gray. Looking at the fat figure, Gray felt this guy was a little lonely.

"Wait! Are you all right?" Gray said loudly.

"I'm fine. Yun Village won't let me off. I'm doomed."

The large black figure moved out of the gate. Gray heard his mother speaking: "Here's some food I've prepared for you. Take it. You'll need it."

Gray sighed and felt relieved at once. He couldn't communicate with people from Deserted Village, but his mother could. It seemed that Mia had asked him to go to the village not to help her but to help himself! He smiled as he remembered the enchanting herb hill.

He lay down, and soon he was asleep. That night, he had some sweet dreams.

"Gray, I ran into Mia. She told me that people in Deserted Village thought highly of you," Dad said.

"She said that to please you."

"But there must be something to it."

"The fact is that I did go to the village, but people there didn't comment about me."

"Oh, let me see—no comment, isn't that also a kind of evaluation?"

"Maybe. But that wasn't a strong evaluation, was it? I'm still growing up."

"I'm happy about your progress. Are you going to the mountains?"

"Yes. I haven't been there for days. Some of the herbs will get tired of waiting."

"You're speaking much better than you used to."

With a basket on his back, Gray walked through the village. The villagers paid close attention to him, as if they felt something uncertain lay ahead of Gray. Gray felt the same way. But when he thought of the herbs in the shadows, his horizon opened up.

"Gray, go early and come back early!" Mrs. Yi waved her encouragement.

Before long, he was halfway up the hill. Now he was full of strength, and his vision was penetrating.

Beside the stream, he saw the goldthreads, so many! He rolled up his trouser legs and went down to dig. There was a spot of bright light in the stream, and his figure was reflected in it. Looking at it again, he was startled. It was not his face. It was someone else's. The man gave him a thumbs up and a toothy grin. Gray turned and saw no one. Was the man in the water an aboriginal? Gray couldn't help but grin back at the man in the water. As he worked, he looked at the man: the man was retreating slowly into the depths of the water. Now there was only a big blue sky in the water.

He hadn't dug up all the herbs. His eyes lingered: he wanted to remember this place and come here again next year.

Someone in the water was talking to him.

"Who are you?" Gray asked.

"I am Tauber. Have you heard Mrs. Yi speak of me?"

"Yes, I have. You're a highly respected ancestor."

"You woke me up when you were digging herbs. This is a beautiful place to stay, but I always like to talk with people. How's Mrs. Yi?"

"She's very well. Grandpa Tauber, will I be able to talk to you again next time I come to Niulan Mountain?"

"Next time? No, you mustn't think of doing that. My dear boy, I'm in the most beautiful place, but in this kind of place we can't make appointments to see people. People meet only by chance. Well, just as we did. We had a pleasant talk about our mutual friend. Are you happy?"

"Ha, I'm so happy! Grandpa Tauber, I hope you're always happy!"

A pebble flying from somewhere fell into the water, and Gray regarded it as Tauber's messenger.

Carrying the herbs and the two-toothed hoe, Gray walked down the mountain. He was not a bit tired, and he even hummed a folksong.

As he passed by the cliff, he heard Tauber's voice again.

"Oh, how I'd like to chat with Mrs. Yi again under the pear tree!"

"You will, Grandpa Tauber. I promise."

Gray honestly believed it would happen.

16
Mia and Her Patients

With Grandpa Onion's guidance, Mia was successful in planting herbs. Again and again she was surprised by the young people from Deserted Village who volunteered one after another to work at her herb hill. Everything was going well. Lohan was now happy from morning to night.

"Milan, your mother is a barefoot doctor now!" he said to his son.

"Mom is wearing shoes."

"But she goes barefoot to the places where neither you nor I can go for the time being."

"If I took off my shoes, could I go?"

"Ha-ha, ha-ha, Milan, you little imp!" He burst out laughing.

Mia produced more herbs than her clinic needed. When the harvest season came, three men wearing black clothes and straw hats showed up at Mia's house. Mia talked with them quietly in the back room, which she had made into a pharmacy. When they left, they were each carrying a large burlap bag of herbs. One of them patted Milan on the head.

Mia blushed with excitement as she told Lohan, "They're from Blue Mountain. The girl Angelica broke through all the obstacles, and her career is prospering."

"What obstacles did she break through?" Lohan asked.

"I don't know. It's just a feeling I had. It is so enlightening. Angelica is remarkable!"

"I think so, too," Lohan said. "I often tell myself that Mia is a miracle."

"Come on! You should see this girl. You don't know how extraordinary she is."

"Anyway, it's great that there's so much demand for our herbs. Are those men in black members of the medical journal staff? I think they must be."

This was a good day, and they decided to go to Yang's place to celebrate. Milan cheered and ran wildly around the room.

When the three of them arrived at Yang's home, he was busy in the kitchen.

The kitchen was spacious, and the walls were darkened by smoke. The smoked fish and bacon hanging from the beams smelled wonderful. As soon as Milan went into the kitchen, he squatted at the edge of the little water tank next to one wall, where Yang was raising two tortoises as pets.

"Yang, we brought *maotai!*" Lohan said.

"I smelled it as soon as you stepped out your door. You see, I'm preparing our meal. The men who visited you are not ordinary people; they can almost be regarded as mountain gods! They used to show up around here about twenty years ago, when Mia was a little girl. The day they've been waiting for finally came! I've been watching that road since August. I knew they would come."

They ate and drank in the kitchen. Milan stood by the water tank with a bowl of food. He tried to feed bacon to the tortoises, but the tortoises weren't interested. Milan was disappointed.

Yang asked Lohan if he had noticed that one of the men in black was wearing a badge on his chest. Lohan said he hadn't. Yang said that the one with the badge was the group leader, who must have been more than a hundred years old. Yang was surprised that the man could still come to Deserted Village.

"But they all looked middle-aged," Mia shouted.

"You can't tell their age by looking at them. These reclusive people on Blue Mountain always look young. These three men often came here twenty-eight years ago, and they look just the same now as they did then." Yang sipped the maotai happily.

Lohan and Mia were a little dazed by Yang's words. Milan's excited screaming brought them back to their senses.

"I read their medical journal, too. It's very profound. The journal is actually one person's work, but it seems to have a large editorial staff."

Mia drank very little. But for some reason, she kept falling into a drunken state today. The moment she recalled the voices and expressions of the three men in black, she was so afraid that she broke into a cold sweat. Her career had reached a turning point, and she was always afraid of making a fatal mistake. The leader had looked stern as he sniffed the herbs; he had even frowned. Was he dissatisfied with her?

Oblivious to Mia's concerns, Yang clinked glasses with Lohan, his moist eyes shining.

"To Mia! The centenarians visited her, and good luck will follow. In the past, nobody knew there was a Deserted Village. But now, because of you and Mia, everyone knows. So the centenarians came down the mountain to visit. What a great achievement!"

"Yang . . . Yang, do—do you think they saw our herb . . . herb hill from Blue Mountain?" Mia stammered, blushing.

"Of course, that's always the case. There's always communication between here and there. Information comes and goes from underground and from the air."

"But there's no proof yet that the herbs are effective."

"They're experts, they can tell just by looking at the herbs."

"Good heavens!" Mia murmured. "I feel cold. Let's go home."

When Mia reached the gate, she heard Yang saying, "Mia hasn't gotten used to her new environment yet. The domain is expanding so fast."

Milan rode on Lohan's shoulders, exclaiming joyfully, "Look! There's the moon! Can you see it?"

Mia looked up, and saw only blackness. Why couldn't she see the moon?

"Everything will be fine . . . ," Lohan comforted her.

"They and we . . . ," Mia muttered blankly. "Lohan, do we have a good chance of succeeding this time?"

"We've already succeeded, Mia. Yang is connected with the people of Blue Mountain. I think he is one of them."

"Good point. It seems that Yang has been staying in touch with them. But why am I so nervous? I keep worrying that something will go wrong."

"When a great change is coming, people do feel anxious about it. Look at that phosphorescence, Mia. It keeps the same distance as it follows us."

"Ah, that's the old director! He thinks of me as his successor!"

That night, Mia slept soundly. The old director's encouragement warmed her heart. She felt she could face any situation. In her dreams, she filled several prescriptions of herbs for her patients, and was quite pleased with herself.

At dawn, Yang woke Lohan and Mia from outside the window.

"Did something bad happen? Is something going wrong . . . ?" Mia asked nervously.

"No, it's supposed to be a good thing," answered Lohan. They opened the door and let Yang in.

"Important visitors are coming! I couldn't sleep. I wanted to share this good news with you as soon as possible! They've reached Dragon King Harbor now, and will be in the village in half an hour!"

"Are they the same people who came yesterday?" Mia asked.

"Yes, and besides them, there is a girl."

"Angelica, Angelica! Lohan, Angelica is coming!"

"How strong we've become!" Lohan said.

Rubbing his eyes, Milan came out of the inner room. He tugged at Mia's arm and said, "Tortoise, my tortoise."

Yang handed the tortoise to Milan. Milan pressed his little face against its back.

"Look at your son," Yang said to Mia. "He was born to be related to Blue Mountain. The two tortoises are from Blue Mountain. They came to my house and stayed."

"Great, great . . . ," Mia said through tears. "Will these people come to our house?"

"Not this time. Today they're coming to pick up the old director. We can watch from a distance."

"The old director! Oh, how exciting!"

"Listen, they're entering the village. But they aren't taking the main road. They're taking the tunnel, because the director is down there during the day."

"Great, great . . . ," Mia said, as if moaning. "They should have come a long time ago to pick up my dear old director. Director, oh . . ."

Sitting at home, Mia and Lohan saw the group of people moving in the tunnel. They were talking excitedly while probing their way forward. One of them struck a match. Mia recognized him in the light . . . It was the old director! Tears ran down her face.

"Mia, your day is coming," Yang whispered.

Mia nodded vigorously.

The party drifted away.

"Why am I sad? I shouldn't be sad!" Mia said loudly, "We have our business and it's growing!"

"Good for you, Mia! I'm going home now. I'll have another drink there to celebrate. Tortoise, why don't you spend some time with Milan and I'll pick you up this afternoon."

Yang went home satisfied.

"I'm so happy, Mia," Lohan said.

"We're having a run of good luck," Mia said.

Before Mia's clinic had officially opened for business, a patient sought her out.

He was a man in his fifties but looked older. He sat down at the table with his head bowed.

"I'm a buffoon left behind by history. I hope the herbal medicine will calm my soul."

"Chinese herbs can help you in just this way," Mia said.

Mia's heart pounded. She heard something familiar in his tone. She couldn't believe her first patient had such expectations for herbs. Did this happen thousands of years ago? Or is this how the world was made? Mia told him that she wasn't yet able to practice medicine on her own, but she knew some of the properties of herbs, and she could give him some to try. If they didn't work, she advised him to go to Yun Village to see Mrs. Yi.

"You must have heard of Mrs. Yi, haven't you?" Mia said.

"Yes, of course. But I think, I live in Deserted Village, so I should see our village's doctor. In the beginning, didn't doctors become doctors because patients went to them for help?"

"Uncle Ling, I can't thank you enough. You bring me hope, and all good things will begin today. Just a moment, I'll get the medicine for you."

She went to the back room and came out with some herbal powder.

Uncle Ling smelled the herbal powder.

"It's so intoxicating. Just a sniff, and I'm half-healed."

Watching Uncle Ling's figure disappear in the misty rain, Mia said to Lohan, "Chinese herbs do have feet. They can walk into people's lives by themselves."

"He often came to the herb hill to watch the herbs growing," Lohan remembered.

"Is that the difference between a barefoot doctor and a doctor in the city?"

"Yeah, this means you have to learn by yourself."

Mia thought about "to learn by yourself"—had she actually learned? Sometimes she thought she had, but most of the time she felt that she was only blindly fumbling around without yet reaching the essence. Chinese medicine was a huge system; she was still shut out from it. The fact that the elders of Blue Mountain had been here today didn't indicate that she was gifted in medicine; they were probably here on other business.

What was it about Mrs. Yi's kind of medicine—if it could be called medicine—that attracted her to it? Was it just some kind of folk art that Lohan said one had to learn by oneself? Of course he didn't mean that. He thought so highly of her work that even she felt that he was exaggerating. Mia realized through her experience that it was indeed an old skill that had almost been lost, and only a small group of people still insisted on demonstrating its effectiveness. The strangest thing was that the plants played a central role, conveying messages in silence with a variety of expressions, and never failing to do so. She had heard the story of the volcano erupting, and she wondered how the herbs and people had developed their difficult relationship over thousands of years. Did the relationship need a breakthrough now? She felt that Uncle Ling knew something about this. He came to her not for treatment but to talk.

"Is Uncle Ling sort of a prophet?" Lohan said.

"Yes, I think so. Is he from Deserted Village?"

"Yes."

"Lohan, the first time I came to Deserted Village, I saw a tiger lying on a rocky hill in the distance. I didn't tell you because I thought maybe it was a hallucination. But that impression is engraved in my mind. A scary beast, so beautiful."

"Later, your determination to study medicine had something to do with the tiger."

"Deserted Village is a place with lots of hidden talents. The elders are all a bit like prophets."

At this moment, Mia felt very lucky. She and Lohan had fallen in love, and she had married him in Deserted Village. Then one day she had come up with the idea of studying herbal medicine. It all seemed predestined. She saw now that she could have a brilliant future in this unassuming village. People of this village had disguised faces, beneath which were ancient instincts. She hadn't known this in the past. Perhaps the villagers like Yang, Ling, and some others were in frequent contact with Blue Mountain and Yun Village, but she hadn't noticed it before. Was Blue Mountain the birthplace of this particular medical practice? It seemed so. That medical journal was published there. This small journal with simple covers had changed so many people's destinies! Mrs. Yi, she herself, Gray, and Angelica—their obsession with this journal wasn't at all misplaced. From the start, she had felt that the messages in the journal were coming from somewhere dark. Perhaps a mysterious editorial office and printing house were in the belly of Blue Mountain.

"Here comes your cousin," Lohan said.

Milan threw himself at Chunli. After playing with him for a while, Chunli took a seat.

"Mrs. Yi asked me to tell Mia that her herb hill project won the grand prize—in the entire industry."

"How wonderful!" Lohan exclaimed.

"It's just an honor, no trophy, no medal, and no money."

"It's great!" Mia said, "Because it's a prize in the industry! Chunli, I'm so proud! I've never ever been so proud of myself!"

"Let's go to the herb hill!" suggested Chunli.

So they all went to the hill.

The hill was bare again because the herbs had just been harvested. Yang was sitting on the hill smoking a cigarette. Next to him were Uncle Ling and Grandpa Onion.

"Mia, we're here to celebrate with you," Yang said.

He handed the tortoise to Milan as a reward for him and his parents.

"We owe you a thousand thanks, Yang," Mia said.

Milan was playing with the tortoise.

Everyone's expression grew serious, for they heard the whistling in the air. They turned their faces toward Blue

Mountain. The whistling went round the hill and away again. Old Onion nodded his head and repeatedly said, "Good, good . . ."

"Grandpa Onion, whom do you see?" Mia asked nervously.

"Who else could it be? Dr. Lin Baoguang, the father of Chinese herbal medicine," Onion answered. His eyes were closed.

Mia remembered that Angelica had been looking for an old doctor named Lin Baoguang. She craned her neck to peer into the distance. She felt herself standing on a pontoon bridge, her hand clutching Lohan.

"Dr. Lin Baoguang is a legend in this area," Yang spoke up. His eyes were closed, too.

They sat for a long while on the hillside, feeling an aura building up around them, then fading away. It was a long time before they woke up.

Onion was the first to leave, saying, "Shameful, shameful . . ." He soon disappeared in the distance.

"He was speaking of himself." Yang explained, "He was ashamed because he couldn't understand the message that Dr. Lin Baoguang was sending. In fact, I didn't fully understand, either. Nobody can."

Yang thought for a moment and then added, "He is sort of a mountain god."

Mia was excited by this, and her face reddened.

"I really want to meet Dr. Lin Baoguang," she murmured.

"According to the information I've received, the girl Angelica has contacted him. Of course she can't meet him in person, for they're in two different places . . ."

Yang seemed to hesitate when he said this. Now as they walked down the hill, they all lowered their voices talking about what had just happened. There was no more whistling in the air, but there was stirring again inside the mountain. Everyone heard the noise—the cries and shouts of people and animals. Milan was beside himself with joy, for his precious tortoise was silent at the sound of the noise inside the mountain. Probably it was also listening.

Mia's second patient had migraines. She was about thirty years old and had a pretty, baby-doll face. She didn't seem to care whether she would be cured or not. She was observant and analytical. She described her medical history this way: "Illness hits me like an avalanche and then subsides, like spinning silk. This is my life."

Mia asked her if she wrote poetry, and she shook her head. Mia went into the back room and took out a bag of herbal powder for her. The patient, Plum, beamed with joy.

"This medicine won't cure you, but it'll make you feel better," Mia said.

"Very well. That's exactly what I want. I'm not really sick, am I? The truth is, I'm not sick. My illness is a hallucination. The herbs will tell me the truth."

"You're remarkable. I can learn a lot from you. Why don't you study medicine?"

Plum looked at Mia for a long time before saying, "Maybe I'm not strong enough. I'd rather be a patient. That's also a good thing, don't you think, Dr. Mia?"

"Dear, it's my pleasure to have a patient like you in Deserted Village. I even think—I think you're coaching me in the practice of medicine. Yes, that's it."

"Your herb hill has given me joy for a long time. My window faces your hill, and even in the daytime the herbs tell me about diseases."

They parted reluctantly. Mia thought Plum truly understood herbs. She would come again soon, and they would be friends for life.

Mia began to miss Plum at once. "I gained a mentor and a good friend," Mia sighed. Plum's understanding of diseases and herbs was so sophisticated that Mia felt that she herself could not catch up with her. Several years ago, in a small courtyard behind a bamboo grove, Mia had seen Plum tending a few common herbs. As a young girl, Plum had been pale and weak but not at all melancholy. She said she had meningitis as a child.

"I didn't deserve to die, did I? I struggled to survive. These herbs, I think, are always doing their best to help me. I'm not very strong, so I can only plant these few."

In those days, Mia hadn't understood what Plum was saying. Later, Plum took out a small bamboo chair and sat down with her. Stroking Mia's hair, she whispered, "There's a lot of vitality in your hair."

Mia used to think this girl was a little strange and made a point of keeping away from her. Now, recalling this, Mia felt that she wasn't strange at all; rather, she herself had been childish and hadn't understood her. After all these years, she had come calling. This woman had a profound understanding of everything in the world. And she talked about illness in such an original way.

Mia felt a vitality awaken in her from her hair and from her heart. But in that earlier time, it was Plum who had smelled the scent of her own kind from her. She was remarkable.

Mia felt that Deserted Village, where she had lived for many years, was opening secret doors to her, one by one, and beyond them lay the landscape she had long thirsted for.

Why hadn't she noticed these doors before? They had been waiting quietly in their hidden places for her to discover. Maybe you had to stare hard at them before they appeared.

"Plum is actually my doctor, and I've been sick all along," she said to Lohan.

"It would be better to say that she's your soulmate. I sensed this even before she came to you."

"See how slow I am. It seems that I'm the last to become aware of anything."

Mia went out of the front yard and stood in the middle of the road. The west wind blew her short hair, and blew Plum's voice into her ears: "Mia, Mia, I am a patient, you are the doctor . . . Mia . . ."

Mia made a trumpet with her hands and shouted, "Plum, wait for me!"

After shouting three times, she felt much more relaxed. Her eyes scanned Deserted Village, and in the darkness she seemed to see one of the secret doors slowly opening.

Someone touched her shoulder. It was Lohan.

"That tortoise from Blue Mountain—Milan wouldn't part with it even at bedtime," he said.

"In fact, no one has ever been parted, right?" Mia was puzzled.

"I'm thinking about that, too. So many people have been waiting for you to be a doctor, and I didn't know that," said Lohan ruefully.

They saw Gray go by the road to the right, and the young man was radiant—as if he were a different man. Mia remembered his recent visit. It was Grandpa Onion's idea for him to come for nothing. Now she was genuinely pleased to see his maturity. Her work, and Gray's, had changed their lives completely. She heard that Gray was now a warm-hearted young man who often talked about herbs with the villagers. She wondered if Gray was now back together with Spoon.

Gray went to meet Yang, who was sitting on the roadside stone waiting. Mia saw them talking enthusiastically. "All people . . . ," Mia murmured, and suddenly she saw the open door.

The patient who came that day had a malignant tumor growing in his head.

"Occasionally I feel that I have no desire to live any longer," he said, "but I don't want to die when I'm in remission. I'm always in this kind of cycle. One day I suddenly understood my illness. Dr. Mia, do I look calm?"

As he spoke, Mia kept nodding approvingly. His final question made Mia admire him—Uncle Owl sensed the pulse of nature.

"Uncle Owl, no other patients are as calm as you are. You don't need drugs to fight the cancer. I can see from your eyes that cancer is an old friend hiding in your body. But perhaps you would like me to give you some herbs as a balm, so that you'll be more attractive to your old friend?"

"Dr. Mia, I have seen that you're my soulmate. Give me the balm so that I can live like a man. In the west wind of the night, I prayed repeatedly for your herb hill. Because in the hill there is a path for the villagers of Deserted Village to return to their former homes."

"Uncle Owl, you're a wise man, and a real man. Because of your example, we have more confidence in our own lives . . ." She was too emotional to go on.

Uncle Owl's face suddenly twisted. Without losing his calm, he got up, took the herbal balm that Mia had given him, and limped out. Mia was worried and escorted him to the main road. She watched him walk slowly into his house.

After coming back, she sat on the wooden chair and began to imagine Uncle Owl's life. She whispered, "People of Deserted Village are really wonderful. How can I not love someone like him?" Then the tide of love began to rise within her, and she heard the pulse of nature. It was because of this kind of patient that she had become a barefoot doctor. Why was there this kind of patient? Because of a certain great passion.

She began to walk back and forth in the room; in her imagination, she was chatting with her patient. When they talked, the west wind blew between them. They were a little sad, but more evident than the sadness were the passion and the warmth of mutual understanding. In the past, before she became a doctor, she had greatly misunderstood Uncle Owl. At that time, she was full of pity for him and privately thought he was a disabled person. Now he was like a mirror, reflecting her superficiality. In just half an hour, in her eyes Uncle Owl had become the most handsome man. Eager to relieve his pain, Mia decided to get some morphine for him from Mrs. Yi the next day.

"Lohan, can you tell me what Uncle Owl looked like when he was young?"

"He used to be a famous strong man who could lift a stone mill," Lohan said.

"He's stronger now. Cancer has fortified his will."

"I was astonished as I watched him leave just now. He is an indomitable spirit."

"What do you have in your hand, Lohan?"

"Morphine. I picked it up this morning." Lohan looked serious.

"Let's hurry and go to his house now."

As they walked home from Uncle Owl's house, they saw an unusual scene in the sky: the clouds were turning as red as blood, and lightning flashed in the west.

"To live, to the last minute for loved ones and things . . . ," Mia whispered.

"I promise!" Lohan hugged his wife tightly.

Mia listened attentively. She heard the long, lingering sound of a bell from the direction of Blue Mountain. The men, she thought, had heard the news that a brave man was fighting in Deserted Village. My God, this means of communication and transmission was so touching! When the last bell fell silent, Mia heard the door of Uncle Owl's home creak. He was listening!

Lohan heard it, too, and they were greatly comforted.

As soon as Yang appeared, Mia began to sob.

"Don't cry." Yang patted her on the back. "It is a solemn moment."

"You're right. I'm sorry." Mia stopped crying.

17
Spoon and Gray

Carrying a basket of herbs and a two-toothed hoe, Gray walked home with his head down. Someone was standing on the road, blocking his way. It was Spoon. She pointed at the basket in her hand, which was full of stonecrop—*Sedum aizoon*.

"Where did you find them? This is a rare herb," Gray said.

"In a place not far from my home. Seeing you going to the mountains all the time inspired me."

"This is exactly what we need, and Mrs. Yi will be very pleased. Thank you for doing this. I heard someone calling me when I was on the mountain, but I didn't think it was you. Are you sure you want to do this?"

"I can try. It's fun."

"My goodness! Spoon, I love you so much!"

"Hush, someone over there is looking at us."

"I don't care! Spoon, let's go home!"

They went back to Gray's house.

Gray's mother braised fish and cooked beef and potato stew for dinner, and everyone drank some wine.

In the evening, Gray asked Spoon to talk about her experiences picking herbs, but Spoon said she couldn't remember.

"I wasn't very clear-headed. In the past, I hardly ever

went up the mountain alone, so I was scared. When you're afraid, you don't remember anything. Fortunately, these *Sedum aizoon* kept nodding to me from a rock. When I was a child, a woman in the village showed me this herb and told me how it was used. I was interested in it then, but later I forgot about it. Well, I saw them—so many!—and picked some, and came back in a daze. Gray, what's wrong with me?"

"It's because you're going through a major change in your life," Gray asserted.

"Now I feel good. I'm getting closer to you. Oh, our mountain! Why didn't I go to the mountain more often? There must be something wrong with me. I was a problem teenager. Did you know that?"

"A problem teenager? That's okay. Tomorrow, let's go to Niulan Mountain together. You said when you were a child, a woman in the village taught you about herbs. Do you remember what she looked like?"

"It seems she wasn't from our village . . . What did she look like? Let me think. Ah, her face is blurry . . . Maybe everyone is a little like her."

Caught up in her memories, Spoon looked as if she were walking on a cliff. She held Gray's hand tightly, and her lips quivered.

"Spoon, Spoon!" Gray gently shook her arm.

Gray felt that Spoon was being tested: Perhaps she was on a glacier? So he led her to the closet, and took out a blanket and wrapped her in it.

Spoon fell onto the bed, and her voice was muffled under the blanket: "Gray, I walked a long way. I need to rest. Thank you."

Gray took off her shoes and tucked her in.

In his excitement, he gasped for breath. Then he took a cold shower.

When he came into the living room, his father did, too.

"Gray, you can get married now," said Dad kindly.

"She knows more than I do!" Gray was very happy.

"You two will do some great things."

Dad invited Gray to go outside for a walk. By the time they reached the threshing ground, the stars had come out.

"Gray, listen: Yun Village is particularly happy tonight."

"Perhaps because someone has come back? I heard some old people talking."

"They're the ancestors. They always come to talk when a major change takes place. Let's go to Yellow Slope. You haven't been there for a long time."

After walking for some time on the raised path between fields, Dad and Gray turned the corner and came to Yellow Slope. It was a barren slope, full of rocks and no vegetation. Gray wondered why his father wanted to bring him here. A gust of wind blew over and Gray almost fell.

"Have a seat." Dad patted the ledge.

Sitting there, Gray felt an unusual quiet all around. He could even hear Dad's heartbeat. He felt that the humble Yellow Slope might be an important place. Dad called his attention to some figures in the distance.

"The Yun villagers often come secretly in twos or threes to this quiet place. They want to ask questions of Yellow Slope, but its answers are always silence. Maybe people like the way it answers questions, and that's why they keep coming back here. They come here furtively because they don't want to destroy the silence. Have you noticed that?"

"No. I never used to pay attention to things around me.

You know me, I'm a loner," Gray said shyly. "I have just asked Yellow Slope a question, and I think it has answered me."

"Great. Let's leave in order to make room for the devout disciples."

Father and son walked slowly down the slope. They saw the figures prowling in the distance, all hunched up like black bears.

"Was your question about Spoon?"

"Dad, you always know what I'm thinking."

"I'm happy for you, and so is your mother."

"I'm never sure. I never dreamed things would turn out this way."

"You should come to Yellow Slope often."

Gray and Spoon went up Niulan Mountain from the north slope, because Gray wanted to take a new path to start their new life. He used to go up the mountain from the south.

Along the way, he told Spoon how to identify the herbs which were often seen, such as snake-beard, purple ginseng, lily of the valley, and so on. While doing this, he felt his vision sharpening. Whenever an herb was found, Spoon clasped her palms, closed her eyes, and said, "Oh!" It became a ritual for her.

"I heard them squealing with joy when you picked them," she said.

"Maybe they feel lucky because they're entering the world of humans."

"Gray, I kind of worship you now. You know everything."

"You're worshipping the wrong person. I don't know anything yet. Only Mrs. Yi and Mia know everything. Of course, my dad knows a lot, too. And you understand more than I do."

Spoon asked Gray to look up at the tree. Gray saw the

python. Hadn't he smashed it? Why was there no trace of wounds on its body? It was for sure the same python: he remembered its eyes.

Gray told Spoon to greet the python spirit.

"Hello there, we've come to see you," said Spoon graciously.

The python glanced amicably at Spoon.

The two of them went around the tree, and Gray saw crystal flowers. Gray caught his breath at the sight of the beautiful, long-lost herb. They picked the herbs carefully, each acquiring a large handful. "How beautiful they are! I'm so happy!" Spoon whispered.

"The python spirit was there to show us the herbs," Gray suddenly realized.

"I like the python spirit. It's like my family."

"Thank you for saying that, Spoon."

Gray suggested going to the stream; perhaps they would have an unexpected harvest over there.

So they climbed up. Suddenly Spoon stopped. She said someone was calling her.

Gray listened carefully; indeed, a faint voice was wrapped in the wind. It might have been calling Spoon but it might have been the whistling of the wind. Looking nervous, Spoon said something.

"Spoon, what are you saying?"

"It's her, it's her."

"Who?"

"The woman who showed me the herbs."

The woman approached, carrying a load of firewood. She was also a Yun villager. Her name was Jade.

She set down her burden and said with a smile, "I saw you from afar. Niulan Mountain is very happy today because a new guest has come."

"Thank you, Jade," said Spoon. "Did you meet anyone there today?"

"How did you know? I did meet a friend from years ago. It is said that she died of lymphatic cancer, but she appeared in the stream and smiled at me. She is an experienced herb farmer. Spoon, are you cold? You don't look right."

"I'm just overcome with emotion, because you've met her. I'm so excited today."

After they parted from Jade, they didn't find any more herbs. In a trance, Spoon uttered "ah" now and then.

"I remembered her appearance now. How could I have forgotten her? Very strange. In fact, she didn't ever really leave me, did she?"

"In fact, you've been looking for her all the time on a winding path, but you were unaware of this."

Gray felt feverish, and suddenly he was dazed. For a moment, it seemed they had forgotten each other's existence. They were taking different paths and they were about to be separated. Gray awakened from this trance when he heard Spoon shouting.

Spoon pointed at the giant spirit mushroom at the edge of a graveyard. Her voice shook: "Who is it?"

Gray said with a smile, "Spoon, you are blessed. It is here for you. We need it for treating patients!"

Kneeling on the ground, Gray picked it carefully and placed it in the bamboo basket. He said a convalescent would need it. He went on to say that Spoon was a lucky star, and Niulan Mountain must be very fond of her. Otherwise, why would it have sent her such a precious gift?

Completely refreshed, they went down the mountain joyfully. But Spoon was a little uneasy. Every now and then, she checked on the bamboo basket on Gray's back. She was afraid the spirit mushroom would fly away. She kept saying, "It's not a dream. It's not a dream."

"Of course it isn't a dream!" Gray shouted.

Gray finally had a chance to perform acupuncture on Old Onion. He let Spoon watch.

Onion lay down in the back room of Gray's home. Gray was going to insert the silver needle into the acupuncture point called "life-gate."

"You were there last time. You know the way, just go ahead," Onion said.

His words immediately reminded Gray that when he got lost in Deserted Village, he had had a similar feeling—a little excited and a little scared. When he noticed Spoon's encouraging expression, he plucked up his courage and inserted the needle.

"Oh, yeah! It's like coming home! Good for you, Gray!" Onion said. "Don't hesitate. You always do it right, because you're Gray."

Gray's tears gushed out, and he hurriedly wiped his eyes with his sleeve.

Although the needle was in Onion's body, Gray himself felt a shock—he was almost numb all over. When he finally came to his senses, Spoon had disappeared.

Before Gray could stop him, Onion sat up with a needle still in his body. Not knowing what to do, Gray stared nervously at the old man, who seemed perfectly at ease.

"Relax," Onion said as he got dressed. "I've had acupuncture before. The silver needle is an old friend of mine. It doesn't bother me at all."

"But I should pull it out."

"No, don't pull it out. It's doing very well inside me, and my back doesn't hurt anymore. I'm going to work now."

Watching Onion walk out the door, Gray was puzzled. Then Spoon came out from behind the cupboard.

"Why did you hide?" Gray asked.

"I was scared. When you weren't looking, Grandpa Onion took the longest silver needle from your bag and stuck it into his body. He did it skillfully, but it made me feel dizzy and I couldn't stand still, so I hid. Just now I've been wondering, What is this silver needle therapy all about? Can you explain it to me?"

"I don't know. I'm just a novice. The human body is full of acupuncture points, and silver needles can be inserted anywhere . . . It isn't only the patient who feels an electrical sensation; people nearby feel it, too . . . Sorry, I don't know what I'm talking about. Spoon, please forget what I just said."

"But I think you're explaining it really well. Gray, I must have been electrified—the left side of my face was numb. Amazing!"

Spoon was so excited that her face reddened. She asked Gray to insert a needle in her "shoulder well," because her shoulder sometimes ached.

Gray sterilized the silver needle, and stuck it into Spoon's shoulder well.

Spoon yawned, "I woke up."

Gray asked how she felt, and she said again, "I woke up."

Spoon suddenly saw the woman Qiu who had taught her about herbs. So this was what she looked like! Spoon realized that she hadn't seen Qiu because she'd been sound asleep all along. As soon as the needle entered her body, she woke up and saw Qiu. In fact, Qiu had always been there, busy with her work in the fields. The herbs clung to her as if intoxicated. Spoon burst out, "Auntie Qiu, I can see you!"

The needle still in her body, she ran out of the room, her eyes searching all around.

Gray was happy for her: how brave she had become! He finally realized that Spoon had been sheltered since childhood, just like him. That's why she had come to Yun Village to find him, and that's why they had fallen in love at first sight.

Gray wanted to pull out the silver needle for Spoon, but Spoon shook her head firmly.

"Don't, I'm very comfortable with it. I don't want to pull it out yet! Auntie Qiu, let me take another look at you! Oh, how cruel of you, Gray—you've pulled it out!"

Spoon shed tears, and she scolded Gray for not letting her see Qiu.

"She's always there," Gray said, "and we shall see her again tomorrow."

"Promise?"

"I promise. You'll definitely see dear Auntie Qiu tomorrow."

They went home arm in arm. Spoon whispered to Gray, "Don't you think Auntie Qiu and Grandpa Onion are actually the same person? People in this line of work can have several personae."

"You mean the work of herbalist?"

"Yes. They're all psychics. And so is Mrs. Yi. I have to apologize to Mrs. Yi. Do you think she'll forgive me?"

"She forgave you long ago. She's been urging me to reconcile with you."

"Really? Why?"

"Because she's not an ordinary person like you or me. She's psychic."

"I sort of understand it now, Gray: there's always a psychic in the crowd, and that person subtly influences and changes everybody."

"You're so smart."

"I am so happy! But in the past, I was inwardly sly and couldn't help doing evil things. I don't think Mrs. Yi should forgive me."

"But she did, long ago."

"I—I will work hard."

"Thank you, Spoon. Look, you have a visitor."

The woman's face appeared at the window. She was a thin, middle-aged woman.

"Hello, are you Auntie Qiu? I'm Spoon. Come on in, please."

The woman shook her head and smiled sadly.

Spoon whispered to Gray, "Auntie Qiu is disappointed in me. I let her down. What have I been doing for the past twenty years!"

Gray raised his voice: "Spoon has great potential. She'll do great things if she ever wakes up, and no one can stop her."

As soon as Gray said this, Qiu disappeared.

But Spoon was still staring at the window. After a while, she heard Gray invite her to go to the herb garden, so she stood up and walked out with him.

Without any moonlight, it was very dark outside. Gray lit the road with a flashlight. Spoon said she was afraid. Gray hugged her tightly and walked on. From a distance, Spoon saw a light in Mrs. Yi's house, but she could see only the outline of the house. Spoon felt herself being dragged along, yet never getting any closer to the house.

She didn't know how much time had passed when she heard Gray mutter, "We're here."

"You mean the herb garden?" she asked.

"Yes. Mrs. Yi is studying medicine at home."

"But I can't see the herbs. Isn't this nothing but sand? I grabbed a handful of sand."

"Maybe it's like that for a novice. Beginners can't always see herbs with their eyes, especially at night." Gray spoke calmly.

"Let's go. We shouldn't disturb Mrs. Yi. I'm sort of worshipping her now. I need to hone my eyesight."

Walking back with Gray's arm around her, Spoon still saw only the light and the outline of Mrs. Yi's house. Slowly, she began to smell a rare faint herbal fragrance floating on the wind. She blurted out, "I wish I could die on a night like this." Gray said she was so young, she shouldn't think of death before doing something for the world. Spoon apologized and said she felt ashamed.

"Mrs. Yi is looking at us," Gray said.

Spoon glanced up and saw that the light had been turned off. Although she couldn't see, she had a distinct feeling that Mrs. Yi was watching, and at the same time she felt her shoulder well throbbing. A warm current rushed to her brain.

18
Revival of the Director

The old director did not die, he revived. He said he was a
"phoenix rising from the ashes." "I can't die yet," he said to
himself. "My students need me, even if only for the sake of
thinking of me sometimes." He remembered Kay, whom he
had seen recently, and he smiled.

He had been hanging around Yun Village these days. He
could see other people, but they couldn't see him because
alcohol had diluted his body and he had become a shadow.
His favorite student was in Yun Village, so he couldn't help
coming here. A few days ago, he discovered that another
long-lost student was also here, so he was even more determined to stay alive. His health took an unexpected turn for
the better.

"Kay! Kay!" He raised his voice.

But Kay couldn't hear him and couldn't see him, either.
She was walking to her clinic, carrying vegetables she bought
at the market. The man walking with her said, "Why is it so
noisy here?"

Kay comforted the man: "It's the wind. Ignore it. Let's
speed up."

The old director stopped in his tracks. He thought, It was
because of her profession that she was so kind to people.
She had become a good doctor. There were always so many

patients coming to her clinic. He had thought Kay was dead, but she was not only alive, she was leading a wonderful life. The director's face reddened, though other people couldn't see this. He was ashamed. He said to the air, "I must . . ."

At night, the director curled up in Aunt Yossi's lean-to. Chunxiu had set an empty bed next to many dried herbs in the room. He thought, Chunxiu prepared this place for me to spend the night. She's very thoughtful.

The director lay down among the herbs, thinking of what he had seen and heard in Yun Village. The mixed scent of all kinds of herbs stimulated his brain, and his body began to stir. He had an urge to launch.

"Here I am," he said kindly to the window. "The two of you just go ahead without looking back. Chunxiu, haven't you now gotten in touch with the Blue Mountain people? This should reassure you. And Kay, you're now so composed. I'm overwhelmed by your grace . . ."

His train of thought was broken because someone pushed the door open and came in.

"Did Mrs. Yi send you?" The woman stood still; she was bewildered.

"Mrs. Yi used to be my student," replied the director.

"Oh, how lucky you are! No, I mean how lucky both of you are! And I am also very lucky because I happen to live in Yun Village. I don't know how to say it. I wish I could bite off my clumsy tongue! I was blind . . ."

"May I have your name, please?"

"Don't ask. I am the daughter-in-law of the dead old lady Aunt Yossi. Mrs. Yi gave my daughter a second chance at life . . . Where was I?"

"You were saying you love Mrs. Yi, right?"

"I would give my life for her!"

"Why? She doesn't need that. She loves you dearly."

"Really?"

"Of course. I've often heard her speak of you. She says you're the most loving person."

"Oh, I'm feeling unsteady on my feet. I have to go."

She abruptly disappeared.

When the director awoke in the middle of the night, he heard a sigh.

A young man was sitting on a stone bench in the moonlight.

"Are you sitting here because you miss Mrs. Yi?" asked the director.

"Yes, every day after leaving her, I feel nervous. Who are you? I can't see you, I see only a halo. Are you the old director? I've heard a lot about you. My name is Gray."

"Gray. That's a good name. But why on earth do you feel nervous?"

"Because my wife is moody. Sometimes she has a goal in life, sometimes not. When she loses her goal, she becomes a different person. That's why I'm always rattled."

"I see. So there is happiness in this kind of panic. You want freedom. You and your wife have set your sights high. Am I right?"

"Absolutely right! Director, the moment I looked at you, I felt I had found the answer. Thank you, and I thank you on behalf of my wife."

Excited, Gray stood up and embraced the halo. He shed tears of happiness. In his whole life, he had never embraced a halo. How extraordinary!

All the way home, Gray felt the light of the halo shining on his back.

The old director was also very excited. He could hear the

herbs rustling restlessly in the darkness. "What a beautiful night," he said. "It turns out I can still be useful to others." Thinking about his favorite student becoming a major figure in Yun Village, his heart warmed with pride.

Before dawn, the director was awakened by the calls of various birds. He went out to look for the birds. He took the road straight into the mountains. Standing at the door of her home, Mrs. Yi saw a small dot of light swinging on the mountain road, as if immersed in a certain artistic scene. She smiled with relief, and inwardly called out, "Director! My teacher . . ."

Not long after the old director entered the mountains, he saw Dr. Lin Baoguang sitting on a rock. The director circled around him. He thought that Dr. Lin had lost some weight and that he looked a little dejected. Could it be that his undertaking wasn't going well on Blue Mountain?

"You needn't go around me," said Dr. Lin. "I can't see you, but I can hear your footsteps. My hearing is okay."

"Hello, Dr. Lin. It's great to see you here. It's a good omen for Niulan Mountain. How's everything going over there on Blue Mountain?"

The director noticed that when Dr. Lin spoke, he looked very young and radiated good health.

"Do you mean our work? Never better. Blue Mountain is bursting with creativity because of the new generation joining in."

"You mean the girl Angelica?"

"Yes, this girl is the spark. Because of her, the people of Blue Mountain are changing their outlook on life."

With that, Dr. Lin stood up. The director hurried over to embrace him, but he held only air. Dr. Lin had disappeared.

The director noticed a swarm of ants on the rock where Dr. Lin had just been sitting. The ants were now scurrying down the mountain. The director thought they were rushing to Yun Village to spread the message that the saint had brought here to the villagers. What a wonderful message! The director still remembered that a poisonous snake had bitten his leg when he was collecting herbs in the mountains that afternoon more than forty years ago. It was this Dr. Lin Baoguang who had saved his life with herbs. It was then that the director learned of the existence of the Blue Mountain medical institution. He had gone to Blue Mountain to find his savior but never succeeded. Instead, Dr. Lin had come to the county seat twice to meet with him. Both times he came and left in a hurry, saying he was just passing by. From his brief visits, the director knew that his benefactor was satisfied with his work in the county. Oh, so many ants! Perhaps the leaders had already arrived at Chunxiu's herb garden?

The director sat on the rock because he wanted to experience Dr. Lin's spirit realm. By this time the last ant colony had hurried away. As soon as the director sat down, he saw his own halo illuminating the rough rock. He was taken aback, for he had never seen light coming from his body. Slowly he saw the beauty of the rock. Some of the patterns on the rock, though vague, were particularly vivid in the light, reminding him of his many years of practicing medicine. He couldn't tell what the changing patterns meant, but the more he couldn't tell the more emotional he became. It seemed to be about his first love, but the core of it had something to do with Chunxiu.

He fell in love with this rock. He felt himself fusing with the rock. Opposite him, the python was dancing.

"Hello, director. Mrs. Yi sent me."

Close by, the woman named Mia whispered to him. She

looked like a mermaid, with the mountains as her sea. The director looked at Mia in surprise and thought to himself, How smart and mature she's become in such a short time!

"I can't see you, but your glow feels familiar," she said.

There were several kinds of herbs in her basket. Evidently she had become an expert on herbs. She sat down on the rock without noticing its patterns. But the director saw a huge golden flower splash up from where she sat.

"Thank you so much for coming here, director. It's nice to sit here, but I can't stay long. I have work to do at home. I'll tell Mrs. Yi that I saw you, and she'll be delighted."

Unhurriedly, she lifted the basket onto her back and swam down the hill.

The director remembered what had happened that night, and—ashamed—he said to himself, "She is the pearl of night and I am unspeakable filth. How lucky I have been in my life."

His glowing light blinded him. It was some time before he saw the rock again, and the patterns on it were still shifting. The director felt strongly that something was hidden in the patterns, but he couldn't figure out what. When a blurry image of a river appeared, he almost caught the word, but what came out of his mouth was a syllable, *kui*; he did not know what that meant. If Chunxiu were here, he thought tenderly, she would know what it meant, and she would know what object was hidden behind the shifting patterns. Chunxiu and Mia were real practitioners.

An old man came by, and the director could see only half of his silhouette.

"How do you do? I am old Tauber. You must have heard of me. I've heard so much about you."

A little excitedly, Tauber smiled at the director.

"Can you see me?" the director asked.

"Only your head. You're wrapped in a halo. Do you like the local chestnuts? And the herbs—do they look the same as they used to?"

"The chestnuts taste great, but the shapes of the herbs are much different from the way they were before. Of course, I can still recognize them. They've changed for ghosts like us, haven't they?"

"Exactly. The herbs always come out from the same place as we do, in all kinds of shapes. Have you seen Mrs. Yi yet? You have? Oh, how lucky you are! I've been waiting here for three days, but I still haven't seen her. I'm longing to talk with her under this Bodhi tree," Tauber said wistfully.

"It makes me feel good to hear you speak of my student like this."

As they talked, they drew close to each other. The director couldn't touch the other half of Tauber's body, and Tauber couldn't touch the director's whole torso. But they felt they had achieved a kind of authentic interaction, and they both blushed.

"Instead of seeing Mrs. Yi, I'm meeting with her teacher. This is immensely satisfying."

Their eyes fell simultaneously on a big clump of lily turf behind the rock.

"Could they have been growing here for more than a thousand years?" Tauber asked. The director noticed Tauber's right eye staring blankly.

"Absolutely possible," the director said.

"I'm shivering all over at the sight of these ancient friends. I hear them calling me. I'm so excited. What about you?"

"Yes, me too."

"Why don't you stroll around some more on the hill? I'll rendezvous with them down below."

With these words, Tauber sank down and disappeared into the soil.

The director turned away. When he sat on the rock again, he heard humming. It was not a common rock as he had assumed, but a living thing. The numerous patterns were shifting so rapidly that he couldn't see them clearly, but he was very excited. He didn't want to leave the rock. Could this rock be Dr. Lin Baoguang? The sun was setting, and the shadows grew thicker around him. The rock suddenly "hummed" again, startling him. He stood up and said to the rock, "I have to go now. I'll come again soon."

As he walked down the hill, he kept hearing Tauber whisper in his ear, "Roam around some more. They all love you! Because you're meritorious!"

The director thought to himself, Why did Tauber say I was meritorious? Chunxiu and Kay are meritorious, but I'm just a useless old man. True, I've done some work in the past, but in the last ten years or more I've lost my willpower and I've led a befuddled life.

It wasn't long ago that he had realized that he couldn't die. As long as he was alive, Chunxiu and her colleagues would feel hopeful.

The lean-to was in sight now—this was heaven on earth— and he needed to return to it at once to rest and reflect on the wonderful moments he had had today. His life had changed a great deal since he came to Niulan Mountain, and it was as if he were driving a carriage speeding ahead—he was now as active as he'd been in the old days when he was practicing medicine.

At night the screeching of chickens woke him from his sweet dream.

The weasel scurried away, and the hen twitched and bled.

The moonlight was clear, and the flowers' shadows were quivering. The scene was breathtaking, and the director was numb all over. Suddenly he sensed a small animal moving in a nearby bush. Ah, it was the weasel coming back! Was it returning to observe its prey? Why didn't it eat the chicken? What kind of relationship did the two of them have?

"Director, it's so late, and you're still outside. Isn't the lean-to comfortable enough?"

It was Chunxiu coming back from a house call. She was as beautiful as before.

"The lean-to is a paradise of herbs. I don't think I deserve to stay in it. I came out because of the tragedy here."

When he said "tragedy," he heard Chunxiu giggle.

"That's just a facade. You don't have to worry about it at all. In Yun Village, all misfortunes conceal blessings. Director, you are a lucky star."

While they were talking, the weasel and the chicken disappeared without a trace. Though the director searched carefully, the blood on the ground could no longer be found. He heard Chunxiu say good night to him.

The director returned to the herb storage room and lay down, his chest heaving. A moment ago he had exchanged a glance with the weasel, and now he understood its meaning.

Passion did not keep him awake; he fell asleep in the midst of it. In his dream he composed a nursery rhyme about a weasel and a chicken, and sang it until tears came to his eyes.

"I finally met with the old director," Mrs. Yi said to her husband. "I couldn't see him, but I felt clearly that he was beside me. This is a blessing for our Yun Village."

"The director doesn't want to be dead. He wants to be a

guardian of his students. Our Yun Village is becoming more and more prosperous. Our future is inspiring," her husband responded.

While the director was wandering about on the raised path between the fields, the young man Gray and his wife came up to him. They looked very happy. Their baskets were full of herbs. The director realized that he wasn't glowing now, so they couldn't see him.

"When I walked up the hill, my heart was murky, and I felt as if I were moving about in the dark. By the time I came down the hill, I felt refreshed. Through the branches of the big pine trees, I saw the stone bridge next to the old market. The woman, I mean the herb farmer, appeared on the bridge for just one second."

As Spoon spoke, the director dodged to one side and let her pass. The director was very happy to overhear Spoon talking to Gray, for this told him that Chunxiu now had one more student.

"You'll see her again and again all your life. She's been waiting for you in the same place for years, and now you've finally seen her." Gray laughed heartily.

"So do I love her, or do I love you?"

"You love both. Aren't I she?"

"Oh, I forgot. See how silly I am. Just now, when I saw *Sedum aizoon* on the hill, I immediately remembered that she had once told me how to recognize this herb!"

The young couple walked away. The director saw smoke rising behind them, but he wasn't worried. The smoke would invade their bodies, but it wouldn't kill them. The cuckoo cried. The director felt a tingling in his chest, and then he saw the light. He was the one who was shining. He heard cheers in the distance. The people of Yun Village were cheering him on.

"Director, sir, now everyone has recognized you! Take good care of yourself!" Chunxiu said.

She was behind him. She was on her way home from a house call.

"I'm just an idler."

"You are our constant ideal."

The old director was hanging around. He had been lying under the big banyan tree and talking with Tauber for a long time, and then they went to dinner in a little café. As they took seats at a table, the waiter looked away from them. The director figured that he had stopped glowing when he entered the café. So in the eyes of the waiter, he was probably just a dark shadow.

In the evening, he went to Chunxiu's herb garden. He was transfixed by the sight.

Spoon was frantically destroying the plants. Spoon had turned over the soil of about half the garden with a spade: ruined herbs were everywhere. What an appalling sight! As soon as the director appeared, Spoon dropped the spade and ran away.

The director knelt at the edge of the garden and began to weep.

Head drooping, Gray approached him. Gray said, "Director, I can't entirely blame Spoon; I have my own doubts about life. I suddenly felt that these herbs were driving me crazy! Spoon did what I wanted to do."

"But you're not mad now, are you?"

"Well, no. That makes me worse. Spoon and I are devils. We don't deserve to live in this world."

"You're good kids. It's okay to go mad sometimes. Feng-shui and the people here will heal your trauma. I've heard your Mrs. Yi say—"

"Don't mention her, we hate her! Ah, what am I saying?"

"You have no idea what you're talking about . . . It's all right. Go home and rest, son. When you wake up in the morning, you will see a different world."

Gray howled like a wolf and ran away.

The director ached all over, as if his joints were dislocated. He huddled on the ground, moaning. It was quiet all around. The ruined herbs must have died or fainted. Chunxiu's house was dark. Where had the couple gone?

It was a long time before he regained his strength.

He didn't want to go back to the lean-to tonight. He went to the brookside, chose a comfortable place, and lay down. The moon was red, the stream was bright, and there was a noise under the water. It was a night of passion. But whose passion? Did it belong to Gray and Spoon? Of course, it should belong to them. They were struggling, and struggling people were passionate. Look, Chunxiu was coming. Her hair was a little messy.

"Director, I have confidence in this young couple—they will survive," Chunxiu said.

"Yes, that's youth." The director groaned.

"All the signs point to a bright future."

"Chunxiu, I feel that the brook water is rising for you."

"And for you, dear director. Please go back to the lean-to; it's too damp here."

"Okay, you go first. I'll return in a moment."

She left. The stream calmed down, becoming so still that it seemed a little sad. The moon was no longer red; it had become a thin shadow.

As the director walked on his aging legs, he felt a power still lurking inside him. This is the way he had felt for years. "For me too!" he said, his voice loud and strong.

He had almost reached the lean-to when he saw Kay and her husband. The man held Kay so tightly that she became a pillow in his arms. The director remembered Kay's unyielding appearance when she was young. What was she made of? His two female students had shown up one after another, causing the director's heart to blaze. The light he gave out lit up the path at once.

Inside the lean-to, he lay down amid the fragrance of the herbs, and an incomparable peace began permeating the air.

In the morning, the director returned to his place in the county seat. To his surprise, the half-collapsed house was restored. Someone was talking in the room when he entered.

"One side is bright, the other is dark—that's a good sign!" He heard a hoarse female voice.

He turned on the lamp and stood in the lamplight. He saw no one in the room.

"Long time no see!" he said loudly.

No one answered him.

Looking out the window, he saw the sun rising and a thin woman walking toward him in the sunlight. The director hurriedly washed his face and combed his hair.

When he came out of the bathroom, the woman was nowhere to be seen. Something had been placed at the door. It was a stick of incense. He found a match and lit the incense.

Then he sat down on his recliner. The adventures of these days in Yun Village were like a movie being replayed in his mind with a lot of dialogue. Some of the speakers he had met in Yun Village and some he had never met, but they looked familiar. He closed his eyes gratefully, listening carefully through the mist of incense, and clicked his tongue, making *tut tut* sounds now and then. Before long, he fell asleep. In his dream someone brought him some yogurt, and he drank his fill.

When he woke up, he saw Tauber sitting in the living room.

"Are you returning to the village tomorrow?" Tauber asked.

"No, I'm going to reopen the clinic."

"Great!" Tauber smiled. "The cause you and Mrs. Yi are working for is blossoming everywhere."

The director was about to speak when Tauber disappeared. Looking down, he saw that the incense had burned down to the end. The director remembered the power in his body, and suddenly he realized that it was for doing this thing. He would take the plaque out from the storage shed tomorrow and have it repainted and hung on the front door. He could open a medical training workshop.

The director sensed someone standing outside the door.

"Who's there?" he asked.

"It's me. I've come here several times today."

The director knew the voice, and he felt birds singing in his chest. This guy hadn't been here for twenty years, had he? His name was Wang. Wang used to be his patient and a close friend. Ever since the director was defeated by the devil in his heart twenty years ago, Wang had disappeared from sight. Occasionally, in a drunken haze, the director would think of him and worry about the tumor in his head. Wang was so young back then. When he came to see him for treatment, a major hospital in the capital had diagnosed the thing in his head as a malignant tumor. But as long as the pain didn't flare up, Wang looked like the happiest man in the world.

He stood in the light. Very strange—even after twenty years, he still looked so young, not a bit sick. The director remembered their customary conversation.

"Is it behaving today?" the director would ask.

"Yes, it's very obedient. Now it's always good, because I've learned to tell it stories. I've come to tell you that I have been traveling around the world for twenty years, and now I'm back. I will never leave home again. I want to work with you to renew our undertaking."

"I understood, Wang, as soon as I heard your voice. Did it urge you to come to me?" The director smiled.

"Sure it did. You used to treat it well, and it will never forget your kindness. See this bulge on my head—it is swelling excitedly inside. It pushed against my skull, but I didn't feel any pain. I know how much it loves you."

The director touched the protuberance on Wang's head, and affection welled up in his heart.

"That's right, Wang, I can't leave you, or it."

"Director, please touch it again, and listen to what it says."

The director brought his ear close to Wang's head, and heard a soft whispering sound—the same sound that rice straw sometimes makes as it dries in the sunshine.

"Wang, you have succeeded."

"Yes, I've been carrying it around the world," Wang said proudly. "Now we're here again, not just one but two of us, right?"

"Yes, that's right. Not one, but two. How wonderful! And I'll do my best to—"

He was too ashamed to go on.

Saying he would return the next day, Wang left in a hurry. The director looked out the window, and he saw Wang, followed by a dark shadow, walking with his chin up. The director remembered that in an earlier time it was he who encouraged Wang to hold his head high and go on living. The director knew the black shadow didn't trouble Wang but supported him. Life was wonderful! Look, Wang's thin figure was almost silvery in contrast to the shadow. He was almost the moonlight incarnate! The silvery Wang was obviously living an elegant life, but he, who had called himself Wang's mentor, had been wasting his life for years. The director slapped his head angrily. He heard a clatter in his head, and a wrenching pain made him squint. At the same time, a grateful feeling rose from the bottom of his heart.

Someone came in without knocking and sat down on the table.

"A knight always takes his enemies with him, doesn't he?" the man said, sneering.

The man was a neighbor, and a drinking buddy of the director's. He looked sharply at the director, and said firmly, "You've become two as well."

The director nodded, feeling that it was becoming clearer.

19

The Cause Is Expanding

It was midnight. Mrs. Yi had just delivered a baby for Zhu's family. When she came out of Zhu's house with her husband, she saw a group of people in black approaching, floating like shadows with flashlights. "Hi!" the leader shouted, waving his hand.

"Tomorrow is doomsday. Are you ready?" the man said.

"Are you sure? Where did you hear this?" Mrs. Yi asked. She was calm.

"Absolutely. Listen, headquarters is sounding the alarm."

"Our Yun Village is always ready. It won't faze us," Mrs. Yi responded coldly.

The crowd went past and left the village.

Mr. Yi's left arm felt a bit numb where they had bumped into him, and he was dazed.

"Are these people from Blue Mountain?" he asked his wife.

"I suppose so. I recognized one of them. Darling, you're shaking. Is it really that terrible?" She clung to her husband.

"I'm not as strong as you are, and I'm not only scared, I'm also excited. What are you thinking about?"

"I'm thinking about the baby and its mother. No matter how long a person's life is, it should be considered complete."

"Indeed. Even if she hadn't opened her eyes, she would

have still been in this world. It's so strange—I'm now kind of looking forward to it," Mr. Yi said aloud.

"It's not strange. You're part of Yun Village."

When they reached the gate of their house, the cooped hen screamed once in alarm and then fell quiet again. Mrs. Yi muttered, "Even the chicken is . . ."

Unable to sleep, they held each other in the dark.

At dawn they simultaneously breathed a sigh of relief and fell asleep.

Gray and Spoon came over in the afternoon. Head drooping, Gray approached Mrs. Yi. Suddenly he looked up, his eyes determined, and said, "We need to replant all the herbs before that happens."

"Good, that's good," Mrs. Yi said, puzzled.

The young couple worked very hard. Mrs. Yi didn't want to disturb them, so she left with her medicine box.

When Mrs. Yi passed by the tofu shop, she unexpectedly saw Tauber.

"Hi, Tauber. Why did you come down the mountain?" she asked.

"I felt the passion of Yun Village. The scenery before doomsday is splendid. I couldn't stay on the mountain any longer; I had to come down here. Don't worry. You're the only one who can see me."

And then Tauber disappeared. Sitting on the bench where Tauber had just sat was Zhu's daughter-in-law, holding the newborn baby in her arms. They both looked very happy.

"Mrs. Yi, how lucky I am!" the woman said, holding back tears.

"Did you hear about that?" Mrs. Yi couldn't help but ask.

"Yes. But baby and I are so happy now. You see? She loves you . . ."

"She's a wonderful little girl. She has the air of a heroine!"

Mrs. Yi waved good-bye to them and then hurried to Grandma Mao's house.

Grandma Mao greeted her from the front yard. Holding her hand tightly, the old woman was listening closely to something. Mrs. Yi saw that Grandma Mao already knew it was coming. Mrs. Yi gave Grandma Mao a massage treatment. Grandma Mao groaned and stammered, "My dear daughter . . . I wish I could die in your arms . . . But . . . that won't happen. This is just a rehearsal . . . What a good idea!"

Her old eyes suddenly glittered like a leopard's.

"You're right, Grandma Mao. Now rest for a while." Mrs. Yi helped the old woman into the room.

Leaving Mao's home, Mrs. Yi was in a much better mood. She thought, This experienced old woman of Yun Village could instantly see destiny's intention. With these old people here, Yun Village could only become stronger. The coming of the end would never threaten Yun Village but rather it would inspire the village.

"Mrs. Yi . . ." Behind her, a low voice called.

"Gray? Have you finished your work? What a beautiful day! Where is Spoon? You look well. Has the crisis passed?"

They walked side by side. Gray was a little shy, and he didn't speak until they had walked for a long time.

"Everyone in the village is talking about doomsday. Spoon and I are the only ones who are scared out of our minds— we're shaking and don't know what to do. You know, we developed late. We're barely adults, and we're stupid. Suddenly . . . We're not ready to die. I said to Spoon, 'Instead of waiting for disaster to strike, we have to take action!' If I'm going to die, I want to die like a hero."

"Good for you, Gray! You're showing your true colors.

You're a spiritual youth who has seized the opportunity promptly. This is great!"

She and Gray parted reluctantly. She noticed the change in his eyes—they were now rather similar to Grandma Mao's. Gray's heart seemed to be overflowing with love. "This is an exercise in wisdom," she said to herself. The crimson setting sun was sinking slowly, and Mrs. Yi mused that the joyous clouds encircling it were making its expression more profound. In that moment, Mrs. Yi's body and mind were relaxed, and she felt very comfortable. "I'll die like a hero!" she shouted happily.

When she saw the replanted herbs, she was even more elated.

A small animal rustled through the herbs. It was the weasel, followed by a black-and-white chicken. What a miracle!

Mr. Yi came out of the house and said, "They're like my own children, and when I see them suffer, I suffer too. I've never felt like this before."

"Well, the signal we received last night at midnight turned out to be good news. The world disguised itself perfectly!"

The couple stood there watching the weasel and the chicken in the last light of the sunset. The two animals were also observing the two people. Mrs. Yi felt that the weasel's gaze was cold. When the couple tried to get close enough to talk to the little creatures, the other two jumped up and ran away into the thick growth of herbs. Mr. Yi laughed and said, "They are really rude!"

"They understand more than we do," Mrs. Yi said.

They had just finished eating when Kay knocked at the door and came in. Mr. Yi went to the kitchen to tidy up, giving the two women some privacy.

Mrs. Yi was surprised to see that Kay looked twenty years

older, as if she had one foot in the grave. She sat Kay down on the sofa and offered her a cup of hot tea.

"Kay, is your work going well?"

"Yes. I've become one with the villagers, and they all respect me. It's about my husband. He's leaving me."

"Doesn't he love you anymore?"

"He loves me. Yet he says he doesn't know why he keeps thinking of leaving me forever. He made up his mind last night. He's packing now, and he plans to leave at midnight. He said if he walks at night he won't see his own body. I'm so worried! What shall I do? I have no idea. I have an ominous foreboding about his going . . ."

"I think—" drawled Mrs. Yi as she paused to consider, "you can look at this matter in a different light. You don't have to worry too much about him. He loves you. That's enough, right? You can stay in your clinic quietly exploring his love while you treat patients."

"Chunxiu, do you think he will be all right after leaving me? He's sick . . ."

"Perhaps he's recovering."

"You're right. I feel the same way. I wonder if I was holding him back."

"You'd better leave him to his own devices. He'll never give you up. How could he ever give up someone like you?"

They fell silent. They stared at each other, and saw exciting events from the past in each other's eyes. Kay broke the silence: "I decided to come here and join you when I left the seaside because I knew I could always count on you. Honestly, you're half the reason I'm the way I am today. Whenever I despaired, I said to myself, 'Chunxiu is holding up there, how can I just give up?' Chunxiu, I'm going back to work now. I'll miss him and wait for him as I work."

It began to rain. Watching her friend disappear, Mrs. Yi thought, Kay's husband would leave in the rainy night; how sad that scene would be. What a strong heart it takes to replace one's feelings with work. Of course he would come back after he had fully recovered. She kept thinking about what Kay had been through. She knew Kay was sad, but she wouldn't despair, because Yun Village had given her a new opportunity. Perhaps there was no such thing as depression in Yun Village. Just think: so many years had passed, yet neither of them had changed her original intention. They still lived passionate lives. Yun Village, the director, the Blue Mountain men in black, and the medical journal: all of these were connected . . .

"Kay has a vital energy," Mr. Yi commented. "It was a gamble—a life-and-death struggle for her man to choose to leave her at this time. That's understandable: in a doomsday atmosphere, his illness might suddenly take a turn for the better."

"I'm not worried about them at all. Everything is going well."

"Yes, Kay is the kind of woman who continually gets happiness."

In the place next to the tofu shop, three men in black invited Mrs. Yi and her husband to the top of Blue Mountain to "discuss matters of vital importance." They also gave Mrs. Yi a map of Blue Mountain, and told the couple to follow the map after getting off the bus. After they left, Mrs. Yi and her husband stood there for a long time reading the map. The map didn't show any mountains, but only a few tangled dotted lines and black dots, and neither of them could guess what the pattern meant.

"Is this some kind of humor?" she said, laughing.

After going home to pack food, water, and flashlights, they set off on the long journey.

Sitting on the bus, Mr. Yi appeared very nervous, while his wife was calmly enjoying the scenery outside the window. They exchanged a word or two now and then.

"It's getting dark," the husband said.

"It may rain. Or maybe not," said Mrs. Yi.

"It's hard to climb a mountain on a rainy day."

"Once we reach the foot of the mountain, we should be able to climb it. Isn't there a shortcut?"

"Oh, I forgot about that. I can't wait to get there," Mr. Yi said.

Before long, the bus stopped at the foot of a mountain. Mrs. Yi and her husband knew this wasn't Blue Mountain, yet all the passengers got off the bus.

"Don't you want to get off?" the driver asked.

"We're going to Blue Mountain. Can we get there from here?" Mrs. Yi asked.

"Sure, it's just the same. Didn't you notice that it's raining? There's a pavilion ahead where you can shelter from the rain."

A heavy rain was falling. As if escaping from a disaster, the couple dashed to the pavilion at the foot of the mountain. A man was sprawled asleep on the ground in the middle of the small pavilion, so Mrs. Yi and her husband could only huddle at the edge. Whenever the wind blew, the rain drifted over to them. Mr. Yi squatted down and tried to wake the man up, but the man was still sound asleep. Fortunately, the rain didn't last long, and suddenly the dark clouds dispersed. They heard people making a lot of noise.

The man yawned and sat up. He looked at them for a few seconds and suddenly laughed.

"You two," he said, "have heard the noise, and you're not following it?"

Mr. Yi blanched. Taking Mrs. Yi's arm, he scurried out. But the crowd in front—about a dozen people—moved faster and disappeared into the mountains. Mrs. Yi noticed that she and her husband were on an indistinct path spiraling up the mountain. She wondered if they should choose a direction. When she looked around, roads seemed to be everywhere, but she couldn't be sure that they were really roads.

"It doesn't matter," Mr. Yi said.

Mrs. Yi was surprised by her husband's resolve. She could see that he was very excited.

There were grass and trees on the mountain, and many wildflowers, but she noticed no familiar herbs. If there were any herbs, they weren't ones that she recognized.

The couple walked in silence until they heard the noise again. This time it was closer, but the dense grove blocked their vision. It was as if men and women were viciously cursing each other. Mr. Yi listened attentively, mesmerized.

"What are you thinking about?" Mrs. Yi whispered to him.

"I think they're longing to reach the destination."

"Well, so are we. We just aren't making any noise."

In such a noisy crowd, they felt their own footsteps becoming lighter and quicker.

"Maybe I'm mistaken, but I think I heard Kay's husband among them," Mr. Yi said.

"Quite possibly. We will 'discuss matters of vital importance' with him." Mrs. Yi thought for a while and said, "If Kay knew this, how happy she would be!"

"Someone is crying." Mr. Yi lowered his voice.

Mrs. Yi had given up on choosing a road. It was as if she and her husband were always on the same road no matter which direction they took. As they neared the summit, she noticed that her husband's eyes were glistening and asked him what he saw. He said he saw the destination, but it wasn't the mountaintop: it was inside the mountain.

"Do you see people holding a meeting inside the mountain?" Mrs. Yi asked.

"Yes, I do. But I know we can't get in there, and we don't have to. All we have to do is sit on this tree stump and wait."

"Are you sure they need us, dear?"

"Absolutely. They need you. It's written on their faces. I heard someone ask, 'Why are we having this meeting?' Another person immediately replied, 'Because Mrs. Yi has revived the traditions of this part of the world.' You can see how important you are . . ."

Before he finished talking, they felt something moving in the soil under their feet. A yellow halo vanished in a flash. Oh, it was the weasel! "What an auspicious little animal," Mrs. Yi said.

While they were sitting there, Mr. Yi said he saw many scenes, and he said that all the people in the meeting looked familiar. They were expecting a lot of Mrs. Yi. Mrs. Yi asked curiously why she couldn't see these people and these scenes.

"Because you are a doer," Mr. Yi said. "The first thing the doers see is their own undertaking, while their families sometimes first see the secret meeting inside the mountain."

She looked at her husband in surprise, as if he had become another person. But she was happy for him. She fantasized that one day she and her husband would wander about in the mountains and then go into them. Anyway, it was better to "discuss matters of vital importance" face to face. Mrs. Yi's heart ebbed and flowed: based on what her husband was seeing and telling her, she tried to communicate inwardly with those people in black. Surprisingly, this word-less communication worked. Mrs. Yi felt absolutely sure of this. For example, when her husband said, "A man is stand-ing on the edge of a cliff, leaning out . . . ," a huge windmill which she had seen many years ago appeared in her mind at once. The image of the windmill swept her off her feet for a while. If Mr. Yi suddenly stood up with a wave of his hand and said, "Okay, we've reached an agreement," she would see a sea of herbs and unfamiliar pink flowers in full bloom. At the moment she felt filled with youthful ambitions. But now her husband fell silent, and his willpower sank into the deep darkness. His silent message lit countless lamps in her heart. The lamps were all over the mountain. She saw a figure on the hill approaching her. It seemed to be Tauber. This Tau-ber said nothing, but what a wonderful passion he brought to her. Look, weren't the pear trees blossoming in the light?

"I am willing to 'discuss matters of vital importance' with my peers on Blue Mountain from time to time," Mrs. Yi said sincerely to her husband.

"I'm as excited as you are, for I saw it first and commu-nicated it to you. I never dreamed I would have this kind of ability. Now they're gone, and the cold wind is blowing in the empty theater. Let's go home. It's been a great day."

As they descended the mountain, they heard the noise of the same crowd fading away, but their song could still be faintly heard. Mr. Yi said they were ancients, and some of them were Yun Village's ancestors. He also said that when he thought of Kay's husband being among these ancestors, he was proud of him. Yun Village was so powerful in being able to revive the collapsing human spirit. Mrs. Yi held her husband's hand tightly and walked on. She was very proud of her husband.

"The day he comes back, we'll 'discuss matters of vital importance' with him," Mr. Yi said.

"You mean Kay's husband?"

"Who else? He won't go far, he'll be hanging around here."

"We found out the truth. I'll tell Kay tomorrow."

When Mrs. Yi came in, Kay had finished treating two women's feet. Neither of them could bear to leave. They were talking loudly with Kay and laughing heartily.

"Ha, here comes Dr. Kay's good friend. We should go," Mrs. Liu said as she stood up.

They thanked Kay profusely and left.

Mrs. Yi heard a small animal running around on the roof, and asked Kay about it.

"It's the weasel. It came to tell me the good news." Kay lowered her head and smiled. "But I already know where he is."

"Your reunion is just around the corner."

"This place has magic power. That's why I rushed over here without giving it a thought."

Kay went to the inner room and returned with an old photo for Mrs. Yi to identify. From the picture, Mrs. Yi saw the rolling waves of the ocean and a few small black dots on the shore. The arrangement of black dots reminded her right away of the map of Blue Mountain that she had seen before. Her hands trembled.

"This is the fishing village. This photo used to be kept at the village office," Kay said.

"Ah!" Mrs. Yi sighed.

"Of course you know what's in this picture. I am so thankful to God that I made the right choice—I came to your village. Now my husband is as fortunate as I am because you're our light."

"Thank you for saying that. But don't be too lavish with your praise—I think you're the light for me and my husband. Look at you, you're full of life!"

"Great—let's encourage each other now and then."

Mrs. Yi picked up the yellowed photo and looked at it carefully.

"Who was there?" she murmured to herself in bewilderment.

"Can't you see? It was the old director."

"Yes, that's exactly who it is." Mrs. Yi sobbed, tears rolling down her face.

They went outside, looking up. What a pure night sky. Kay told Mrs. Yi that it was the director who brought her the good news. The director had not appeared but had spoken vaguely outside her window, and she knew immediately who it was. And she understood at once that he had brought good news of her husband. So in the middle of the night, she had a wonderful interaction with her husband. "It was head over heels," Kay said a little sheepishly.

Kay pointed out a woman who was passing by in the distance and told Mrs. Yi that it was her patient. Kay enjoyed treating her. Once, in Kay's clinic, they both heard Kay's husband talking to them during the treatment, and they chatted with him for about five minutes. During this short period, Kay became an entirely different person. She couldn't tell which stimulated her more—the work she was doing, or listening to her husband, or seeing the patient's response. She had reached the pinnacle of her happiness. "He has become so perfect and so helpful to my work that I never expected his departure to turn out like this." As Kay spoke, she embraced Mrs. Yi tightly, trembling with excitement. "After the fishing village was destroyed, I was the only family he had. I always thought I was his rock, but now our relationship is reversed."

"Great," Mrs. Yi said with a smile, "this is what you deserve. What you've said has aroused waves of excitement in my heart."

"Did those people from Blue Mountain want anything from us?" Kay asked.

"They said they wanted to 'discuss matters of vital importance' with us, but I think they are letting us consult with each other."

"You're right. But don't we do this all the time?"

"We need to do better. I have to go back now. Kay, what's happening here is so inspiring. Look, there's a lone star in the sky. But it is not alone. It's in the midst of a boundless nebula."

They hugged each other tightly and parted.

Mrs. Yi walked to the road. She saw a number of women going to Kay's clinic, probably for treatment of their feet. A cloud of happiness floated above the roof of the clinic. Just then, Mr. Yi appeared. He said he had just attended a meeting on Blue Mountain. Mrs. Yi asked him where Blue Mountain was, and he replied that it was in their own herb garden. "We can have a meeting in the midst of the isatis bushes," he said. "I've come to take you to the meeting."

The couple walked into the herb garden and sat down on a familiar rock. Mr. Yi asked his wife to listen carefully in the direction he was pointing out. "They're all here," he whispered. Mrs. Yi did sense that several people were sneaking into the herb garden, but she couldn't see them. "Gray!" she cried, "Are you here for the meeting, too?"

Embarrassed, Gray said, "I didn't expect them to invite me. I haven't done much work. And I did some damage."

Mr. Yi hugged Gray to stop him from talking.

Another person arrived and stood outside, hesitating.

"Spoon, come in and join us for the meeting!" Mr. Yi shouted.

The four of them stood there embracing, each saying the same thing: "I can hear, can you?"

Everyone felt an inner warmth. Spoon said, "I always thought I didn't have a home, and now I've found one."

It was late at night, and the four of them were still in the meeting. They heard everything. They were thinking hard. Their minds were as lively as rabbits leaping around.

"How did you discover this meeting place?" Gray asked Mr. Yi.

"I tried to listen, and one day I heard. The weasel, of course, and the black-and-white chicken have been of great help to me."

Now they all felt a small animal moving between their legs.

"What an industrious messenger," said Spoon.

Over there, the Yis' house had been dark at first, and then suddenly the lights came on. From a window came a baby's cry, very loud.

"It's the Zhu family's daughter-in-law—her baby girl," Mrs. Yi whispered.

The four people in the herb garden trembled as the baby's cries rose and fell.

Then they filed out of the garden, came to the door, and opened it.

Inside, all was dark again.

"They left after passing on a message," Mr. Yi said. "In Yun Village, even the newborns come to our meetings with their mothers."

Mrs. Yi brewed tea for everyone.

"It's midnight," said Gray uneasily.

Mr. Yi put his hands on Gray's shoulders to comfort him and said, "Tonight is an important occasion. We Yun villagers, along with friends from the surrounding area, are gathered together to 'discuss matters of vital importance.' Did you hear your father's voice?"

"Yes, I did! It really was my father. What a heated discussion."

When the young couple left Mrs. Yi's home, they no longer looked lonely. As Mrs. Yi watched Gray walking away, she was recalling the first time he came here.

The Yis weren't at all sleepy. They heard ebullient bubbling in Yun Village. Mrs. Yi said, "Now I know hearing can also be trained. You'll have to train me more."

"Where do you think Yun Village is heading?" Mr. Yi asked.

"I guess maybe it's at a turning point, and it's going to become completely different."

20
Footsteps of the Times

Mrs. Yi prescribed medicine for Ginger's two daughters, and she herself helped them take it. The girls had measles but were not in danger.

Ginger was grateful and insisted that Mrs. Yi stay for dinner. Ginger made a delicious dish of long beans with rice, and Mrs. Yi enjoyed it very much.

"I don't have a mother, and my mother-in-law has gone. You're my mother now," Ginger said.

"I'd love that, though I always feel that your mother-in-law is still around."

"It's true. I heard a voice calling me one night, so I got up and went outside. My mother-in-law was standing in the moonlight wearing a white scarf on her head. When I walked over, she looked at me and said, 'Go to Mrs. Yi, go to Mrs. Yi.' She said this twice. But she didn't come in. She went behind the house and disappeared." Ginger looked a little worried.

"Oh, she thought of everything. It's all right now, isn't it? We're always together."

Mrs. Yi hugged Ginger to comfort her, and assured her that her daughters would be okay.

"I'm afraid you'll leave us," Ginger said tearfully.

"Nonsense. I would never leave you. I promise."

It was late when Mrs. Yi left Ginger's home, but she still

wanted to gather herbs on Niulan Mountain as she had planned. She went home, picked up a bamboo basket and a two-toothed hoe, and set off. Mr. Yi told her not to go too far, so he would be able to find her if something happened to her. Mrs. Yi knew that her husband worried about her safety. She thought she wasn't that old yet and should still be able to go to Niulan Mountain, at least this year and next. Later on, she would turn this work over to Gray and Spoon.

It was afternoon already. Mrs. Yi planned to dig some goldthread in a pit halfway up the mountain, because two villagers diagnosed with malaria needed it.

After entering the mountains, she sensed that Niulan Mountain was a little restless. This was most noticeable with the rocks. For example, the rock in front of her, which was mostly buried in the earth, made slight explosions as the sun's rays fell on it, as if expressing its impatience or a warning. Mrs. Yi went around the rock and climbed up. She longed to run into Tauber, but she was going in the opposite direction from his cabin. She thought Tauber would always hang around his cabin.

After climbing for half an hour, she noticed that the sky was overcast, and a large dark cloud was moving toward her from the northwest. Fortunately the pit with goldthread was nearby, and she quickened her pace. Just then she heard a noise from a tree. It was a python. Her legs went limp. She decided to go around this big guy. As she ran nervously, she wondered if this was the one Gray had encountered. After she detoured and thought she had finally distanced herself from the scary python, she saw that the mountain before her was now unfamiliar. It was a place she had never seen before, and the woods were so dense that they blocked every way out. Even the path she had taken had disappeared. This was a banyan tree forest. Mrs. Yi had seen this ghostly tree only in books, for it was not a local species. Mrs. Yi was cut off in the dark banyan forest. It was difficult to take a step in any direction, and she suddenly felt exhausted.

She heard rain falling—at first, only the pitter-patter of rain in the woods, but soon such a heavy rain that she couldn't keep her eyes open. Mrs. Yi stood against a big tree, holding herself together. She thought, Will I die here today? She thought of her husband, she thought of the director, and she thought of Kay. But she was quite composed. The cold rain had cleared her mind. "So there have always been two Niulan Mountains," she said with a little laugh. Ah, the python was the serpent of fate which had led her to this place! But what did it mean? A strong force grew within her—she must struggle. "Darling, my dear! Help me!" she shouted wildly.

Ah, her husband answered her from afar. His voice was barely audible, and she didn't know what he said, but she knew he would come for her, no matter what. Mrs. Yi kept shouting as she looked for a way out. The rain was lighter, but there was no way out. The aerial roots of the banyan trees were dangling above, like evil spirits. Cornered, Mrs. Yi suddenly started digging in the ground with her hoe. She didn't know how she came up with this idea—as if it were premeditated. After digging up the surrounding weeds, she found that the rain-soaked mud was easy to dig. She dug a few times, and shouted a few times to her husband again. It was strange: there were no roots or stones in this spot, only beautiful red earth, and so she easily scooped up the earth and threw it aside. Soon she had dug out a waist-deep pit. Mrs. Yi was energized now and thought this might even be a tunnel. Before long, the pit was the depth of a person, and inside the pit she could no longer hear her husband's voice. As she was reinforcing the wall of the pit, a man behind her said, "Why do you keep beating me on the back? I have a herniated disc." Mrs. Yi looked up, and saw that the pit was now spacious and at least five meters deep, so deep that she couldn't climb out by herself. The man stood in front of her and looked at her curiously.

"I want to get out of here and go home. Can you help me?" she asked.

"You can't go home from up there. Why don't you try to go down?" he scoffed.

"Down? You mean continue digging down?"

"Yes, you're very smart."

He gestured toward a spot on the ground, telling Mrs. Yi to dig down from there. Mrs. Yi dug gently just once, and the mud crumbled. Before she could see anything, they sank several meters together. The pit was not at all dark. Mrs. Yi suddenly burst into laughter.

"All right, all right. Laugh as much as you like. Do you see the door?" the man said.

"Door?"

"It's a door that you dug out. Isn't that what you wanted to do?"

Mrs. Yi thought, This man makes some sense, but what about this pit? She looked up and saw that the ground had risen to a faraway place. It was as if she were inside a coffin so spacious that she could run about in it. The glare from far above lit the pit. "Did I dig this up?" Mrs. Yi couldn't understand this kind of thing. Hadn't she simply felt afraid and wielded the hoe a few times and removed a little soil with her bare hands?

"Look, this is the goldthread that you were looking for," said the man, pointing to a tuft of plants in the corner.

"Ha-ha, here it is!" Mrs. Yi shouted happily.

She dug up some of the goldthread and put it into her bamboo basket. Then she faced the problem of how to get back to Yun Village. The man read her mind, and said in a teasing tone, "You may stay here waiting for a miracle. Think of some ways to amuse yourself while waiting."

"But I just want to go back to Yun Village."

"Well, then, you're on your own. I have to go," said the man angrily.

The man went behind the cluster of goldthread and disappeared. Mrs. Yi ran after him and saw that the mud where he had stood was a little loose. She retreated timidly to the center of the pit. She wanted to dig again, but she was afraid of causing a disaster. She hesitated.

"What are you afraid of? Haven't you already thrown caution to the wind?" It was her husband talking.

Mr. Yi's voice seemed to come from the goldthread. She went over to check, but found nothing except traces of her digging.

"Where are you?" She was wrought up.

"Don't shout!" Mr. Yi sounded sullen. "If you want to go back, go right now! The patients are waiting for you. You're their only hope!"

He was right. She had to dig her way out. Wasn't the drumbeat coming from Yun Village? So she continued to dig at the spot behind the goldthread where the soil had loosened.

"Good, that's good. You've almost cured my herniated lumbar disc," said the man. "You're really a New Age hero!"

He stood up in front of her and wrote a big "O" in the air with his hand.

Mrs. Yi straightened up to look around, and found that the pit no longer existed. She saw familiar houses and chimneys: she was standing on the threshing ground in Yun Village. She picked up the basket and the two-toothed hoe, and headed home in high spirits. On the way, she ran into Mia's cousin Chunli. Chunli said, "Mrs. Yi, you've been away for a long time—two days and two nights! They're crying up a storm in your house! Are you hungry? Go home and get something to eat!"

"Who's in my home?"

"Mia, Ginger, and Spoon."

She opened the door and went in. Mr. Yi and the three women looked at her in surprise. They were afraid to touch her, as if she were a piece of fragile china.

"Darling, when I was on the mountain, I heard you talking to me. You encouraged me."

"I did, but only in my heart. Anyway, I'm glad you heard it all—It was a dark time . . . Then I ran into a man from Blue Mountain who told me to go home and wait. Did you meet him? You must have. He said he would bring you home."

"The man accompanied me, but he ran away midway here."

"Cheers!" said the three women in unison.

"Cheers!" Mrs. Yi drained her glass.

A lively conversation began. Halfway through the meal, Mrs. Yi suddenly put down her chopsticks and went out . . . She had remembered the malaria patients.

"Director, your training workshop is well known," Mrs. Yi said to the old director.

"It's strange. I never advertised, but these young people came to me one after another."

"They were waiting for you all along. The young man named Simon, who subscribes to the medical journal, has been asking me for the past year when you would start taking new apprentices."

"Simon is very promising. Like you, he loves helping others. He'll be a pillar of the future."

The director took Mrs. Yi to see his new classroom, which was built on the ground where part of the building had collapsed. It was capacious and light.

"At present there are two teachers here, Wang and me," the director said. "Do you remember Wang? The one with a tumor in his head? He takes the tumor with him to class. He told the students that for every word he said, the tumor said something different. He asked if they wanted to hear the tumor's words, and the students responded enthusiastically. Wang didn't have a formal education. He discovered the secrets of cutting-edge medicine by learning from his own illness."

"Director, what's happening here is so moving!" Mrs. Yi said.

"I'm old and useless. All I have going for me is my teaching experience."

"You're a respected senior who's a model for newcomers! Don't ever stop your work again, I beg you!"

"Of course I won't. Chunxiu, you gave me a second shot at life."

As they were talking, the room was very quiet. A big bat flew in through the window and out again.

"You see, even the animals are teaching me. I've recently become more and more studious. Wang's tumor was the most enlightening. Ah, what a fantastic way to communicate!"

Mrs. Yi nodded in agreement. She said that she would like to sit in on Wang's class in a couple of days, hoping that she'd be able to spread Wang's experience and knowledge. She was particularly interested in the details of the reactive communication between the brain tumor and Wang. And she was moved by the tacit understanding between Wang and the director.

The director beamed. Then he asked if she had run into Dr. Lin Baoguang on her way to the county seat. At a loss, Mrs. Yi shook her head and said no.

"I wouldn't recognize him even if I did. He's a legendary doctor who hasn't left the mountain for a long time. Do you think he'll come here today?"

"According to the message I received this morning, he should have come. Why do you think you wouldn't know him? On the contrary, Chunxiu, you will recognize Dr. Lin as soon as you see him. I'm sure you will."

"Do you think so? That's wonderful! He's the miracle-working doctor of Blue Mountain."

"You'll learn more and more about the secrets of Blue Mountain."

"I've already learned some things. The time when I went to dig up the goldthread—"

"Hush, you mustn't say anything about that. You can only hold it in your heart."

"You are so kind. I love you, and I always will."

Before leaving, Mrs. Yi walked in a circle around the empty classroom. The silence of the classroom carried her thoughts far away, and a voice kept whispering to her, "Do you have everything with you? Did you forget something . . . ?" The question seemed to ask her to dig deeper into her memory . . . the faraway memory.

After leaving the director's place, as she walked on the main road in the county town, the sadness she used to feel when she was missing the director had vanished. Feeling an impulse to fly, she stretched out her arms. Then she thought of Wang and his heroic life—living with his brain tumor.

"Ma'am, what's happening with malaria control in Yun Village?"

The speaker was an unusually small old man, his back bent almost to the ground.

"It's almost over. The disease is under control." She bent down to speak to him. "Where are you from? You look familiar."

"You have to ask? You already know," he said reproachfully.

"Oh, this is incredible. I'm so fortunate!" Her voice was shaking a little.

The old man waved her away, saying, "Let's go our separate ways."

On her way to catch the bus, Mrs. Yi thought, Dr. Lin Baoguang! How serious he is! Perhaps he's not satisfied with my work? She felt uneasy.

Oddly enough, she saw the old man again in the station. He was talking with a young man. Mrs. Yi distinctly heard the shy young man call him "Dr. Lin." On the bus, the two of them sat a few rows in front of Mrs. Yi and talked on and on. Mrs. Yi managed to catch some fragments of their conversation, such as "The one from Lubi's family scattered grass seeds everywhere . . . ," "There are indications . . . ," "The vegetation problem . . . scarlet fever is not scary," "Animals are infected . . . ," ". . . The veterinary station on the hill . . . ," "Experiments are occurring spontaneously everywhere," ". . . Yes, mountains and lakes." Mrs. Yi thought, Perhaps a big plan is brewing. How inspiring! Had her experience in the banyan forest actually been fate urging her on? Her face was hot.

The two men got off the bus midway. Mrs. Yi watched them disappear on a barren slope.

As soon as Mrs. Yi got home, she shouted, "I saw Dr. Lin Baoguang!"

"Great! I always had a premonition that you would meet him," her husband said.

"Before I had said very much, he said, 'You already know.'"

"I thought that's what would happen. Actually, you've been in touch with him for years."

At dinner, Mrs. Yi talked about Wang's tumor. Mr. Yi listened so attentively that he even forgot to eat. At last he sighed, "A miracle! If only I can do the same one day! It was a perfect time for him and the director to open this workshop."

"If I had known about Wang when I was in the banyan forest, maybe I would have been calmer? Wang . . ."

"With the passage of time, you'll be calmer and calmer," Mr. Yi said with a smile.

Mrs. Yi smelled medicine, and asked her husband, "Are you taking precautions again? Are there signs of a new epidemic?"

"No, but we'd better be vigilant. Yun Village is growing, so there could easily be an outbreak of any kind of disease. Do you think that's a good thing?"

"You already know the answer," Mrs. Yi said.

They went to the back room to look at the prepared herbal decoctions. When the light came on, the decoctions danced in the glass bottles and made a beautiful sound.

"They can't wait," Mr. Yi whispered.

They immediately turned off the light and returned to the front room. She cleared the table and said, "You're remarkable!"

That night, Mrs. Yi read an article in the medical journal that had recently arrived. This article didn't seem to have anything to do with medicine. It was an ethereal argument on regional personality traits. Mrs. Yi was fascinated and involuntarily sighed, "Ah! Ah!" The writer's pen name was "Guard." Somehow, Mrs. Yi thought this article was very likely written by the girl Angelica in Blue Mountain. Mrs. Yi was sure—why so sure, she didn't know—that the writer was describing a hero of the times, a woman who specialized in cultivating exotic plants. She couldn't keep from shedding tears.

"Have you ever met Angelica?" she asked Mr. Yi.

"Yes, I met her today. She asked after you," Mr. Yi said quietly.

"Why didn't you tell me?"

"I thought you had seen each other. She said she had an appointment with you this afternoon at the lean-to."

Mrs. Yi jumped up and said she had to go to the lean-to at once. Then, grabbing a flashlight, she rushed out.

No one was in the lean-to where the herbs were kept. She lay down on the wooden bed in the middle of the room. The herbs stirred softly, and their exotic fragrance enveloped her. Thinking of the director having slept in this very bed, Mrs. Yi couldn't help becoming emotional.

Someone knocked on the door. It was Ginger.

"Has she been here?" Mrs. Yi asked.

"Yes. She's really a beautiful woman. She told me not to disturb you. She said you work too hard and she cherishes you. She's such a considerate girl."

"How are your daughters doing?"

"Very well. I've brought you a rose cake. Doesn't it smell good?"

"Yes, wonderful. Why don't you have some, too?"

"I've already had some. Mrs. Yi, I saw that Angelica keeps your photo in her breast pocket. She said you're her sweetheart! I'm a little jealous."

"Why are you jealous, Ginger? You know you're my sweetheart, too."

"Mrs. Yi, I'll have wonderful dreams tonight. See you later."

Mrs. Yi tried a piece of the rose cake: it was delicious. She sighed. Aunt Yossi had a gift for understanding people. She had seen the essence of her daughter-in-law. She stood up to go home.

The moment she opened the door, she saw a man in black from Blue Mountain.

"We Blue Mountain villagers want to thank you," the man said.

"Why?"

"For many, many things—things that started a long time ago."

"I see. Dear sir, are you leaving now?"

After the man in black left, Mrs. Yi remembered that Angelica kept her picture in her breast pocket. How could Angelica have a picture of her? She didn't have a camera and was rarely photographed. Not long ago, however, she did go with Kay to see the director, who had a very old camera. They took some pictures with the director, and also a few individual photos of themselves. Angelica must have gotten her picture from the director. The director, Kay, Angelica, and herself—magically connected, as if by a predestined bond! No wonder the man in black said many things had begun long ago, but she hadn't been aware of this.

She was emotional on the way home. She noticed many of the villagers loitering like shadows.

"Yuan, what are you doing?" Mrs. Yi asked.

"Just walking around. I've been burning with passion for days, and I love it. Mrs. Yi, you cured me of malaria, and now I have a vision that I shall never die."

"That's good. It's fine to think of it that way. What are you carrying?"

"Fried fish. When I set out today, I had a hunch that I would run into you, so I brought it for you."

"You had that kind of hunch?"

"True enough. I also heard your footsteps. I became familiar with them when I was sick. Oh, those days and nights!"

Mrs. Yi went home. When Mr. Yi asked if she had seen Angelica, she said no but that it had been more real than seeing her in person, and even more thrilling.

Her husband nodded and said approvingly, "The girl Angelica is just like you when you were young. She looked familiar the first time I saw her."

"Perhaps our Yun Village, Blue Mountain, and Deserted Village are the same clan, but geological disasters later scattered us. We're still together . . . Actually, we never scattered."

Mrs. Yi had never again found the banyan tree forest on Niulan Mountain. But she knew it wasn't a dream; her experience in the forest was real. She had dug hard with that hoe, hadn't she? Wasn't her arm sore when she got home? Her husband's memory agreed with hers. Mrs. Yi felt that after that incident she had become more broadminded and more confident. One afternoon she remodeled her henhouse and built a small passageway so that the weasel could visit the black-and-white chicken whenever it wanted to. Mr. Yi appreciated his wife's idea. Afterward, the visits did take place, but quietly, without struggle or bloodshed, and it was only by careful examination that Mr. and Mrs. Yi could find any traces of the weasel. The black-and-white chicken became more lively and alert.

Later, Mrs. Yi went halfway up Niulan Mountain to pick goldthread once again, and nothing strange happened. Life was once again peaceful, and Mrs. Yi and her husband were very happy.

As she sat in the herb garden under the moonlight, Mrs. Yi's thoughts flew far away. She said to her husband, "The director and Dr. Lin opened up this homeland when they were young." Without missing a beat, her husband said, "Now it is you, Kay, Mia, Gray, and Angelica as well as many other people who are making our homeland prosperous." Mrs. Yi added, "And you, and Lohan, Tauber, Spoon, Yang, and Grandpa Onion . . . We are all the masters of this land."

In the lilac night sky, they heard the continuous humming of a soft *zizi* sound. The couple listened and nodded. They understood intuitively: it was a message from Blue Mountain.

21
An Invisible Network

This patient was named Kim. Mia's son Milan brought him home. Kim had been standing on the side of the road watching Milan play marbles for more than half an hour. When Milan stood up to go home, he said, "Little brother, may I go with you?"

Milan nodded, and they went home together. Kim wanted an appointment with Mia.

". . . just not interested in anything, and I feel like I've lived too long," he said.

Mia looked at his face, nodded gravely, and went into the inner room.

She came out with a packet of dried lilies.

"Take two at a time. Soak them in water first. You have to watch them unfold in the water. Then steam them with a little water and rock sugar for about half an hour."

"It's quite a bit of trouble," Kim said, frowning.

"But you'll feel better after taking them. Look how beautiful they are." Mia smiled knowingly.

Three days later, Kim came back beaming. He looked much better.

"Amazing, absolutely amazing!" he said, shaking his head sheepishly.

"Did it work?" Mia asked happily.

"Not only did it work, you guided me to use my brain to cure myself. The lily is usually used in food therapy; people mix it into rice porridge. I've never taken this herb seriously before. This time I did what you advised every day, watching the whole process and then taking a dose of it. Afterward, my mind was full of flowering lilies and their wonderful bulbs . . . Oh, my goodness, I'm a lily! Who has ever seen a lily suffering from depression? Never! And I really felt that they were in my body to support my recovery. Mia, I am so ashamed to face you. I have to go now to help my mother with the garden."

He came and went in a hurry. As she looked at his receding figure, Mia nodded slowly.

Mia had not known before that the Deserted villagers had a long history of kinship with plants just as the Yun villagers did. It was after she became a barefoot doctor that this truth began to dawn on her. She'd been ignorant, too, when she had first entered Mrs. Yi's garden. That's when she had discovered this vast world of vegetation. She said to herself, "Brother Kim, maybe you and the lily are in love with each other. The lily can cure you!" Seeing someone at the door, she cried out, "It's open, come in!"

It was Lohan's fourth uncle, a wizened old man, who entered.

"I want to—I want to ask you for some lilies, too . . . ," he said hesitantly.

"No problem. What's the matter with you?"

"I just don't feel right. I know it's not an illness—Kim told me that. I don't want to feel sick all the time. I want to be healthy."

"Uncle, you're wonderful! I think you're teaching me about life. I'll get it for you."

She took out some fresh lilies, some fresh *Poria cocos,* and some dried patchouli. The room was filled with the fragrance of the plants.

The old man smiled.

"So this is life, isn't it?" He shed a cloudy tear. Milan threw himself into the arms of his granduncle. The old man took two water chestnuts out of his pocket and gave them to Milan.

"Try walking more, digging more, and planting more. You'll feel better," Mia suggested.

"Yeah, yeah, I'll try it. Mia, you're the pride of our family! I never thought . . ."

He went out with the herbs in his hand, sniffing them and laughing.

In the golden sunlight, Mia leaned against the door. She heard the nearly inaudible mezzo-soprano folksongs coming from Blue Mountain. Accompanied by the songs, Yang came into her garden. These days Yang was always cheerful.

"Our herb hill is dancing. This has never happened before! When I was halfway up the hill, it vibrated. I lost my footing and rolled down the hill, but I wasn't hurt. The strange thing was that I felt so refreshed as I rolled down, and I heard Lohan clapping and cheering. So I've come here. Where's Lohan?"

"He went to the village to distribute a flu vaccine. I think he's on the hill now. Let's go over there and take a look," Mia said.

They walked to the herb hill. The hill was quiet in the sun, and a big green lizard was squatting motionless beside the path.

"The gatekeeper won't let us by. Let's go up from the west," Yang said softly.

Mia followed Yang to detour around to the path on the west. She was a little nervous.

Halfway up the hill, they ran into Lohan, who seemed drunk.

"The bell rang from Blue Mountain," said Lohan. "It was the bell of the new era. Our herb hill was completely revived. I rushed over here as soon as I heard the bell . . . How thrilling! All kinds of small animals ran out . . . Is it because we grow herbs that the hill has changed? What do you think, Mia?"

"This hill belongs to our Deserted Village. Yang has been its guardian for decades, and now we're dancing with it and with the message from Blue Mountain. This hill must be feeling a new lease on life!" Mia said.

The three of them sat side by side on the big rock. The sun was shining, and it was quiet all around. Something was moving in the grass—the lizard again. Mia thought that perhaps it had climbed up so quickly to express its joy. The lizard looked seriously at the three of them—the only way it could express its joy. Mia could understand it. She crouched down and looked at it, passionately communicating her feelings with it. Yang moved closer and crouched down, too. He was emotional as he lowered his voice to say, "This greenwood guy is in love with our doctor Mia. I know it."

"Can you talk to it?" Mia whispered to Yang.

But Yang just heaved a long sigh.

The lizard turned away slowly and disappeared into the grass.

"The lizard is the most stubborn species among animals. It has a dreadful mind, but it's dangerous only to itself. That look . . . Who wouldn't be moved by it?"

Yang was meditating. Mia ran a few steps ahead, trying to track the lizard. Then she thought for a moment and returned.

"I love it. Lohan, you won't be offended, will you?" Mia blushed and stuttered.

"Of course not. I'm going to cry," Lohan said softly.

Yang felt the hill dancing again. This time, though, it wasn't moving physically but spiritually. Yang bobbed his head to the rhythm of the dance.

"How old is it?" Yang asked suddenly, as if waking from a dream.

"It is said that in ancient times there were no mountains here. It must have risen up over time from the ground."

Lohan answered Yang unhurriedly. As he spoke, he heard a man inside the mountain saying the same thing. So he said, "Ah!" The man in the mountain also said, "Ah!"

"That is to say, it has been looking forward to this. Now it has come to us at last. Because it saw an opportunity. Isn't that right?" Yang looked over at Mia.

"The three of us created this opportunity!" Mia shouted.

Mia's suddenly raised voice led to a buzzing in the mountain's belly, and it shuddered slightly.

"Oh, let me die in bliss!" Yang said, closing his eyes.

"Yang, your time isn't up yet," said Lohan. "I heard the hill say you will enjoy still more bliss. If you hadn't bought this hill, we wouldn't have had such good luck."

When the three of them went into the village, the villagers, who were usually a little indifferent, gathered around eagerly. They seemed to have something to say but they couldn't.

"Dear, you want to tell me something, don't you?" Mia asked a little girl kindly.

"Well—I want a pet. It's a little green lizard. It's very small. My parents told me to ask you if it's okay . . ." The girl looked at Mia with tears in her eyes.

"It's a great idea! The lizard is out looking for a job, and you can give it a lot of work."

On hearing this, the villagers said, "Oh," and dispersed.

Mia stood where she was, puzzled.

"Mia, this is how our villagers are repaying you," Lohan said.

The next morning when Mia woke up, she heard Lohan talking loudly with someone.

"She will not leave Deserted Village—there is much to be done here!" Lohan said.

"That's what I thought. I was just sounding you out," said a familiar voice.

Mia dashed to the door and found that her husband was alone.

"Who was with you?"

"It was Dr. Lin Baoguang from Blue Mountain." Lohan shrugged.

"Why did he leave so soon?"

"I spoke to him ten minutes ago. Did you hear us only now? If you just heard us, it means Blue Mountain people's time is different from ours. I was in their circle of time just now. How mysterious!"

"It is. Does he think I should leave here?" Mia asked.

"He came to see if you had any intention of leaving. I think he's the kind of saint who watches the sky and the earth at the same time. Is he pressuring me or encouraging me?"

"We Deserted villagers also look at both the sky and the earth," Mia said with a smile.

Lohan was silent. He sensed the ancient feeling, as Mia did.

A man who was one of Mia's patients came in.

"My ears are buzzing all the time. Should I just get used to it?" he asked.

The patient was a man of forty. He was troubled, but he seemed to be in high spirits.

"Try to get used to it. Things will get better," Mia said, looking him in the eye.

"I see. It means I still have some kind of power, doesn't it?"

"You still have a lot of power. I'll give you a tea mushroom that you can brew at home."

Holding the jar with both hands, the man left.

"You're right," said Lohan, nodding appreciatively at Mia. "The Deserted villagers have the same blood as Dr. Lin. This gives us freedom in life."

"I have more work than I can handle every day; there just isn't enough time."

"Dr. Lin got the answer he wanted."

They saw their son Milan watering the several castor oil plants. Joy rose in Mia's heart when she saw Milan concentrating on what he was doing.

Someone came in. It was Fourth Uncle, looking very vigorous today. Milan ran to his granduncle, and they hugged each other.

"Mia, I have a life of my own now!" he said huskily.

After Fourth Uncle left, the family stood listening in front of the door. They heard a suspicious sound. Suddenly, they ran to the backyard.

The dried-up well in the backyard was bubbling, and a large patch of sparse grass was being watered. Milan clapped his hands in ecstasy and shouted, "Mom, he's coming!" He raced over to the little boy standing in the shallow puddle and took his hand.

"Whose child are you?" Mia asked the little boy.

"I came from the other side. I just came to check on this well. I'm leaving now," he said as if he were an old hand.

"Mom, he's going away!" Milan was downcast.

The boy shook off Milan's hand and ran quickly out of the garden.

"How did you know he was coming, Milan?" Mia asked gently.

"We had an appointment. He came to see if I had grown up yet." Milan stared blankly.

Lohan and Mia felt like crying.

Through the tree branches, a ray of sunlight fell on Milan's small profile. Milan stood motionless on the spot. He had shown fortitude.

Lohan was remembering. He remembered that the well had run dry in his boyhood. He used to lie by the well and dream of water rising from the earth. But the miracle had never happened, probably because of his temperament. "What momentum! It's all because of Dr. Mia," he said.

"Because of me? You have too high an opinion of my abilities," Mia said. "It's because of the prosperity of this place."

"Mia is a true Deserted villager."

"Thank you, Lohan."

The water dropped in the well. All three of them stood at the edge of the well and looked down. They saw that the water was moving farther and farther away from them, and that the well had become an unfathomable bottomless dark hole, though they could still hear the wonderful sound of water.

"It will come often in the future," said Lohan.

"My tortoise!" Milan shrieked.

The tortoise had rolled over the edge of the well and fallen, making a sound like waves at the bottom of the well.

Milan was quiet, sitting at the edge of the well.

After a while, Mia whispered to her son, "Milan, have you thought it through?"

"Yes, Mom. The tortoise went home from here. It will come again. It likes to play with me. Mom, let's go back and eat dinner. I'm hungry."

The family went to bed early that night. But in the middle of the night, Mia heard a noise in Milan's room.

"Milan, where are you going at this hour?" Mia asked her son seriously.

"I thought I heard my tortoise coming back. It was crawling in the mountains. Mom, do you remember it promised me?"

"I know, my dear, but I don't think he'll come again so soon. Tortoises are slow, aren't they?"

"How long do I have to wait?"

"First, you have to learn waiting, Milan, and then you'll know how long you have to wait."

"What is waiting?"

"Waiting is thinking of all the fun, happy things."

Milan put down the flashlight, and also the sack, which he had prepared to hold the tortoise. Then he took off his hat and coat, and went to bed again. Soon he was snoring.

Mia and Lohan returned to their bedroom. They stood in each other's arms in the middle of the room, thrilled and nervous, for they also heard the sound: the tortoise was crawling this way from Blue Mountain.

"This movement has been going on for tens of thousands of years," Lohan said softly.

22
Gray

Spoon left him. Every time Gray thought of this, his heart ached. Sometimes he felt that he understood, but the next minute he didn't.

It was a cloudy, windless day. Gray was in high spirits as he and Spoon went up Niulan Mountain. He had been thinking of the slope next to the cliff, where wild lilies grew. He had gathered many of them last year. Spoon didn't look as cheerful as usual, and sometimes her thoughts wandered. Gray thought she was simply tired from hard work. He blamed himself for not taking good enough care of her. Today was a good example: he should have let her stay home and rest, but he took her up the hill just because *he* was in a good mood. He still hadn't learned to be considerate of other people.

Just then, Gray saw a big yellow beast. "Tiger!" He grabbed Spoon to stop her from going any farther.

The tiger paced contentedly up and down in the pine grove ahead. It was hard to tell whether it noticed them or not. One thing was certain, though: it did not intend to attack them.

For some reason, Spoon fought to break free of Gray.

"What are you doing, Spoon?" Gray asked anxiously.

In the fierce look that Spoon gave him, Gray saw the old

Spoon from the past. He was so shocked and depressed that he felt he was falling into hell. Just as he was struggling in the dark, Spoon angrily broke away from his grip and ran recklessly toward the Amur tiger.

The tiger immediately snatched Spoon up with its mouth, and dragged her into the bushes. Gray raced over madly to hit it with his two-toothed hoe, but the tiger dodged away each time, and his hoe connected only with the ground. The tiger carried Spoon off, and soon ran out of sight. Only Spoon's excited voice echoed in the air: "Gray, I'm leaving you, I will not come back! You're on your own now!"

Gray stood there alone. He saw the cliff, and he saw the wild lilies on the slope and some other herbs across from the wild lilies. But now the herbs no longer attracted him; he seemed to be looking at them through another man's eyes. What had happened just now? Maybe it was a show that Spoon had put on to get away from him? But it was a real tiger, and he could distinctly hear it stepping on the dead leaves. Spoon wouldn't have been so excited if it weren't a real tiger. He knew this much about her temperament. She was tired of their work and had impulsively joined the tiger. As Gray imagined scenes of Spoon with the tiger, he unexpectedly felt excited, too. The excitement was followed by frustration. He alternated between excitement and despair for a long time. Finally, he slowly calmed down. "I will be someone like Mrs. Yi," he said to himself. It was as if his voice were coming from another person. He dug up some wild lilies and trudged down the mountain.

It was late afternoon when he got home. He didn't understand how time had passed so quickly. It should have been just a little past noon.

While he was eating dinner, Dad was doing his book-keeping. Gray didn't pay attention to his father, but his father was observing him. No sooner had he finished his meal than his father came over and sat down at the table.

"Spoon said good-bye to us this afternoon. I wished her luck. She's a brave girl, and she will be okay in the outside world. We don't have to worry about her, do we? "

"No, we don't. But what's going on?" Gray asked blankly.

"There's always something in life that you can't explain at the moment. Earlier this afternoon, your mother and I sat here looking out the window. We saw the you of twenty years from now. Can you believe it?"

"What do I look like? Tell me!"

"You're dressed in black, and your face is covered by a large cloth hat."

"Like the men in black from Blue Mountain? My goodness!" He asked again, "Why did Spoon dump me?"

"She's struggling. You've struggled in the past, don't you remember?"

"I see."

He went into the kitchen to wash the dishes, and slowly started feeling less depressed. On the kitchen wall by the water tank a little green lizard was crawling at an imperceptible speed. Gray stared at it, deeply moved. He said to himself, "I must be as strong as it is . . . Today is Wednesday. Let me remember this day."

"It's getting late. It's midnight already. Go to bed, Gray." Dad's voice came from his bedroom.

Gray was taken aback—how time flew! Would his own time go by faster and faster? This was the last thing he wanted! He had to rest now or he wouldn't have energy to work tomorrow. Gray made up his mind: he would put aside all thoughts and feelings, and learn from the lizard.

After taking a bath, he went to bed. He forced his thoughts into the darkness, and after a while he fell asleep. At dawn he heard Spoon's laughter and woke up with a start. He crept out of the house to the yard, and then he felt completely refreshed.

With a hoe on his shoulder, Gray went to Mrs. Yi's herb garden to do some work before breakfast.

Gray's parents stayed up all night. It was not until his father saw from the window that Gray had gone out that the couple breathed a sigh of relief and lay down to sleep. When they woke up, the first thing the mother said was, "Our Gray is a late bloomer." The father replied, "That's okay, isn't it?" Then they started laughing.

At the same time, Gray was weeding in the herb garden. He looked up and saw Mrs. Yi.

"Spoon is gone," Gray said.

"I know, she came by. Gray, you're a grown man now. You're one of the best-looking men in Yun Village. Mr. Yi and I were just talking about you."

"Thank you for saying that. Don't worry, I won't be as shallow as before."

After she left, Gray continued working for a while. His pain had vanished. "I'm very secure now!" he said to himself. He had weeded about half the herb garden.

On the way home, he heard someone talking about him behind his back.

"He was always good-looking but we didn't notice him. He's a barefoot doctor now. All of a sudden he's remarkable."

Turning around, he saw Dad.

"Dad, who's talking with you?"

"No one. Perhaps you heard Yun Village talking? That's good, Gray, that means you are very important now."

"How can I be important?"

"Of course you are. Everyone in Yun Village should be. You've thought of yourself as a smashed pot. That's why you weren't important in the past."

Gray laughed. Father and son stopped to look at the blue sky, which seemed a little different from the way it was in the past, surprisingly higher and farther away. And they could see beyond the sky. Gray asked Dad why he had acted that way in the past, and Dad said it was because he had not yet been exposed to herbs. Dad said that people who didn't love plants and animals couldn't know their own importance. Fortunately, Gray wasn't that kind of person; he was just a late bloomer.

After thinking it over, Gray realized Dad was right. The ignorant life that he used to lead was terrible. He might have made mistakes at any moment and be dead.

"Now I'm on the right track," he said to his father.

Afterward, they squatted down again and gathered some oxalis and birdweed to use as medicine for the neighbor with a urinary tract infection. As Gray picked them, he realized that because he hadn't paid any attention to these beautiful grasses before, they had also ignored him. And so he had turned himself into a loner, feeling sorry for himself all the time. His self-pity seemed so affected. Oh, thought Gray, the grasses were joyfully welcoming his harvest, for they longed for the journey of life! It would be a great journey.

It was the morning of the fifth day after Spoon had left, and Gray was making herbal medicine in the house. All of a sudden, he heard a landslide.

He ran out at once. His mother chased after him, shouting, "Gray, Gray! Where are you going . . . Danger!"

"I'm going to Mrs. Yi's . . . She went to Niulan Mountain today . . ."

Gray's voice grew weaker and weaker, and was soon blown away by the wind. His mother fell to the ground.

In the herb garden, Gray saw Mrs. Yi and her husband observing Niulan Mountain from a distance. They all smelled the strong odor of sulfur.

"Ah, Mrs. Yi, you've come back . . . ," Gray said. He felt as if his body were about to fall apart.

"Oh my God, the mudslide is so close to our village. Fortunately, we got the message in time. Mrs. Yi is blessed. Don't you think so, Gray?" Mr. Yi said.

"Who sent the message?" asked Gray, pressing his hand on his chest.

"It's Dr. Lin Baoguang. The guard from Blue Mountain stopped Mrs. Yi and told her to go home right away. You can see, she's all right. She said she flew back and the mudslide couldn't catch up with her."

Gray smiled as he imagined Mrs. Yi flying. Then he noticed that he was standing under Mr. Yi's umbrella, and his clothes were drenched.

Mrs. Yi urged him to go inside to change. So the three of them went in.

Gray came out wearing Mr. Yi's clothes, which were too big for him.

"We haven't told you about Tauber." Mrs. Yi turned to Gray. "I couldn't see Tauber on the mountain, but he kept telling me, 'Go home, go home.' He also said that he no longer paid attention to landslides here or there, but I had to be careful. So I came down the hill immediately. You see, there are good people protecting me everywhere. Do you feel the same way?"

Gray nodded with tears in his eyes. Thinking of the recent past, he became emotional.

The rain stopped and the sun shone again. Surprised, the

three of them went outside together. They walked straight in the direction of the mudslide and soon reached the end of the village. Farther on, they saw the debris flow. What kind of debris flow was this? Gray used the stick he was carrying to poke at the thing next to his feet. It looked like mud. Oh my God! It was coal! This great mass of high-quality coal had slid halfway down Niulan Mountain and piled up at their feet. What a generous gift! Gray felt feverish, as if the coal were burning. Soon they heard the villagers shouting.

"Coal, coal! It's coal . . ."

The villagers, men and women, old and young, were beaming. They came running over with baskets.

On the way back, Gray couldn't stop talking because he was so stirred up by what had just happened. For no reason, he started telling the Yis that when he was a child he had mistakenly entered the courtyard of the ancestral house. Now it no longer existed. He ran all around and lost his sense of direction. Though he tried and tried, he couldn't find a way out. The house was very dark, and he was afraid to go in. He dashed back and forth in the courtyard, but no matter which direction he took, he ran into the wall. He wanted to make some marks on the wall, but he couldn't find any chalk. Desperate, he finally remembered to shout for his dad. Dad appeared at once, not at all surprised, took his hand, and led him out the gate. "This is our ancestral home," Dad told young Gray. He noticed that Dad never mentioned this incident to anyone later.

"Does the ancestral home exist?" Gray asked the air, bewildered.

"You are remarkable!" Mr. and Mrs. Yi praised him in unison.

"What do you mean?" Gray asked.

"It's a remarkable thing that you came out of the ancestral house!" Mrs. Yi said.

"But I was muddleheaded, just following Dad out!"

"Muddleheaded!" Mr. Yi laughed heartily.

Mrs. Yi was also laughing. Gray wasn't able to follow their train of thought at the moment, and he felt embarrassed.

After returning to his own home, Gray couldn't calm down for a long time. Outside, the villagers passed by carrying coal and singing folksongs, as if celebrating a festival. Gray thought he should get some coal, too, so he picked up his basket and went out.

Standing at the gate, Dad smiled at him and said, "When you dig coal, you'd better keep watch all around!"

"Will something happen, Dad?"

"Wait and see. This is always the case, you'll see. It's the same as when we gather herbs . . ."

Dad didn't finish what he was saying. Gray thought Dad wanted him to figure something out by himself. So he began to pay attention to his own action.

Gray met the security guard Xiaoqiang, who was on his third trip. Xiaoqiang said he needed more coal because his wife would soon give birth.

When Gray reached the place, he looked about. He heard a wolf howling from underground. He tried to move aside, but the wolf howled at wherever he was standing. This frightened him, and he didn't dare dig down. He looked at Xiaoqiang beside him and saw that the guard was doing just the opposite. Xiaoqiang dug like crazy at wherever the wolf's howls came from. Soon his basket was full.

"Gray, are you thinking of your sweetheart?" Xiaoqiang asked mockingly. Then he walked steadily home with a full load of coal.

Gray stood and watched him blankly. The howls of the wolf in the earth gradually subsided into whimpers but still followed Gray wherever he went. Gray kept listening to them, tears streaming down his face. He couldn't dig down, for the wolf was right under the coal. It was a mountain spirit. He had dug at the python before. He had been so cold and unfeeling because he didn't recognize the mountain spirits. As it grew dark, Gray looked around and saw the coal quietly piling up at his feet, as if waiting for him to make up his mind.

He turned and went home, carrying an empty basket.

Looking up from his ledgers, Dad said, "Our Gray has matured."

Then Dad turned to fetch wine.

The family of three drank silently, to Niulan Mountain and to Gray.

As Gray drank, he looked intently at the window. There was a dark shadow—the head of a wolf. What a handsome wolf!

Though Dad's back was to the window, he somehow felt the wolf approaching, too. He said to Gray, "This is a unique gift for you from Niulan Mountain. See how lucky you are."

Gray went outside and saw that the wolf had retreated to the yard; in a few seconds it went out the gate. The breeze blew on his face and he smelled the animal.

"Did it come down the mountain?" Gray asked.

"I think it probably came from where Spoon is," Mom said.

"That's very possible," Dad said.

When the moon rose, the faint howls of the wolf brought Gray happiness. He no longer expected Spoon to come back to him, nor did he think that was very important.

"See how earnest he is now. His manner reminds me of the ancestor," said one villager, pointing at Gray from behind.

Gray's acupuncture treatment became so popular in Yun Village that patients now came to him almost every day. Ever since he had practiced acupuncture on himself, his view of the human body had changed. Or rather, he was completely fascinated by the human body—God's exquisite creation. When the silver needles entered a body, his vision followed them into the body. Holding a silver needle, he could actually "see" what was going on in the dark places—the movements of the internal organs, the reactions of the nerves and the muscles, and so on. And so he adapted his needles to bring relief to the patients and to improve the way their bodies functioned. Occasionally, a patient would test him by asking, "Dr. Gray, do you think I'm sick?"

Gray would smile and ask him to lie down on the treatment bed. He knew the patient was ill. After leaving several short needles in his body, he used a long needle to pierce the key acupuncture point. The patient groaned at once.

"Gray, Gray, you saved me!" he exclaimed.

Gray observed calmly from one side. He could clearly feel the patient's nerve respond to the needle, and he was satisfied with this response. When relief came, Gray uttered, "Ah," which was his way of sighing. In his first twenty years, he'd been befuddled, like someone who was blindfolded. Now he had learned through practicing acupuncture treatment that one could actually feel the other's physical pain. For example, this man who was the same age as he: through the silver needles, Gray became familiar with his body at once. Bodies were so sensitive—why hadn't he known this earlier?

"Gray, you are really a good and considerate doctor," the patient said as he dressed.

"It's just an ordinary medical treatment," Gray said shyly.

The patient couldn't resist giving him a hug before he left.

Something strange happened at midnight. When Gray woke up, he felt the familiar physical pain. He got dressed right away. Carrying his medical kit, he groped his way out in the dark, for he didn't want to disturb his parents.

"Gray, where are you going?" Mother asked from her bedroom.

"I need to go to Dr. Kay's clinic," Gray answered vaguely.

It was a very dark night, and all kinds of insects were making a great deal of noise in the grass by the roadside. It was ominous. Kay's clinic wasn't far away, but Gray walked for quite a while. It was as if the road under his feet were extending automatically. Filled with anxiety, he was drenched in cold sweat. While he was still struggling on the road, he suddenly heard someone talking, and an outstretched hand pulled him into a room.

"Ever since you arrived at dusk, I expected Gray to come," said Kay to Spoon, who was curled up and moaning on the diagnosis cot.

Gray opened the medical kit immediately and took out the silver needles. He began sterilizing them.

"Help me, Gray! The pain is killing me! Ah . . ."

When the silver needle was inserted, Spoon flipped up, and then dropped down, and didn't move anymore.

"Gray, my dear, how could I have left you?" she cried softly.

About an hour later, after the acupuncture and moxibustion treatment, Spoon felt that the pain in her back had almost completely disappeared.

"Spoon, only Gray can see your pain through his fingers. Go home with him."

Spoon blinked her eyes—still wet from tears—and said, "He's an angel, I'm a devil. I'll kill him if we're together. I need to be far away from here before dawn."

She quickly gathered up her things and left without so much as a glance at Gray.

"Gray, don't lose heart. See how much she loves you," Kay said, looking at him.

"You're right. We were in love with each other. That should be enough for me. It never occurred to me that I'd be able to help her as a doctor."

"Are you really okay with it?"

Gray nodded his head earnestly. He meant what he said. As he gave Spoon the acupuncture treatment, something had flashed through his head, and he could even see the outline of his ancestral home.

He walked out the door, then turned to Kay: "I do love Spoon, Dr. Kay, and I love you, too. I was on top of the world tonight."

It was still dark outside, and insects were still making a big disturbance in the grass. Gray stared hard into the darkness, and suddenly he saw two things inside his ancestral home—a square dining table with a delicate teapot on it. The sight flared for a second and then was extinguished.

"Are you coming again, Gray . . . ," asked an old man hoarsely.

Then the old man's figure faded away.

Of course he would return eventually. He was destined to meet Spoon again in this way. The wonderful silver needle connected her to his destiny. Now he was beginning to see the significance of his profession. He quickened his pace.

He wasn't depressed at all. On the contrary, he felt proud. From a distance, he saw the light in his house. He knew how much his parents loved him and how much they worried about him. Now he could reassure them.

He was whistling when he went inside.

"Gray, you still have time to get some sleep. You'll have sweet dreams!" Dad said from his bedroom.

"Yes, Dad, I'm looking forward to that!"

He fell asleep easily in the grass. The insects swarmed around him, and he returned to the depths of darkness. He began his journey to the ancestral house. Someone gently took his hand, and he knew who was walking beside him. He wanted to keep going without turning.

He did not think he was an angel. Instead, like Spoon, he often thought he was a devil. Now, despite his enthusiasm and dedication to his medical practice, on a rainy day he would suddenly feel the urge to kill. The objects were often snakes, lizards, and the herb with the local name of seven-leaf flower, or dandelion—this weed that grew everywhere drove him crazy. The strange thing was that despite his urge to kill, he never actually harmed the plants or animals. And as he grew older, he felt less and less likely to do evil. He crouched down and looked at a little green snake. "I'm getting a little older. It's a good thing . . . What do you think?" The snake didn't move. Although it was motionless, Gray felt it communicating with him. Gray was moved by the wild thing, and—through it—he saw his own foolishness.

On rainy spring nights, Gray often heard a woman walking toward him from far away. The woman didn't look like Spoon, but she was the type he longed for—flexible, strong, and not too young. Her eyes were penetrating, like his. She could see his unmentionable disease but not worry about it. She sat at his bedside, put her arms around his neck, and told him that his illness was benign. Not only would it not harm him, it would be beneficial. Gray was very pleased. He remembered sneaking into the back room in the dark with her once and fiddling with the herbs. Gray said to her, "You're not Spoon. You look nothing like her."

"But I am," the woman said.

When Dad coughed in the next room, the woman vanished. Gray tried repeatedly to grab her but missed. He knew she wasn't far off, and he knew she wasn't Spoon, only a little like Spoon. He hoped the rain would stop, so it wouldn't soak her clothes and hair.

"Gray, have you found a new girlfriend?" Father asked him in the morning.

"It seems so. But no—no," Gray said.

Gray began to pay attention to the old villagers, whom he had completely ignored. In the past, he had refused to interact with old people, not even looking at them. Though Grandpa Onion had caused him to reconsider his attitude, he still seldom associated with seniors.

The transformation was brought about by an old man whose nickname was "Beard."

Gray called him Grandpa Beard. He was very thin, only skin and bones, and he had phlegm in his throat all year round. It was strange that his eyes were so bright, as sharp as knives. Gray used to stay away from him.

"Grandpa Beard is related to us," Dad said. "Gray, you look like him. I noticed this long ago."

Gray disagreed. He had a square face, but Grandpa Beard's face was like a loofah. Maybe Dad meant something else. Dad asked him to ease Grandpa Beard's pain with acupuncture. In fact, the old man seemed to be in no pain at all, and he always smiled when he saw Dad.

"How do you know he's in pain?" Gray asked Dad.

"Those things in his chest communicate with me," Dad replied.

Gray was ashamed because he hadn't noticed that Grandpa Beard was in pain.

He carried the medical kit to Grandpa Beard's home. Grandpa Beard had built a rockery in front of his house. The rockery was big, and two little monkeys were jumping in it. They were Grandpa Beard's pets.

Gray chose several acupuncture points. As he thrust the needle down to the "Tiantu" point, he was startled, for he could clearly see not only Grandpa Beard's lungs, but also his pulsating heart. He felt a little dizzy.

"It's okay, Gray, I have nothing to hide," Grandpa Beard said clearly.

After a while, Gray's vision returned to normal. He inserted needles into other acupuncture points and left them there. He didn't dare examine Grandpa Beard's internal organs for fear of fainting.

When he twirled the silver needles, the phlegm in Grandpa Beard's throat disappeared. Gray took a quick look, and saw that the bronchi and lung lobes were clearing. Unable to speak, Grandpa Beard held Gray's hand to convey his gratitude. After the treatment, Grandpa Beard exhaled a long breath and said, "The roses of those days, you could smell them from a mile away. Will you come with me to see the roses of the olden days?"

"Let's set a time, Grandpa Beard."

"No, it can't be done that way. But we'll meet again. Really, I can't bear to part with you, Gray."

When Grandpa Beard walked Gray to the door, Gray smelled the heavy fragrance of roses. When Gray asked if he had planted roses in the backyard, Grandpa Beard said no. Then he laughed and said, "If a man thinks of a plant day and night, the plant will linger around him."

When Gray passed the rockery, the little monkeys jumped up and disappeared behind it. The movements of the two monkeys stirred a puff of wind, which Gray called rose wind. Gray felt refreshed. He believed that the old man who thought of roses day after day was living in happiness even if he suffered from chronic diseases. In his mind, he saw the old man's clear lungs again.

"Which dynasty was he born in?" Gray asked himself aloud, his voice humming in the air.

Gray told Dad, "He had nothing to hide. I saw everything."

"Of course, he's an old man with a big heart. Do you like him?"

Gray nodded vigorously.

"Once, he led the villagers out of a sea of fire," Dad said.

"Now he's surrounded by roses . . . an old man, who was leading such a wonderful, pure life, is right next to us . . . I had never realized that! Dad, do you think he is a kind of mountain god?"

"What else could he be?" Dad was lost in thought.

Every day, Gray thought about going with Grandpa Beard to see the roses of the past. But the old man never brought this up again during his daily treatments. The day that a course of treatment ended, and Grandpa Beard's staph infection was much improved, he held Gray's hand, pointed to the window, and asked if he noticed anything. Looking out, Gray didn't see anything.

"Just sniff it," Grandpa Beard said. "The roses of the past are coming."

He sniffed hard for a while, but he couldn't smell the roses.

Grandpa Beard patted him on the shoulder and said,

"Don't lose heart. Keep trying and you'll smell it. The roses always come in from the windows. When you sleep at home, if you're alert at dawn, they'll come. This is something you can learn through practice, especially a young guy like you."

Gray began staying alert. But the roses did not come in the hazy dawn; they came in broad daylight, under bright sunshine—it was a complete surprise.

It was like daydreaming; Gray couldn't remember the details. He was working in the herb garden, and Mrs. Yi and her husband were out. The weasel suddenly ran directly toward him. Gray rubbed his eyes in bewilderment, and then he was horrified to see a paring knife in its back. Holding the weasel, he ran to his medicine kit which he had set down in a corner of the garden. He opened the kit, pulled out the paring knife, sterilized and bandaged the wound, and gave the weasel some medicine. He did all of this mechanically. The weasel was weak and its eyes were half-closed, as if it were dying. Looking into its eyes, Gray was overwhelmed by a sadness which he had never experienced before. After a while, Mr. and Mrs. Yi returned. Gray had no memory of anything after that. He didn't even remember how he got home. Dad made him sit in a recliner in the yard. Sitting there in the sun, he remembered the weasel and sniffed his hand to see if it had left a bad smell. But no. When he sniffed again, he smelled the roses. He looked at his hands over and over, wondering how that stinky little animal could smell like roses. He turned and saw his father smiling at him.

"Gray, let's go to the backyard and take a look," Dad said.

They went together to the backyard. Gray saw a row of roses in full bloom along the fence. The air was fragrant. Gray asked Dad if he had planted the roses, and Dad said no one had planted the roses—they had just grown on their own.

"There are seeds everywhere. Besides, aren't you thinking about them?" Dad winked at Gray.

"Yes, I am. I'm thinking of our weasel, too . . ."

"In fact, the weasel came in the night. The weasel and the roses belong to the same family."

Gray understood what Dad meant. He thought that he and Spoon also belonged to the same family. They weren't together now, but they responded to each movement the other one made. Would roses grow where Spoon lived, too?

Father and son squatted to look at the roses and listen to the footsteps. No one passed by, but there were footsteps. They both knew what was going on, and they were immersed in the scene.

When Mom approached, they stood up at the same time.

"You're accomplished now, Gray," Mom said with tears in her eyes. "When I saw the roses growing, I remembered things from your childhood."

"Mom, I'm sorry I gave you so much trouble."

"That's a silly thing to say."

The sun was still bright and there was no wind. But the flowers were nodding along with the steady footsteps!

"Oh, my God," Gray whispered.

Then they heard a knock at the courtyard door.

"Beard!" Dad exclaimed, and strode over to open the door.

As Gray sat down in Grandpa Onion's room, he felt a little absentminded. Grandpa Onion told him that he had recently taken a rare herbal medicine, and his lumbar spine had become much stronger. As proof of this, he even demonstrated a few martial arts moves. Gray was astonished. When Onion stopped moving, Gray noticed that the upper and lower parts of the old man's body were separated in the air. Gray was scared, and he couldn't help but probe the gap between the two body parts.

"Ah! Ah . . . ," he gasped.

"Ha-ha, this happens often," Onion said.

"How could you—"

"So can you! Suppose you are ill—everyone can be ill—you can make room for your illness, as I did. Gray, this is the method your father taught me in the past! Before you were born, your father was paralyzed with a strange disease. He was bedridden. When I went to see him, I found that he wasn't depressed at all. He was playing games with his illness. He was so excited playing these games that he kicked and waved—not a bit like a paralyzed patient! He played all kinds of games, and he was so engrossed in them. And then one day, he stood up."

With this, Grandpa Onion told Gray to have a look outside.

He opened the door and smelled the wind from the mountains. Grandpa Onion said that the black-clad guard was passing a message to him. It was out of the ordinary for Grandpa Onion to do something like this, and once he did, those black-clad guards immediately knew and hastened to contact him. Onion asked Gray how he felt at the moment, and Gray said he felt very comfortable—he could hear bees humming on Niulan Mountain.

"What kind of herb have you taken?" Gray asked.

"In fact, it's an ordinary herb. It's the big blood vine, which I gathered in the mountains. There's something special about this vine, though. Sometimes a special growing environment can change an herb's medicinal property completely and produce unexpected results."

"Grandpa Onion, can you pass your experiences on to me?"

"I can't. You have to learn from your own experience."

"I hope I'll have the opportunity!"

"You'll have many opportunities."

Gray walked with his head bent, a little depressed. It had been more than two years since he started practicing medicine, but he hadn't made much progress. What would Mrs. Yi think of his work? His faltering had wasted a lot of time. What kind of man would he turn out to be? Suddenly he heard Tauber talking to him.

"Gray, you really are somebody now. Incredible. Now those roses are blooming for you!"

He looked around but saw no one. He smiled, and his mood brightened. At the end of the road the weasel hurried by. He said to himself, "I'll go on gathering herbs and making medicines, and I'll plant herbs. I'm happy to be an herb farmer." Even the dead Tauber could see his happiness. His happiness was related to his father. He'd never known what kind of person his father was; he had only known he was Yun Village's accountant. Today, he had been overwhelmed by the story of Father and his illness. His parents were so remarkable, and it was under their subtle influence that he had become interested in herbs. Just then, he thought of something: This was work that he could enjoy for a lifetime. What was this work? The work that he had just spoken of— being an herb farmer.

Ginger walked up and said loudly, "You look great, Gray!"

"Did Tauber come just now, Ginger?" asked Gray.

"Yes, but he's already returned to the mountains."

"Yun Village is wonderful: the quick and the dead live together!"

"I only found that out this year. It seems that you knew it before I did!"

"No, I just found out."

There were footsteps all around, and they looked at each other in silence.

After saying good-bye to Ginger, Gray went to Mrs. Yi's house. On the way he met another person.

It was the black-clad guard of Blue Mountain, but he was wearing the clothes of an ordinary farmer. He wasn't wearing a black hood, either. Even so, Gray recognized him.

"Where are you going, sir?" Gray asked.

"I've been waiting for you. Here you are. I'm leaving."

"Why? Since you were waiting for me, you must have something to say to me."

"No, I never talk much."

The guard left hurriedly. Looking at his figure receding into the distance, Gray shed tears. He thought of the first time he had seen the guard: when the guard bent to tie his shoelaces in a crowd of people, the men behind him pushed him down and stepped on him. Gray still remembered his pained expression. Today the guard had waited for him on the road. What did this mean? He looked around and saw wild roses by the side of the road where the guard had been standing. Many buds were slowly opening, one after another . . . Gray was dumbfounded. Obviously, it was not he but the guard who made the roses blossom—for him, Gray! He crouched down, pressed his left cheek against the flowers, and then he heard the footsteps again. He looked up and saw a group of black-clad guards heading toward Niulan Mountain. One of them seemed familiar.

"Wait! Hello!" cried Gray, waving his hand.

The men stopped, seemingly unable to decide whether to go on. Then they moved on, and soon were out of sight in the mountains.

In the fragrance of the roses, Gray's mind became very clear. He murmured, "Sir, many years ago when I was a boy, we met at the foot of Niulan Mountain, didn't we? Will you come and see me again?"

Epilogue

Spring was coming. Standing on the road in Yun Village, one could see the flowers in full bloom on Niulan Mountain.

As she was enjoying the mountain flowers, Mrs. Ma decided to visit her husband's grave. Mrs. Yi had just given her a bottle of herbal medicine. Somehow, Mrs. Ma wasn't sad at all: she was animated as she dressed up and put on the embroidered shoes she had made for herself. Her daughter Yungu stood watching; she was also happy.

"Your dead daddy is full of tricks. He enjoys staying beside the cave alone!" said the mother.

"I think Daddy will be very happy today!" Yungu said. Then she lowered her voice and asked, "Uncle Mud won't be jealous, will he?" She was referring to her stepfather.

"He can't wait for me to go, so that his friends can come over for drinks. He said that he also wanted to be buried next to the cave when the time comes. It will be easy for your family to visit if the three of us are buried in the same place. More and more families in this situation are buried together now."

Mrs. Ma put the medicine bottle into her sack, and set out joyfully.

When she went out of the gate, she noticed something. Calling for Yungu to come out, she pointed at the top of the fence. "Where is the mirror? Have you moved it? Put it back where it was! Your daddy will definitely return today, don't you remember?"

Yungu ran into the house to get the mirror. Relieved, Mrs. Ma left.

It wasn't long before she heard the song. She was blinded by tears—her dead husband was singing, not very loudly but with deep emotion.

"You damn fool! You damn fool!" said the woman. She nodded along with each line of the song.

As she neared the cave in the mountain, the singing stopped and everything became quiet.

"Dear, take your medicine," Mrs. Ma said as she poured the liquid on the grave.

The scent of the herbal medicine pervaded the air at once.

"Mother, mother . . . ," Yungu shouted. She came up panting.

"What's the matter?" Mrs. Ma asked.

"The mirror . . . I think Daddy has come home!"

"What happened to the mirror?"

"There were many sika deer in the mirror! It must be Daddy who invited them. Daddy never shot sika deer when he went hunting. I looked toward the woods: I definitely saw no deer. They were just running in the mirror! I was thinking of Daddy's last year: Daddy often made gestures and whistled to the mirror . . ." Yungu looked distressed.

"I see. Let's go home. This damn fool!"

Though she scolded her dead husband, she was very happy. She imagined that on this beautiful day, her late husband was singing mountain songs and coming home.

Mother and daughter descended the hill in silence. But when they came to the fence and looked in the big round mirror, they saw nothing but the woods.

"Daddy must have grown tired of waiting," Yungu said, downhearted.

"Nonsense." Mud came out with a cup in his hand. "After you left, I drank a few cups with Mr. Ma! Didn't I say I would have my friend over for a drink? He's the one I meant. I was afraid Yungu would be in our way, so I flimflammed her into leaving. Ha. What a beautiful friendship!"

Mrs. Ma kept wiping away her tears, and then she laughed.

"He said he would return often," Mud announced.

"What about the deer?" asked the girl.

"Your father and I summoned them. I used to hunt, so they also know me."

At dinner that night, they saved a seat for Mr. Ma.

"You never know when he'll show up," Mud said.

Over time, Ginger became prettier, and her sallow cheeks turned rosy. Ever since her late mother-in-law, Mrs. Yossi, came to visit her at home at midnight, she had grown more self-assured. She was no longer suspicious of others, and with Mrs. Yi's encouragement she began to study medicine. "It's never too late to learn," Mrs. Yi said to her. "Besides, you can help others with your medical knowledge." Ginger thought that helping neighbors was now her favorite thing to do.

She was a happy young woman now. She attributed her change to Mrs. Yi and her late mother-in-law. Sometimes she would wake up at night and say aloud, "I love Mrs. Yi so much!"

"Good, that's very good. Mrs. Yi is all right . . . ," her husband replied sleepily.

"But you don't understand that kind of love. I often wonder how Mrs. Yi communicated with your mother. My memories burrow into one dark hole after another, where I eavesdrop on their conversations. Sometimes I hear, sometimes I don't . . . Alas!"

Now fully awake, her husband said, "My mother loved you and was a little worried about you, so she asked Mrs. Yi to look after you."

"You're right. Yun Village is really a good place. Now I'm sleepy."

In her dream, she laughed and laughed.

When her elder daughter left for school, Ginger followed her, shouting, "If you run into a weasel, be sure to stay out of its way! It is Mrs. Yi's pet, and everyone else's, too. Be kind to it!"

Ever since seeing the weasel in Mrs. Yi's herb garden, Ginger had been in love with it. It had lost a patch of hair on the left side of its belly, so it was easy to recognize. She had seen it in the vegetable plot, by the toilet, in the lean-to, and in the woods. In order to lure it to her home, she raised several black-and-white chickens, hoping the weasel would fall in love with one of them because Mrs. Yi had told her the weasel had been in love with her black-and-white chicken. Ginger watched her own chickens closely, but never saw the weasel approach them. The weasel was elusive, solitary, beautiful, and arrogant. Ginger sighed, "What a devoted lover!"

Ginger began to gather herbs in the hills. She decided to improve her medical skills by identifying herbs. Mrs. Yi had told her it was the easiest way. "Sickness and herbs are lovers," she used to say. Ginger considered this and found it meaningful because it reminded her of her mother-in-law and of her mother-in-law's illness. With this thought, she took great pleasure in picking herbs on the mountains.

For example, one time on the north slope of Niulan Mountain when she found a large clump of diamond thorn, she was so excited that she repeatedly called out to her mother-in-law. She felt that the diamond thorn was her mother-in-law's lover! Gathering herbs was a wonderful process, and now she knew dozens of herbs. Some were precious but most were ordinary. For Ginger, even common herbs were one more kind of lover in addition to the weasel. Now that she was courting them every day, why wouldn't she be in a good mood?

"Niulan Mountain," Ginger murmured as she worked in the garden, "with you, my mother-in-law won't be lonely. She lives in your belly and watches our family from there. She said she would protect us." As she said this, the wind from Niulan Mountain relayed a vague murmuring. Ginger listened ecstatically. After a while, she heard the footsteps of Mrs. Yi and her husband, so she quickly brushed the dirt off her clothes and ran to the gate.

"Ginger, did you gather a lot of herbs on the mountain yesterday?" Mr. Yi asked with a smile.

"Not bad—I found a lot of diamond thorn."

"Good for you. The wild diamond thorn was your mother-in-law's favorite," Mrs. Yi said.

Mrs. Yi's words reminded Ginger of the night when her mother-in-law came to visit. She stood in the dark, and she herself stood in a bright place, both talking loudly. Later, her mother-in-law made a strange gesture, as if she were holding a gift for her in both hands. Ginger stretched out her hand but couldn't reach it. Then her mother-in-law disappeared into the shadows. Ginger was a little depressed because she didn't receive the gift from her mother-in-law. She told Mrs. Yi of this, and Mrs. Yi said that actually Ginger had received it and that this was typical of Aunt Yossi's behavior. Ginger would know this in the future. By repeatedly pondering the meaning of her mother-in-law's gesture, Ginger was imperceptibly reassured.

She realized that her life was being enriched day after day because she had indeed received what her mother-in-law gave her. In her eyes, everything now was in love and confiding in one another. Sometimes she tried to overhear the murmurs—the whispers of love—but she never really succeeded. For example, when she saw the weasel make out with the sunflower, why did her heart pound? It seemed Mrs. Yi was right about the gift from her mother-in-law. Mrs. Yi was the same type of person as her mother-in-law. Ginger hadn't been deliberately waiting for her mother-in-law to visit, but when it really happened last time, she was extremely excited. After that, she thought Yun Village was great. This custom was remarkable—dead relatives were never far away. They lived in the bodies of living people. Was it because of this custom that she had set her heart on studying medicine? She couldn't sort out such complicated things, but she felt much better about herself now.

One day Ginger noticed her elder daughter observing the herbs she had planted in the yard. The eyes of this nine-year-old revealed a girlish love, and once more Ginger's heart beat faster. She flushed and slipped away in a panic. Ginger walked a long way, but when she turned around, her daughter was still squatting motionless beside the herbs. "The world is possessed . . . ," Ginger said to herself. She thought she should plant some more roses in the corner. Why not? Now she had something to give to her relatives and neighbors. When had this begun?

———

Winter was coming, and more and more people came to buy Widow Liang's roasted sweet potatoes. The sweet potatoes she kept in the cellar were improved varieties: mellow and extra sweet, they were mouthwatering. With more customers, she and her son were now better off. When she was alone, she would say, "Liang Shan, how happy you would be if you had lived to see this day!" But Liang Shan had gone. This optimistic man had endured a lifetime of hardships in order to lay the foundation for a better life for his wife and child. Every time she thought of this, she wanted to cry, but her tears had dried up. Some days ago, a relative told her that Yun Village was a blessed place. Everyone who stayed here would achieve happiness in the end. Had Liang Shan achieved his happiness? She guessed so, and Mrs. Yi thought so, too. Mrs. Yi was no ordinary person. She was a saint who could see through to people's hearts. Of course Widow Liang wanted to stay in Yun Village. She had never thought of going anywhere else. Besides, her husband was buried here, and sometimes he came to visit her. If she went away, they would never see each other again.

She also thought about remarrying, for after all was said and done, it was too hard to get through the long nights. After considering it carefully, she felt that perhaps she could find a companion among the out-of-towners. She had no sooner come up with this idea than she thought of a man who had just come to Yun Village the year before. He was a bachelor with light eyebrows and a cheerful face. This man bought her roasted sweet potatoes every day.

"What do you do for a living?"

"I'm a bricklayer. Do you want your house repaired?"

"Not yet, thank you."

While they were talking, the man took a close look at her hands as she worked, and when she noticed his gaze, she blushed—her hands were rough and old. The man glanced away. Then he looked into her eyes and told her that he had fallen in love with Yun Village and Niulan Mountain. He had made up his mind to settle down in Yun Village. For years, while he was drifting, he had dreamed of spending the rest of his life in a place like this.

"What do you think of this place?" Widow Liang asked him.

"It's hard to say. In short, everything is plump here."

"Plump?"

"Yes." He went on, "My real name is hard to remember. You may call me Peach."

"Peach. That's a nice name. There are some things which only outsiders can see clearly."

Widow Liang didn't expect to make friends with Peach. That day, a long time after Peach had walked far away, she kept thinking: she and Liang Shan had struggled with hardships ever since they had married, and now Liang Shan had gone. Was this life "plump"? The more deeply she thought about what Peach said, the more it made sense to her. Everything that related to her late husband was still everywhere around her and Songbao, and around the Yun villagers, too. She and the other villagers felt it in silence, and she still talked to him in the dark. Wasn't this the plump life? If Liang Shan were still here, he'd be content. There was no improved variety of sweet potatoes in the past; now there was. Liang Shan would have been elated.

Now, in the middle of the night, Widow Liang also began to talk to Peach: "Peach, do you think I should remarry?" She knew the answer, because Peach understood her, and he also knew Yun Village. It was as if God had sent him to re-place Liang Shan.

He looked again at her hands as she worked at the fire-place.

"Are they ugly?" she asked.

"No, they're beautiful. I'm fascinated by them."

She cried softly.

"Let's get married."

"Okay, we'll get married."

Widow Liang's house was reroofed. Friends and relatives came to celebrate the wedding.

Tauber was used to drifting in the mountains and in the village. He didn't feel that being without a real body was a big handicap, because he could always imagine himself with a body. Wandering around in the familiar friendly en-vironment, he would sometimes come across Mrs. Yi. That explained his behavior. He'd had a crush on her for a long time. He knew he would never say anything about his se-cret love, so there was nothing wrong with it. After all, he had carried this love to the grave. Who could be jealous of a dead man?

Now Tauber entered the village joyfully. He was going to examine all the details of Yun Village which he had over-looked in his rushed and rough old days. The day had just dawned, and the villagers had not yet gotten up, but Grandma Mao's big gray horse unexpectedly came out alone for a walk. The horse was astonished at seeing Tauber, and stopped in the middle of the road. Tauber thought, This gray horse re-ally knows human nature, for it noticed that I was different from the people in the village. He tried to get close enough to touch the horse, but it turned and trotted back to Grandma

Mao's yard. The horse's wariness did not affect his good mood at all. He thought the animal was wary because it wasn't yet used to people like him. If it saw him again and again, they would be good friends. Tauber bent down to look at the varied pebbles on the ground. How elegant the stones were. Year after year, they kissed the feet of the people in Yun Village. They were endlessly communicating with people in silence, endlessly compassionate. Look closely: each stone actually had one expression—the profound expression of an eyewitness to history. Tauber discovered one pure white stone which was especially like Mrs. Yi. He couldn't help crouching down: he wanted to talk with it.

"Good morning, Tauber . . ."

The voice came from above. It wasn't the stone, but Mrs. Yi herself speaking.

"I was thinking about you just now. Are you making house calls?" said Tauber excitedly.

"Yes. I was thinking about you, too. What a coincidence! I want to have a good talk with you under the acacia tree one of these days. Now I have to go—a newcomer's wife is going into labor."

She left, carrying the medicine box. As he watched her leave, Tauber felt strong emotions surging in his chest.

Then his gaze rested on the ground again. In the morning light, he saw that each of the small stones looked impassioned. Suddenly, a shadow moved toward him. Tauber looked up and saw the big gray horse.

"Did you recognize me, brother?"

The horse moved close to him, and Tauber immediately smelled the reeds and the lake. He put his arms round the horse's neck, closed his eyes, and murmured, "How did I miss you, man? I'm thinking of you even in my dreams!

We've covered thousands of miles together, and it's true . . . I remember that you were always waiting for me at a fork in the road and never stood me up. There were white locust flowers all over the ground."

The big gray horse fell to its knees. It understood Tauber's words, and a distant memory floated in its eyes.

When Tauber's ceremony with the big gray horse was over, he noticed Grandma Mao standing nearby.

Grandma Mao waved to him. She was laughing, her toothless mouth agape.

"Tauber, it's predestined that you would like this fellow who is dear to me. This guy's been running around for about a week," Mao said. "I knew he was looking for someone who had known him long ago, perhaps known his mother . . . It didn't cross my mind that it was you! I was really surprised. What happened in the old days of war?"

As she spoke, the horse went home on its own. Pondering what Grandma Mao had said, Tauber was puzzled: it was a beautiful but odd narrative. Is it because I'm dead that Grandma Mao is talking to me this way?

"Grandma Mao," said Tauber, thinking for a moment, "your words have inspired me. Perhaps this gray horse is me. I remember now. Extraordinary things did happen! But I had just a few memories, and it was this horse that kept them in my mind. Grandma Mao, I am so grateful to you . . ."

But Grandma Mao seemed unwilling to listen to Tauber's expression of gratitude. Her eyes wandered, and she murmured something as she left.

After meandering all morning, Tauber finally met it by the well. It was at that moment that Tauber realized he had been looking for it. It was an ordinary tortoise. When the well water rose to the opening of the well, it climbed out.

Tauber sat on the edge of the well, and it climbed onto Tauber's knee.

"Hello!" Tauber said.

The tortoise didn't move, as if it had become a fossil.

A song came from Blue Mountain; both Tauber and the tortoise were listening. When the man had finished singing, Tauber saw the water descend in the well.

"You're home now," Tauber said gently to the tortoise. "Where is your home? Is it Blue Mountain, or here? Maybe both? Why don't you come with me to Niulan Mountain? The place where I live may look a little isolated, but in fact it is very lively! Tortoise, Yun villagers now all know who you are—just look how popular you are! Okay, we're going to my place. There's a brook nearby. You'll like it."

Holding the motionless tortoise in his hand, Tauber walked to Niulan Mountain. All the way, Tauber's ears were ringing with the sound of the sea. Tauber thought, Wherever there was a tortoise, you could hear the sound of the sea. The association was so natural.

"Grandpa Tauber, let's keep it." Milan pointed to the tortoise in Tauber's hand.

"Milan, you should know, it chose to stay here. It climbed up out of the well, up onto my lap, and won't leave. Let's take it to Niulan Mountain."

"Great!" Milan flushed with excitement.

Tauber looked up at the sky and saw the eagle circling. It was time to go home. Whenever he stayed out too long, the eagle would come and urge him to be on his way.

Tauber and Milan climbed the mountain excitedly. Tauber knew Milan was too young to hear the underground chorus, but look how enthralled the little fellow was!

———

A swarthy, thin old man was standing in front of the gate of Yun Village Primary School selling flower seeds. He held up a clear plastic bag and shouted, "Roses, jasmine, camellias . . ." His voice wasn't high. In the bag about a dozen different colored flower seeds were sealed in smaller transparent plastic bags. Teacher Zhang heard the flower seeds give off the sound of small stones colliding, and he couldn't help but stare closely at the plastic bag.

"May I ask your name?" Teacher Zhang said nervously.

"My name is Lin Baoguang," the old man said. "Buy two bags of seeds and plant them next to the fence on the campus. Even if the seeds don't sprout, the students will like them, because it is a kind of faith."

"Dr. Lin Baoguang, the saint! Of course I will buy them. Three yuan for a pack? I'll take them all. Can you tell me why these seeds are small stones?"

"They are special varieties that I brought from Blue Mountain. Why are they small colored stones? That's a good question. Because they are handed down from ancient times. Do you like them?"

"Yes, I do! Will they sprout and come out of the ground?"

"Never mind that sort of thing. Students will be patient."

"Oh, of course! Thank you very much!"

Dr. Lin Baoguang left the primary school and headed toward the oil factory. Spring came late this year. In the early spring mists floated images of men laboring in the fields. It was a little hard for him to walk now, and he wondered if this was the last time he would come to Yun Village. He was very glad that he had just sold all his seeds. This was Yun Village, after all, the place that he had been paying close attention to since he was young. Teacher Zhang was definitely

253

in on everything, and he guessed that most of the villagers in Yun Village were insiders, too. He heard someone calling to him.

"Dr. Lin! Dr. Lin! Please wait for me!"

The old man stopped, and turned with a smile.

Dr. Lin Baoguang recognized the man as the old master of the mill. He must have been very old, but he could still run—run and crawl, to be more precise.

"Take it easy, Wu, I'll wait for you," Dr. Lin Baoguang said.

Grandpa Wu stopped, panting. He tried to get a close look at the doctor, but the bright light from the little man blinded him.

"Ah, ah!" Grandpa Wu exclaimed, becoming more anxious. "May I hold your hand?"

Grandpa Wu gripped Dr. Lin's hand. "This is a real person!" he said to himself. He recalled the scene when Dr. Lin Baoguang had given him the donkey.

The donkey was a small breed which he had never seen. It was not much bigger than a dog but better at work than any donkey in the village. A child told Wu that Dr. Lin had left it in the woods for him. It was then that Wu realized the importance of his mill.

"The mill is still operating, and business is good."

"Good to know."

Grandpa Wu went back, satisfied. Dr. Lin Baoguang heard noise from Niulan Mountain. He said to himself, "When a Yun villager lives to an old age, as Wu has done, his every move will be watched by the ancestors." His eyes cleared, and now he could see far, far away. The light of the rising sun shone on a rock by the side of the road. Dr. Lin sat on the rock and began to imagine how this area would have looked in the times before he was born. He reasoned that there was a connection between his hometown and this place. All his previous fears of losing witnesses now seemed superfluous.

He looked up and saw that the people who had been working in the fields in the morning were all gone. The land was quiet, taking on the appearance of the era when it was only wilderness.

"Grandpa Lin, are you going back?" a little girl's sweet voice asked.

Dr. Lin Baoguang turned around and saw a beautiful hoopoe on the empty road. So it was the bird talking to him. The bird hopped along without paying any attention to him, and in a few moments it was out of sight. Dr. Lin felt that his body was congealing with the rock, and the clouds were hanging down from the sky. At that moment, he truly saw how the landscape looked before he was born. The bell of Blue Mountain pealed, as it had before. But this time it sounded a little peculiar, a little overpowering to him. Was someone new ringing the bell? Or had the system changed over there on Blue Mountain? Dr. Lin Baoguang found it difficult to move his body. He was both alarmed and delighted. At every tightening of his aged muscles, the hoopoe which was out of sight uttered a mournful cry. "Ah, my home," he said softly. Ah, his hometown had always been Yun Village. Before his gaze was extinguished, he saw the rosy cloud.

Translators' Acknowledgments

We are grateful to the entire team at Yale University Press, including Abbie Storch, Kristy Leonard, and Danielle D'Orlando for their organizational skills, and Robert Pranzatelli, Erika Lake-Thomas, and Stephanie Lee for their promotion of Can Xue's work. We are delighted with Jenny Volvovski's evocative jacket design. Special thanks go to Susan Laity, senior editor, for her enthusiasm for Can Xue's writing and for her meticulous attention to detail; and to John Donatich, director of Yale University Press, for his vision and for his long-standing commitment to Can Xue's works. Finally, we thank Can Xue for challenging her readers with her spontaneity and creativity and for once again inviting us to render her work in English.

CAN XUE, pseudonym of Deng Xiaohua, has written many novels, volumes of literary criticism and philosophy, and short works of fiction. *Barefoot Doctor* is her twelfth book to appear in English. *I Live in the Slums* (2020) was long-listed for the 2021 International Booker Prize and the 2021 National Translation Award for Prose. *Five Spice Street* (2009) was a finalist for the Neustadt Prize. *The Last Lover* (2014) won the Best Translated Book Award for Fiction. *Frontier* (2017) made the 2017 "Best of" lists of NPR, the *Boston Globe,* and *World Literature Today. Love in the New Millennium* (2018) was long-listed for the 2019 International Booker Prize and the Best Translated Book Award. In 2001, Can Xue moved to Beijing from Changsha, Hunan. She has recently moved to Xishuangbanna, Yunnan, where she continues writing and jogging every day. When she was young, she served as a barefoot doctor for a time.

KAREN GERNANT and CHEN ZEPING have translated six previous books by Can Xue; this is the seventh. It follows *Blue Light in the Sky* (2006), *Five Spice Street, Vertical Motion* (2011), *Frontier, I Live in the Slums,* and *Purple Perilla* (2020). Gernant, professor emerita of Chinese history at Southern Oregon University, and Chen, professor emeritus of Chinese linguistics at Fujian Normal University, Fuzhou, have translated contemporary Chinese fiction for more than twenty years. In addition to their work with Can Xue, they have published a collection of stories by Zhang Kangkang (2011), a volume of stories by Alai (2012), two novellas by Zhang Yihe (2017), and *The Zither,* a collection of short fiction and a novella (2021). They have also published numerous short story translations in various literary magazines.